Carrie Fisher lives in Los Angeles
with her dog and her bird.
She has been known to act in films.

Carrie Fisher

POSTCARDS
from the
EDGE

published by **Pan Books**

Designed by Eve Metz

First published in Great Britain 1987 as a Picador edition
by Pan Books Ltd
This Picador edition published 1991 by Pan Books Ltd,
Cavaye Place, London SW10 9PG
3 5 7 9 8 6 4 2
All rights reserved
© Carrie Fisher 1987
ISBN 0 330 32031 9
Printed in England by Clays Ltd, St Ives plc

For my mother and my brother

CONTENTS

Prologue

<u>BROTHER THOMAS</u>,

You know how I always seem to be struggling, even when the situation doesn't call for it? Well, I finally found a place where my struggling fits right in: the sunny Middle East. Brooding and moping doesn't seem overdramatic in Israel or Egypt or Turkey. Today I stood in a recently bombed-out train station. I looked at the charred, twisted metal and I thought, "Finally my outsides match my insides." Maybe I should take a tour of the world's trouble spots and *really* relax. See you soon.

Love,
Sister Suzanne

<u>DEAR LUCY</u>,

Okay, here's what I think now. Ready? I have to establish an over-all plan for my overboard life. When I cross the finish line of my twenties this fall and that thirty flag goes down, I'd like to be closing in on having some idea of whatever it is that my life is about.

Here's what I've come up with so far: a) I'll get back into therapy, maybe with a woman therapist this time; b) I'll stop coloring my hair and dye it back to its normal color—I'll artificially go natural; c) I'll only date people I really like, so I can feel like there's some point to it; d) I'll fix the eating thing; e) I'm going to slip my hand out of the comforting clasp of chemicals—No More Drugs. Also, get up early every day, read more, keep a journal, talk on the phone less, do less shopping and, eventually, have a child with someone. Obviously, the plan is in a really rough early phase, so I'll keep you posted as this gets honed down.

Honey, I'm honed.

Your elfin buddy,
S.

DEAR GRAN,

Yet another offering to add to your collection of my poetic works.

> *Oh wow now*
> *I've done it*
> *I've made a mess*
> *I feel a fool*
> *I feel obsessed*
> *When we get to the good part*
> *Will I have something to wear?*
> *I know my heart's in the right place*
> *'Cause I hid it there*
>
> *I act so much like myself*
> *It's a little unreal*
> *It's a lot of work*
> *It's no big deal*

My heart's in the right place
Ticking away inside my torso
I'm just like other folks
Only that much more so

I remind myself
Of someone I've never met
Of someone I'd like to meet
Of someone I can't forget

I'm not insane
But I'm halfway there
You can tell from the smoke
Rising from my molten hair

Follow me down insight road
And I'll show you the sights along the way
I'm a flash and the world is my pan
Have a nice day

Give Granpaw a kiss if he remembers me. This is the kind of vacation I might need a vacation after. I'll call you when I get home.

Your ever-lovin'
Suzanne

Postcards from the Edge

DAY ONE

Maybe I shouldn't have given the guy who pumped my stomach my phone number, but who cares? My life is over anyway. Besides, what was I supposed to do? He came up to my room and gave me that dumb stuffed animal that looks like a thumb, and there I was lying in bed twelve hours after an overdose. I wasn't feeling my most attractive. I'd thrown up scallops and Percodan on him the night before in the emergency room. I thought that it would be impolite to refuse to give him my number. He probably won't call, anyway. No one will ever call me again.

DAY TWO

I was up all night with my head full of frightening, chattering thoughts, walking around and around the halls. After about the sixth spin I stopped waving at the night nurse and just kept my head down.

One of the therapists came in to admit me and asked how long I'd been a drug addict. I said that I didn't think I was a drug addict because I didn't take any one drug. "Then you're a *drugs* addict," she said. She asked if I had deliberately tried to kill myself. I was insulted by the question. I guess when you find yourself having overdosed, it's a good indicator that your life isn't working. Still, it wasn't like I'd planned it. I'm not suicidal. My behavior might be, but I'm certainly not. Tomorrow I get out of detox and start group.

I hate my life.

DAY THREE

All of the therapists here seem to be former addicts. They have this air of expertise. Drug addicts without drugs are experts on not doing drugs. I talked to this girl Irene at lunch who's been here two weeks, and she said that in the beginning your main activity is a nonactivity in that you simply don't do drugs. That's what we're all doing here: *Not Drugs.*

The woman who admitted me, Julie, is my therapist. I don't know if I like her or not, but I want to like her. I have to like her, because the way she is is probably the way I'm going to be. I need to make an ideal of someone who did drugs and now doesn't.

Three people here—Carl, Sam, and Irene—have been to prison. We also have Sid, a magazine editor, and Carol, an agent's wife, and several others whose names I'm not sure of yet. Most of them are here for cocaine or free-base, but there's also a sizable opiate contingent. The cocaine people sleep all the time, because by the time they get here, they haven't slept in weeks. We opiates have been sleeping a lot, so now we roam the halls at night, twitching through our withdrawals. I think there should be ball teams: the Opiates vs. the Amphetamines. The Opiates scratch and do hand signals and nod out, and the Amphetamines run around the bases and scream. There are no real rules to the game, but there are plenty of players.

Tomorrow afternoon after the cocaine video, the nurse takes everyone who's not in detox on a Sunday outing to the park.

DAY FOUR

It was nice being outside. You feel less like you're being punished and more like a normal citizen. It's hard not to feel like an outcast in a drug clinic, but then it's hard not to feel like an outcast, period. I seem to be the only one here who had their stomach pumped. It's an interesting distinction.

Carl and I shared a blanket in the park. He's a fifty-five-year-old black grounds keeper and a would-be ex-free-base addict. He looks like a burnt mosquito. I asked him how he could afford to be here and he said he's on his wife's health insurance.

Carl talked so much in the park that I thought I was going to kill myself. His main topic, of all things, was drugs. He talked about cooking up the rock and the feel of the free-base pipe, and how he'd make enough money from Tuesday to Friday to free-base all weekend. I asked him what he took to come down, and he said he didn't like downers. He said, "Shoot, those drugs don't do nothin' but constipate me."

The fat guy Sid seems really smart. He's in for lodes. I asked him what lodes were and his eyes started to shine. When addicts talk about their drug of choice, it's almost transcendental. He said, "You've been a downer freak and you don't know what lodes are?" It turns out lodes are four strong painkillers combined with one weird sleeping pill, which produces an effect like heroin along with a stomach addiction, which Sid had. I can't believe I missed that drug.

The weird thing about all this is that I had been straight for months—the whole time I was filming *Sleight of Head* in London and all through my vacation. But then I got home and *BOOM!* four weeks of drugs. I hated it, I even wanted to stop, but I just couldn't. It was like I was a car, and a maniac had gotten behind the wheel. I was driven, and I didn't know who was driving.

DAY FIVE

I let Irene cut my hair today. It's kind of horrible. She's only twenty, and her skin is all broken out from PCP and heroin. I got so absorbed listening to her stories of blackouts and arrests for prostitution that I didn't notice how badly the haircut was actually going.

Julie is so cheerful I want to punch her. And two guys who get out of here next week, Roger and Colin, almost swagger. They've got it all over us, because they haven't done drugs in almost a month. They *really* know how to not do drugs now. Big fish in a little rehab.

I feel so agitated all the time, like a hamster in search of a wheel. I'm consumed with panic that everyone will find out about this and hate me, or laugh at me, or worst of all, feel sorry for me. Pity me for taking my Everything-That-a-Human-Can-Possibly-Be-Offered and turning it into scallops and Percodan on the emergency room floor.

I can see where people would think that my life is great, so why can't I feel it? It's almost like I've been bad and I'm being punished by rewards—this self-indulgent white chick whose inner voice says, "Look how spoiled you are. Go on, have *another* great thing. What are you gonna do about it, huh? What are you gonna do about it?"

The thing about having it all is, it should include having the *ability* to have it all. Maybe there are some people who know how to have it all. They're probably off in a group somewhere, laughing at those of us who have it all but don't know how to.

The positive way to look at this is that from here things can only go up. But I've been up, and I always felt like a trespasser. A transient at the top. It's like I've got a visa for happiness, but for sadness I've got a lifetime pass. I shot through my twenties like a luminous thread through a dark needle, blazing toward my destination: Nowhere.

DAY SIX

This is hard—I feel like I've got bugs flying around inside of me. I called my friend Wallis today, and I tried to get the operator to say, "Collect call from hell, will you accept the charges?"

After not feeling anything for years, I'm having this Feeling Festival. The medication wears off and the feelings just fall on you. And they're not your basic fun feelings, either. These are the feelings you've been specifically avoiding—the ones you almost killed yourself to avoid. The ones that tell you you're something on the bottom of someone's shoe, and not even someone interesting.

I talked to my agent and ended up in tears, which is not my favorite presentation of myself. Crying to my agent. I tried very hard not to, but I didn't have a chance. I've used up all the Not Cry I was issued at birth. Now, it appears, it's crying time.

I talked to my mom briefly. I was afraid that she'd be mad at me for messing up the life she'd given me, but she was very nice. She said a great thing. I told her I was miserable here, and she said, "Well, you were happy as a child. I can prove it. I have films."

What went wrong between what she gave me and how I took it?

DAY SEVEN

How old do you have to be to get past caring?

Sid looked over at me during lunch and said, "You look so unhappy." I was sort of startled, since the picture of myself that I carry around in my wallet of a head is of a peppy, happy-go-crazy gal. I keep my eye on this picture when evidence to the contrary is all around me.

How could I have gotten all this so completely wrong? I'm smart. I guess I used the wrong parts of my brain, though—the parts that said, "Take LSD and painkillers. This is a good idea." I was into pain reduction and mind expansion, but what I've ended up with is pain expansion and mind reduction. Everything hurts now, and nothing makes sense.

DAY EIGHT

Drama in Drug Ward Six!

Irene got kicked out of the unit for smoking dope in her room. She offered some to Carol, the agent's wife, and Carol came to me crying and asked me what she should do. I told her we should turn Irene in, so we told Stan, the therapist who was on duty.

Stan called Irene in, and she had this real defiant look on her face, like she'd been caught doing something noble for her country and now she was going to be killed for it. Carol was crying and I was sitting and holding her hand. Stan said, "Irene, we hear you've been smoking dope." Irene said, "Well, I didn't know where I was gonna be when I moved out of here, if I was gonna go to a halfway house or whatever, and I was confused so I smoked dope." Stan said, "There are a thousand excuses and finally no reasons to do drugs."

Most of the people in here share the desire to seem cool. They can be aching from heroin withdrawal, but ask how they are and they'll say, "Pretty good, man. Hangin' in there." The answer comes too quickly, and hovering over a grin, a look of desperate loneliness gazes across the abyss. The only thing worse than being hurt is everyone knowing that you're hurt.

DAY NINE

So, essentially I could have died. Not only this time but probably several times, forgetting how much I took and when I took it, not to mention why I took it. Was I celebrating, or drowning my sorrows? Or celebrating my sorrows?

The junkies were up in arms this morning. Half of them wouldn't speak to Carol and me because we snitched on Irene. The other half thought it was pretty stupid for anyone to have smoked dope at a drug rehab. They had to call a special little group session to defuse things. These aren't people with a good handle on their emotions, and without their chemical coping skills it's every man for himself. It doesn't run hot and cold here, it runs hot and *hotter*. Bart, the homosexual triple Scorpio, called me an asshole in the Ping-Pong room.

It turns out Irene got the dope from one of the cleaning men who she was fucking in the stairwell during lunch. My kind of people.

DAY TEN

Three new people checked in today. Marvin, a retired bus driver in his fifties, is probably here for alcoholism. Wanda is a heroin addict who says she's a model and brought the makeup to prove it. And Mark is a crazy kid from Vacaville—I don't know what his drug of choice is, but I don't think it matters anymore. This is a cross section of village idiots from all over the state. Everyone you ever would have thought was too loaded at a party is in one place.

After group, Bart apologized for calling me an asshole and told me a story about the time that he spilled amyl nitrate on his testicles and his balls melted into the sheets, and he had to take the sheets and his balls to the hospital and have them separated. I told him it was a great idea for a TV movie.

We had lunch and watched *The Outer Limits*. Drug addicts pretty much all have the same taste in shows: science fiction and MTV. It's so bizarre. Everyone is acting like where we are is sort of normal, and we're in a *drug clinic*.

DAY ELEVEN

The new people came out of detox today and joined our group. Marvin said he wasn't an alcoholic, but he likes it here. He thinks all of us are interesting. It's like he's on a field trip for *Psychology Today*, or a segment of *Bloopers, Blumpers and Bleepers* where they send a healthy person to blend in with a wardful of addicts just to see if anybody notices.

Wanda was in the hospital recovering from a suicide attempt (carbon monoxide in her car). She called her dealer to bring her heroin because she couldn't sleep. She overdosed in the hospital, so they just transferred her down here.

Mark was brought in by his parole officer directly from Vacaville. He's nineteen, and he looks like he's been on medication of some kind for most of his life. His blond hair is greasy and parted down the middle, and he has very wild eyes. When he walks down the hallways, he hugs the walls, which Carl says is a prison thing. Mark has already been in jail for three years for resisting arrest and assaulting a police officer, and now he's in a drug clinic. His father came in today to bring him some clothes. He seemed disappointed at the way Mark's turned out.

My mom is probably sort of disappointed at how I turned out, but she doesn't show it. She came by today and brought me a satin and velvet quilt. I'm surprised that I was able to detox without it. I was nervous about seeing her, but it went okay. She thinks I blame her for my being here. I mainly blame my dealer, my doctor, and myself, and not necessarily in that order. She didn't like my hair very much, but pretended to. She said it was "interesting." She thinks my life would work better if I got a new business manager. She washed my underwear and left.

In the last few years I've become an accepted eccentric at best, and a fuckup at worst. I feel like I'll let people down if I take away the behavior they've grown accustomed to disapproving of. They try to discipline me, I refuse to be disciplined. They object, I'm objectionable. We all know exactly what to do.

Julie talked to us today about the family and friends of the addict, the Alanons. She said they become very caught up in the whole downward spiral of watching the alcoholic slowly die. It can become their whole lives. Addicted to addicts. "It's like an Alanon jumps out the window and *someone else*'s life flashes in front of their eyes," said Sid. I wished I'd said that, but then, I probably will.

I keep thinking that if I could marry somebody, this would be less embarrassing. I'm so jealous of Carol because she has a husband. It makes it seem less final that she's here. It gives her something to go back to, someone to be with, and someone to be. I have no situation that requires me to be more than I am. It just seems like when you get two people together, and one's in a suit and one's in a dress, how could they be unhappy? Unless their kid murdered another kid or something.

I envy people who have the capacity to sit with another human being and find them endlessly interesting. I would rather watch TV. Of course, this eventually becomes known to the other person. I once told Jonathan that I would pay more attention to him if he got better programming. It always seems that in the beginning with someone, nothing they do could ever be wrong, except that they don't see you enough. And eventually it gets to the point where you just want to say, "Get off my leg, okay?"

What's the difference? No one would marry me with this haircut, anyway.

DAY TWELVE

This boy Brian was checked in this morning by his mother and his aunt. He wore a red knit hat and stunk of beer. He was about eighteen years old, and he did not want to be in a drug clinic. He had a concert to go to Wednesday night.

Brian's brother was killed last year in a car accident. He was lying in the street and someone released the brake on a car, and it rolled over him because he was too loaded to get out of the way.

They sent Carol and Bart and me to convince Brian to stay. He said he was impressed that someone like me actually stayed in the clinic, and that he wanted to be an actor, but he couldn't be persuaded to stay. He said he was too young to stop drinking and drugging. All his friends did it.

He knew he was probably an alcoholic—he drank all day and smoked a lot of dope, and did cocaine when he could get it—and he knew that his brother had, in effect, died of it. Still, he couldn't handle what it meant to be in a drug unit. He wouldn't examine it. It was too heavy and it was definitely too hard. It couldn't be true, therefore it wasn't. And so he split.

The whole thing made me think. I used up so much energy explaining why I was late, why I didn't show up, how I wasn't really loaded, I was just tired, I had jet lag. Avoiding looking people in the eyes because I couldn't stand how I felt when I saw the disappointment in their faces. That ate up a lot of energy. If I could accept that I'm a drug addict, I could have all that energy back.

So, I'm a drug addict. I guess we're allowed just so many drugs in one lifetime, and I've used up my coupon. From here on out, there's just reality. I think that's what maturity is: a stoic response to endless reality. But then, what do I know?

DAY THIRTEEN

This is not necessarily where I envisioned myself when I was young. I didn't stand up in school and say, "My goal when I'm older is to be in a drug hospital, eating cafeteria food and watching *The Outer Limits* and fighting in group therapy and playing volleyball in the park and not dealing with my feelings."

I talked to Thomas on the phone today. He said he's been trying to reach me, but the line is always busy—it's a pay phone. Thomas sounded so calm, so okay, so not me. Somehow I absorbed the world's genetic horror, while my brother inherited the sweetness and patience of someone who befriends birds. He's one of the few people who, when you ask how he is and he says fine, you don't question it. It reminds me of the scene in *The Exorcist* when the priest looks into the devil inside the possessed girl and cries, "Take me!" and the devil leaves the girl and enters the priest. It's like I'm an exorcist, taking all the darkness and letting it gather inside me, while Thomas absorbs—well, maybe not light, but certainly lighter colors. There's some sad buoyance in him. He ambles and strolls, moving through life in smooth easy motions. I told him that the great thing about having me as a sister is that I make him look even better by supplying him with contrast. He said, "The really great thing about having you as a sister is that you're the only adult I know that keeps a bowl of Tootsie Rolls for her guests." I don't know why, but this made me feel better.

Sid said that drugs weren't the problem, *life* was the problem. Drugs were the solution. I think Sid has a crush on me. He gets me up in the morning by coming into my room and holding my feet until I'm totally awake. I like having my feet held, even if it is by Sid.

Marvin still doesn't think he's an alcoholic.

Mark showed me his letter from Manson today. It didn't seem to make much sense—something about redwood trees. Mark says Manson is deeply misunderstood and a "cool guy."

DAY FOURTEEN

Today Mark threatened Sid's life. Nobody quite knows what happened, but Mark was given Haldol, an antipsychotic. Now he has all this mung in the side of his mouth, and he looks wilder than ever. Carol and Wanda say they're going to put trash cans in front of their doors tonight, because there are no locks in drug clinics.

Carl's mad at me because I gave him ten dollars to shut up. He says I'm a spoiled movie actress and I don't know the first thing about real life. Maybe he's right. Sometimes I feel like I've got my nose pressed up against the window of a bakery, only I'm the bread.

DAY FIFTEEN

A lady came in today to beef up our spirituality, AA-style. She told us a couple of great stories. First, she explained why people who bring us into AA are called Eskimos. There was this guy named Harvey, sitting in a bar up in Alaska. Another guy, Tony, came into the bar and started talking to the bartender about God. Harvey said to Tony, "Do you believe all that stuff?" Tony said, "Yeah, I do," and Harvey said, "Aaah, I tried that God stuff. It's a bunch of crock." Tony said, "What do you mean? What happened?" So Harvey said, "Well, I was in this really, *really* bad snowstorm. I mean, I'd been lost for days and I was dying. I was desperate. Finally, I dropped to my knees and prayed. I said,

'God, if you're up there, please get me out of here. Save me!' "
Then Harvey stopped talking, so Tony said, "Well, what happened?" And Harvey said, scornfully, "Oh, nothing. An *Eskimo* came and got me out."

Then she told us this story of how her first AA sponsor had gotten this horrible kind of cancer, and her sponsor believed in God. So this lady couldn't understand how she could believe in a God who would make her suffer like that. And her sponsor said, "God never gives us any more than we can handle, so if he gives you a lot to handle, take it as a compliment. It's because he believes that you can handle a lot." It was such a powerful thought, I wanted to brand it into my brain.

When I got back to my room, there were flowers from the guy who pumped my stomach. The note said that he could tell I was a very sensitive person. I'd have to be sensitive to need all that Percodan.

I'm tempted to marry him, just to be able to tell people how we met.

ALEX

. . . That's it, I've quit. This time I've really quit. I'm not doing cocaine anymore. If someone came up and *offered* me cocaine I wouldn't do it. I doubt that anyone will offer it to me, though. No one offers cocaine anymore. It used to be a way that people got friendly, sharing a few toots, but now everyone *hoards* their cocaine.

My first party without drugs. Interesting. I mean, when I was a little kid I always went to birthday parties straight, but that was a while ago.

I wonder if anyone here even *has* any cocaine. That guy Steve looks like he might, he usually has some. I *loathe* that guy, but he always has great cocaine . . .

No, I promised myself I would not do any cocaine, because that last time was such a *nightmare* and . . . But it was fun in the beginning. Sometimes it's fun. I don't know, Freud took it, so how bad could it be?

But this is the new me. I'm totally on a health kick. I have not taken any cocaine in *four days*. I don't even like it anymore. I never really *did* like it, I just did it 'cause it was *around*. And I don't think I was really heavy into it, not like Steve over there. Steve is really, really into cocaine. I would say *he's* got a problem. He can't stop. Well, sometimes he stops for a while, but he can't stay stopped. I really think *I* can. I think I have willpower, I just haven't used it in a while. I've been kind of on a willpower break, but now I feel it's coming back. I really think I can stay with this commitment of not doing cocaine.

Besides, this healthy life is great. I really love this being straight. You know, you see people jogging and you think, *"Yuuucccchh,"* but I'm getting on. I'm in my late twenties, and I think taking drugs was all part of being young. I don't think I had a *problem*, I think I was just *young*. And that by definition isn't a problem, it's just a point in your life when it seems *okay* to take a lot of cocaine. And then that point passes.

I don't know, I think it was the bad relationship I was in that really determined my drug intake. And now Joan's left me, and I really feel good about myself. I mean I *want* to. And I went to that juice bar today and bought chlorophyll juice, that green drink. It gave me diarrhea, but I really feel good tonight. And I feel like it's a beginning. You go to a place like that and you buy the chlorophyll juice and the carrot juice, and you're making a statement. And I bought some new sneakers, I'm gonna start running . . . I actually got up at nine thirty this morning and moved my exercise bike right next to my bed, so tomorrow morning I *know* I'm just gonna hop on that cycle. Ten minutes is enough for aerobics, I guess. And then maybe I'll go to that Canyon Ranch health spa. Maybe then I could meet a really great girl. I think if I meet someone who doesn't do drugs, then we won't do them together, obviously, and that'll really help me. I think all of these choices reflect where you're at with *you*.

The only thing that bothers me is the idea of giving it up *completely*. I should be able to celebrate every now and again. Like if I stay straight for a while, I should be able to celebrate by getting loaded. I don't see what's wrong with that. Steve does that, but Steve has a *problem*. I think that once I get this under control, I'll be able to do it. And I really feel like I've made a strong beginning. God, my stomach is upset from that juice, though. I wonder if everything good for you tastes awful. I hope not, because I'm really gonna get into it.

Steve looks kind of loaded now. That looks so awful. You see people and they're loaded and ... Look how dumb it looks. That looks *so stupid*. I can't believe I ever did it. I feel so good about being on the other side of it now. It really erodes your self-esteem to make a decision like not taking drugs and then taking them. The thing is, I also think you can take a little bit, and not do it to excess. Not *everybody* can—obviously there are some personality types who can't do *anything* a little bit—but I'm not one of those. There are certain areas of my life where I do a *very* little bit, and I think if I practice, one of those areas could be cocaine.

Well, maybe not cocaine, but maybe I could take a speed pill every so often. I love what speed and coke do to my weight. It's unnatural, I know. I *could* just exercise ...

God, there's that great feeling right at the beginning. If you get some *good* coke. From now on, I'm just gonna do *good* coke. When I do it, I'm gonna make sure. I'll *never* go to the dealer in Brentwood again. *Never.* I think *that* was the problem. His coke hurts your face, it becomes a *chore* to do it. I'll just do pharmaceutical, that's not hard on the membrane, and I really want to take care of my body. I think I'm unusual, because even during all those years when I was doing drugs, I still sometimes went to the gym. Joan accused me of trying to maintain my body so I could destroy it with chemicals, but I think that's a

little harsh. And even if I did, I'm certainly better off than someone like *Steve*, who's just frying himself *and* eating burgers and
sugar. I eat no carcinogenic food, I'm drinking some juices now
... I went overboard today, but ...

I'm *tired*. Who's that girl? She's attractive ... Aauugggh, I
don't want to get into another relationship thing again. God,
I'm *so tired*. I shouldn't be drinking. I shouldn't have started
drinking, 'cause I associate the two, alcohol and cocaine. I'm
just gonna *not drink* now. Oh, he sees me, he's coming over. I
should ignore him so he gets that I'm not interested in doing
any—

"Hi, Steve, how ya doin'? Yeah, yeah. I'm fine. No, I feel okay.
I don't look *that* bad. I have a stomach thing today. How are
you? You seem very *up*. No, I'm ... I'm not doing any right now.
I've quit. Yeah. No, I feel great. No, I'm serious. What do you
mean, that's not a great line reading? *I feel great.* I'm absolutely
committed to this. No, I don't mean it like a judgment on you. I
think it's fine that some people still do coke, you know? I don't
think it's weak ...

"No, I don't think I had a *problem*. It's just that my nose
started ... I don't know. I'll probably end up still doing a little
bit every so often, you know. Not right now. Maybe ... well,
like, maybe ... I don't know, let me just ... Is there food at this
party? All right, maybe like a hit, but *that's*—who is that girl
over there?—*that's* it, though. I'm gonna do ... No, this is ...
I'm not ... All right, give me one hit. But don't give me any
more even if I ask you to. This is good coke, right? It's not from
Brentwood? All right, one hit.

"(*sniff*) Mmmmmmhh! (*sniff*) Ooohhhh, *fantastic*. Oh, *great*.
Shit, that's great! Mmmmhhhhh! It just burns a little bit. There's
not much cut in it, right? Yeah? It's good. No, I really don't need
any more. I mean, I can *handle* it, I just think that was it. You
know, people come to a party and they do one hit to break
the tension, and I think I can really master that now. I can do
a little bit.

"God, I feel so . . . I really feel *good* about my commitment to not doing drugs. I mean, just doing a little bit of drugs. Feel my arm. I feel really good. Well, I *know* I don't look that great, but I didn't sleep that much and I drank this bad juice.

"Let's go over and talk to that girl. I wanna go over and talk to that girl. Who is that girl? Lisa what? What is she, an actress or something? I *loathe* actresses. She looks smart, though. Smart people always wear black. Who's the guy she's talking to? *Craig?* I wanna go talk to her. God, he's such a *loser*. I should talk to her, I'm like a real guy. I have to go talk to her. Give me another hit of that stuff, maybe I'll go talk to her. I *know* what I said, I know what I said. Just give me one more hit. What are you, stingy with the blow now? I'll help pay for it. I'm just gonna do it . . . Like, I'm gonna celebrate not doing it by doing a little bit. (*sniff*) Mmmmhh! (*sniff*) Yeesssss!

"I wish there was something like holistic blow, you know what I mean? That there would be some way in nature you could take blow and it would be *good* for you. I wish my doctor would make me take it for some weird ailment I have. This is *good* coke, though. This is really good. How much did you pay for this? Not bad. That is *not bad*. And who did you get it from? Oh, yeah, I had some once from him that was so great. Remember the night we . . . Give me another hit. Give me one more hit.

"(*sniff*) Aaaahhh! (*sniff*) Ooooww! No, it's not the coke, it's me. I had this cold last week. Actually, I think it was more my sinuses. I have a sinus problem, or I seem to more in the last couple of years. I don't know, I have to go to a doctor at some point.

"Nah, I don't want to talk to that girl anyway. I wanna talk to *you*. I've missed you. I really feel like I can talk to you, I really feel we have a lot in common. I know we don't see each other much socially, but I've gotta say every time that we've spent time together, I've enjoyed it. Remember the night in Vegas when we met? You weren't actually dealing then, were you?

Someone said you were a dealer once, I nearly punched the guy out. You're like a really good guy, man. I really like you.

"Think we can get any more of this stuff? 'Cause, I mean, I'm quitting after tonight anyway because, I don't know, I should start taking care of myself. Whew, my heart is really palpitating. You think if I took one more hit it might calm me down a little bit? I know that sounds like a dumb cocaine question, but I think if you do a certain amount and then taper off, you can *hit that peak* and *really* be buzzing, you know, when you feel like the world is lined up just *exactly right*. God, I sure love life. Can I have another hit?

"I think this is good for me—to test my resistance. I mean, I think it's wimpy to give up cocaine. Master the drug, *that's* the key—the total key to the whole thing. I mean, people who actually have to go and give it up—it just shows they're weak. They go to groups like Cocaine Anonymous and those people, they always fuckin' talk about drugs. You know? It's like all they do is not do drugs. Well, man, I'd rather *do* drugs. Do you have another hit?

"Man, this party's a drag. I don't know, I feel so agitated and, you know, itchy to . . . Can we go to your place? Hey, come over to mine. Well, let's just go outside then, let's walk around. There's nobody here that I like. God, look, they're *eating*. Uuggh, look at that shit, it looks awful. Come on, let's go outside and talk.

"Did I ever tell you I graduated with honors from high school? Yeah, I was a real brainy kid. Very precocious. I don't know, I thought I'd go into writing because it interested me. But I gotta tell you, the environment at the networks is just not that exciting. I'd rather be in music, you know, but I don't play an instrument. Maybe I could learn, though. I feel *now* like I could learn an instrument. Do you play an instrument? That's interesting, that's very interesting. We both don't play any instruments. But, you know, I feel that you, like me, we have the *spirit* of musicians. You know, sitting around communicating. I think *artists* do that.

"That girl in black, maybe she's an artist. I've always wanted to meet someone who wrote poetry and went to jazz clubs, and she'd draw me into her life and we'd become soulmates. I wonder if I have a soulmate.

"Can I have some more blow? One more hit, 'cause I'm like really cresting now. Maybe we could just buy a little, what the hell? This is a party. I have not been getting loaded. This is a reason to celebrate.

"(*sniff*) Aaaahh! (*sniff*) Ooohhh! There is like an edge on this, though, don't you think? Am I sweating? I look all right, don't I? I don't look paranoid, do I? Sometimes I get paranoid that I look paranoid. I don't want anyone to think I'm paranoid. It's not like I care what people think, but sometimes I do. I admit it. I'm a human being. I've always cared a little bit what people think.

"But anyway, I like it when it's like this, you know, and we're just talking. This is a great conversation, man. We should be taping this. So, what do you do? You're writing? What are you writing about? Articles on stereo equipment. That's fascinating. So should we go buy some more of this blow? He's out? Well, let's go to Brentwood. No, that's true, he *usually* has shitty blow, but it's not that expensive and he's *always* there.

"Are my gums bleeding? It feels like my gums are bleeding. I don't know why, I must have cut myself talking. Maybe we could get a lude, too, because I'm starting to feel very . . . *unhappy.* I don't mean unhappy, literally, but it's like I wanna be somewhere else but I don't know where I wanna be . . . Let's go to Brentwood. Let's just, fuck it, let's go to Brentwood. Leave your car here, I'll drive you back later. How many toots do we have left? Shit, well, let's go to Brentwood.

"God, I wish I hadn't had that wheatgrass juice, I feel *awful.* Shit, they really should give you instructions with health food. Anything taken to excess can be unhealthy, even healthy stuff. But forget about excess, I don't even think it's that good for you in moderation. Nothing *green* can be good for you, can it? Uuugghh! Give me some more. Let's just do the last hit, just so we can get into the car and get to the next stop. (*sniff*) (*sniff*).

"What's the matter with you? You look tense. Are you okay? God, what time is it? Sometimes I get so nervous and I don't know why, you know? I heard this phrase once, 'contentless fear,' and I think that's what I have now. 'Cause there's no reason why I should be this jumpy. I mean, I'm comfortable with you, or I *was* comfortable with you. I'm sorry I'm talking so much. I don't know, it just must be the night. God, what a night.

"*Jesus!* Where did that guy come from, I almost ran him over. *Jesus!* Jesus. Okay, okay, I *am* slowing down. I don't know, somehow it got up to seventy-five. Jesus. Let's do the rest of the blow in case we're stopped. What did you do, *hog* it all?

"God, man. I should never have done this. I should never have done all this blow. I *hate* myself. Why did I do this? Now I have an upset stomach from the wheatgrass juice *and* the fuckin' thing with the blow. I wonder if that girl with the black dress is still at the . . . Here we are, this is his block.

"I feel so dumb now. Why did I *do* that? Well, I didn't do anything dumb. It was probably the blow. That blow *did* burn a little bit. Now we'll get some better blow. I hope he has some *good* blow. I hope he has some *blow.* Maybe he has a lude, though. You know, if I could . . . Well, now I'm maybe in kind of a two-lude mode . . .

"What do you mean, I'm talking to myself? Well, obviously I'm talking to myself. I can't talk to *you.* What do I have in common with someone who writes articles about stereo equipment? Jesus.

"All right, let's just get inside, we'll get inside. How much cash do I have? Hundred and ten, a hundred and ten bucks, that's good. Maybe he'll take a check, that'd be okay. I don't like to do that, though. What if they . . .

"Alex. It's *Alex!*"

What is this asshole, deaf?

"Hi! Hi, man, how ya doin'? Yeah, yeah, I know it's late. Yeah, well, we were just drivin' around and . . . You know Steve. Yeah. Well, can we come in? Thanks.

"So, do you have any coke? Half a gram? What do you mean? I thought you were a *dealer*. Can you get more?"

Oh, *shit*. Oh, *shit*!

"Well, do you have any ludes or anything? I'm really on edge now, I'm *so* on edge. Well, yeah, get the half a gram, and see if . . . Whatever you have. Anything you have. I just want *anything* you have. And Steve wants whatever else there is."

Good*damn* it, why did I do this? Just give me that half a gram, and then I'll take the half a gram, and then I'll try and decide what to do. I've gotta figure out how I'm gonna get down . . . I don't want to be with these people. Who *are* these people? I *loathe* these people. Look at the *skin* on that guy, God, it's enough to drive anyone *insane*. What is that, a *bug* on the floor? Look at this place. God, what a dive. What a miserable dive.

I hear people. Why do I always hear people? Wait, now, this is the coke, just calm down. What's the big deal? Just *calm down*. I can't believe this, I'm not gonna be able to drive. I feel like digging a hole in the carpet. Oh, Jesus. Oh, Jesus.

Is that the *sun* coming up? No, it's probably just . . . It is, it's the streetlight. I just hope those *birds* don't come out. I'll kill myself, I will, I'll *kill* myself if those fuckin' birds come out. I've gotta have those ludes, gotta have a set of ludes just to get me down. Maybe I should check his medicine cabinet, but he's a dealer so wouldn't he be smart about that? Nah!

"Can I use your bathroom?"

I *loathe* this guy. Let's see, what's he got? Anacin. Afrin. Actifed. Lomotil—sure, 'cause he's got the runs all the time from the baby laxative in his fuckin' blow. Percodan! *Jesus!* Two. Two's not usually enough, but fuck it, I'll take the two. Endo 333, *oooh*, my favorite. I better run the water so they don't hear me close this. Aaahh, that's good, that'll be good. I've taken so much blow, though. Two Percodan on all this blow won't even matter. Maybe I should go get health food . . . Tomorrow I'm really . . .

That's it, man, this is *it*. I'm gonna remember this, I'm *always* gonna remember this. That I'm sitting here in Brentwood with two loser guys that I have nothing in common with, doing drugs and trying to make conversation. I could kill myself. I *loathe* my life.

I'll *never* feel those Percodan. Goddamn it, I hope he's got some ludes. *Please* let him have ludes.

"Oh, man, I feel a little better after going to the john. Hey, listen, man, you wouldn't have any *ludes* or anything? I mean, I know I asked you already, but I had like a very tense day. I had some bad wheatgrass juice and . . . I don't know, maybe it's an astrological thing, but . . .

"Ecstasy? No, but I've heard of it. Yeah, right, who hasn't? Aren't you supposed to be with girls or something? Really? It just puts you in a good mood? Well, great, give me some. A *good* mood? Oh, great. No, no, I'm in a good mood now, I'm just in too *strong* of a mood. No, let's, let's . . . Give me one of those. Sorry, I didn't mean to grab.

"Great! They're big, aren't they? Do you have anything to wash it down? Any tequila or anything? Yeah, beer's fine. Oh, wow. So how long do these take to kick in? No, not since that juice this afternoon. Really? That quick? What's in it, do you know? Somebody said there was heroin in it. Not this stuff? Okay, good, 'cause that's the one thing I don't wanna do. Well, one time I snorted some, but I would *never* do any needles. I really think that makes you a drug addict, and me, I'm like a neck-up person."

I feel a little nauseous all of a sudden. It's probably the juice.

"Hey, this is a nice place. I've never really noticed that you have a nice apartment. It's like, *kind.* I don't know if that's an appropriate way to describe decor, but it seems so . . . friendly.

33

Particularly for a dealer's house. *What* is this music? This is *fantastic* music. Really? I usually *hate* Led Zeppelin. It's so interesting, *so* interesting. Do you mind if I lie down near the speakers? Do you have a pillow or anything?"

God! I feel like I'm making such a fool of myself. I don't even know these guys and I *love* them. I guess it's gotta be the drug, but it doesn't *seem* like the drug. Maybe this is the Percodan. I know it's not good to mix so much, but this feels like such a good blend. Maybe this is *exactly right*. Maybe from now on I should only do a little cocaine, a couple of Percodan maybe, and then that Ecstasy, and listen to Led Zeppelin. And that'll be my recipe. Like when I've been good, like I have for the past whatever. I've been straight . . . I mean, I was drinking, but I don't count that. When I've been straight for this kind of a while and I really get on edge, the way to take it off is to be with *these guys.* I *love* these guys.

I mean, I don't want to have sex with them, but that idea is not totally repellent to me, either. Steve, even though he has bad skin, is a great guy, and he's got an ass like a girl. I never noticed that before. Oh, I'm *so happy.* I think I've really turned this experience around.

"Steve. Don't ever leave me. I can't imagine being separated from you people. *Ever."*

I want to bond with them on some level. I want to show them how I feel. Maybe this is too excessive. Yeah, I should just get more into the music.

That girl at the party in black . . . Even the party seems nice now. Maybe we should . . . No, I'd have to move. Maybe I could call the party and tell them to send the girl here. *That* would be perfect.

I just feel at one with everything. I remember the time I took acid, and I took the wrong end of the cardboard and it never came on. Maybe this is like acid. But everything looks the same, it just looks *nicer.* Nicer to be with. Maybe I should decorate *my* apartment like this.

My nose still hurts, though. Maybe I should never take cocaine again. Yeah, from now on I'll just take Ecstasy every so often. It's probably better for me. They only just made it illegal, so how bad could it be? And they haven't even said it's bad for you. They just don't really know yet what it does to you.

How could I not have found this before? I'm so happy. Maybe I should just call the party and ask for that girl. What'd he say her name was? No, maybe I'll just . . . Is it rude to jerk off in people's houses? I'll just get up and . . .

"No, no, no, I'm okay, man. I just wanna use your can. What? No, I've snorted heroin, but I would never shoot it. Oh, you would do it for me. Well, I suppose that doesn't count, then, right? But I wouldn't have to . . . ? And it'd just be a little bit, right?"

It seems like it would be good. Heroin's like the natural drug. I don't know, though. This is so weird.

"You wouldn't do anything bad to me, would you? You have such a great expression on your face right now. All right, sure, I'll trust you. But just give me a little bit. And Steve, you're driving us back, right? Well, maybe I'll just crash here then. That's cool, right? I like Brentwood."

I can't believe this. I'm tying off. This is so weird. I never thought I would do this. But I'm just gonna do it once.

"Okay."

Oh, my God! Now I understand everything. This is so intensely great. Smack. It sounds like a breakfast cereal. It sure doesn't feel like a breakfast cereal. Shit, I love this. It's like floating down the Nile in your mind. Deep sea diving in your head. This must be well-being.

Does this make me a drug addict? No, I'm just celebrating tonight. What a great night this is.

I'll never do cocaine again. Uh-uh. Maybe a little Ecstasy, a little heroin, but I'll never do cocaine again. And I'm gonna start working out tomorrow. I'm gonna start an aerobic workout tomorrow on my bike. Maybe tomorrow afternoon. I wish I'd never had that wheatgrass juice, though. I feel sort of nauseous.

"Oops, sorry, man. Let me clean it up."

God, that was the easiest puke I've ever had. I wish I could have always thrown up that way. That felt almost good.

"Sure, take my car. I'll wait here. I'll just . . . be . . . here . . ."

What a nice, kind apartment this is. I think everyone should just love each other. That's what I think.

I don't know when I've felt this rested. I've never truly been relaxed. I'm finally relaxed. I feel like Jesus slipped me in the pocket of his robe, and we're walking over long, long stretches of water.

My parents were so fabulous to have had me. This is just . . . *everything.* My teeth feel so soft. *This* is why people take this. It wouldn't even be so bad to *die* of really good heroin. I wouldn't mind just living two more weeks and dying at the end of it if I could have two weeks like this. Although it would be much better to have years and years. I don't think you can even call this a drug. This is just a response to the conditions we live in.

I wonder what that art student at the party is doing. She had such soft, silky hair. She seemed so invested in everything, like the now was exactly where she wanted to be. And now I know how she feels. This is perfect.

If she were here now, it would be like Adam and Eve. We would make this the Garden of Eden, this apartment. Anywhere we were would be the Garden of Eden. And I could really communicate with my heart. It's just a question of finding the right person. If she were here now, I would just hold her and hold her and hold her, like we were twins waiting to be born out of this apartment in Brentwood.

She's probably my soulmate. What if I met my soulmate and now I'll never see her again? But we met and kissed on the astral plane. We flew in the astral plane, and now I'm flying toward her. If she's my soulmate, and I truly believe she is, we'll meet again. We're always meeting. There is no meeting for soulmates. They're always together and never apart.

We'll have a child, and we'll bring it up on heroin so that it'll have a happy childhood. And I'll buy her lots and lots of black shirts and sweaters. And she'll play the bongo drums in a jazz club in the East Village, while I recite stream-of-consciousness poetry that everyone thinks is brilliant. I am brilliant. I'm everything.

Sometimes I wonder if I really am Jesus, but I just haven't grown into it yet.

I wonder what color Jesus's eyes were. And if he needed glasses.

He had the sweetest face . . .

<u>SUZANNE AND ALEX</u>

DAY SIXTEEN

They brought a new guy in today, Alex. He's very good-looking, in a Heathcliff sort of way. He had a seizure an hour ago. I didn't see it, but Sam said it was pretty amazing.

Carl told me Sam was in jail for rape. My reply was, "Oh." I casually asked Sam about it, and he said he was framed—that his friend had done it. I asked him what he did when he wasn't in jail, and he said he was a scalper. He told me he'd sold tickets to the concert of an ex-boyfriend of mine, as if to say, "What a coincidence that we should finally meet." Sam is homophobic and hates Bart. He calls him "Barf."

Wanda told me she likes to be tied up and have her clothes torn off before sex. She said it really makes her happy. I don't know what makes me happy, but that doesn't ring a bell.

. . . That fucker Steve! How did he find my parents' number? How could they have put me in a drug clinic? This is *humiliating*.

So I overdosed. Well, of *course* I did. I'd never shot heroin before. I told them I'll never do it again. I was on Ecstasy and I thought it would be okay. I was more open to the heroin because of the Ecstasy and the Percodan. So I won't take Ecstasy again. I only took it in the first place because he didn't have ludes. I've gotta get out of here.

How did this happen to me? How did this *happen* to me? I'm in here with *drug addicts*. It's so degrading. I keep telling them I'm not an addict, but they laugh at me. My problem isn't drugs, it was just those two drugs that made the other one possible. I hope they didn't tell Joan.

Detox! I took heroin *once*, what am I detoxing from? My mother—God, she was upset—said something about alcohol withdrawal, but I didn't drink . . . Well, I drank every day, but I didn't drink like they imply I drank. I can't be an alcoholic. That's insane. I'm twenty-nine years old.

And they expect me to go to these meetings, these Alcoholics Anonymous meetings. I don't *like* groups. I like to be alone. I'm kind of a lone animal by nature. I can just imagine the kind of scum you'd meet there. Greg Friedman used to go all the time, and he had to stop. He said, "I never would have taken drugs with half those people. How am I supposed to get straight with them?" He died of cocaine poisoning, but I really trusted him.

It's so wimpy to have to lean on groups of people. Do it alone! It's a private matter. I think it's bullshit to go to a public place to handle a private matter. I don't want someone getting in my face and talking about drugs all the time. It's just *mindless*. And then what happens? You give up drugs, and then you do something else to death. I want to do *this* to death. If I'm going to do something to death, I mean, which I don't think I am. You learn from your mistakes, I think. You're human, you have to fall down a little bit, and you learn from that. Pain is growth.

I wish I had some blow . . .

DAY SEVENTEEN

It struck me today that the people that have had an impact on me are the people who didn't make it. Marilyn Monroe, Judy Garland, Montgomery Clift, Lenny Bruce, Janis Joplin, John Belushi. It's not Making It to be Marilyn Monroe, but it is to me.

In our culture these people are heroes. There's something inside of that—a message that killing yourself like that isn't so bad. All the interesting people do it, the extraordinary ones. A weird, weird message. Most of the people I've admired in show business—comedians, writers, actors—are alcoholics or drug addicts or suicides. It's bizarre. And I get to be in that club now. It's the one thing I cling to in here: Wow, I'm hip now, like the dead people.

Romancing the stoned.

. . . I can't believe Suzanne Vale is here. I never knew she was an addict. She looks a little puffy, but she's definitely cute.

This is so Not Hip. I don't mean everything has to be hip. This is probably good for some people, but . . . *Look* at these people. I have nothing in common with any of them, except Suzanne. She's been here a couple of weeks now. She seems like she's really into this, but she's an actress. Actresses can seem like they fit in anywhere. I'm mainly gonna talk just to her. It would be great if we fell in love. That would show them, if I came back from the drug clinic with Suzanne Vale as my girlfriend.

Jesus, that black guy! If he doesn't shut up I'm gonna put a pillow over his face at night. How can they let people like him in with people like me? There should be different clinics—one for the assholes and one for the people who just have drug problems but aren't assholes. Not that I have a drug problem, but I'm gonna be here for a month so I'd better do what they want me to do. I'll just tell them I think I'm a drug addict, 'cause it's the only way I'll ever get out of here. Hey, if it's good enough for Suzanne Vale, it's good enough for me.

She's got a great sense of humor, which you need in a place like this. I'm really stunned that people like her are addicts. When you hear that somebody famous overdosed, it always sounds like fun when *they* do it. It's just part of the big myth. It's like it happened in the movies when it happens to someone who makes movies. Like, maybe I had an overdose, but it wasn't the same kind she had. I'd like to think it was, though. I'd like to think I had an epic overdose. I wouldn't have minded ODing if I was Suzanne Vale.

Maybe I'll go sit in the park with her. But she's always talking to that black guy, or *listening* to him. God, I just want to run out of the room when he starts . . . That voice of his is like he swallowed weird helium, the kind that makes your voice deep and hollow. He just goes on and on and on. "Let me say this about that." "Let me say this about that." Jesus!

How can she go to those AA meetings? I can understand poor people going. They have nowhere to go and nothing to do, but . . . I don't know how anybody can *stand* each other here. I won't go to an AA meeting unless they let me sit next to Suzanne. I haven't really talked to her yet. I don't want to wreck it. I want to seem cool, I want this to build naturally. It's not like I'm gonna play hard to get, I don't want to play a lot of games with this, but celebrities don't like it when you run up and get in their face and come on to them. It's a turn-off.

I think she'd like me, though. She seems very friendly, and she wants everyone to like her, which could get to be a drag. If we got together, she'd have to stop all that, because it would be too hard on me. Not that I'm the jealous type, but it would be annoying. I'd have to tell her *I* would rather be the priority.

Maybe I was a little deluded about my drug intake. Okay, I accept it. I took too many drugs. But certainly they don't expect me to give up alcohol. I'll give up cocaine. That's not so difficult. I've given up cocaine before. I've done it a lot. I'll just do it again, I don't care. But what happens if I go to a party and they're toasting somebody with champagne? What if my brother gets married? Do they expect me to toast my brother with Perrier? No way! I mean, he's only fourteen, but still, they can't expect me to give up everything.

That woman who keeps tilting her head, Julie, said I was stuck looking at the differences between me and everybody else here, and that I should look for the similarities. Look at her, she's overeating. I don't want to do that. God, when will this be over? Do they expect me to give up wine? It's absurd. This group is absurd. That fat asshole Sid told me if there were no drugs, I would have been an alcoholic. That's absurd, and anyway, there are drugs. Shit, I'm next.

"Me? Yeah, I'm Alex. I don't really know what to say. Uh . . . I'm in here . . . Why am I in here? I'm in here because . . . Well, I took a lot of drugs one night in Brentwood and I had a problem . . . I had a bad reaction to some drugs. I was allergic . . . I never . . . I took some heroin and I had never taken heroin . . ."

God, Suzanne's gonna think I'm such a putz. She comes right out and says she's an addict. Maybe I should just say it. Maybe there's something manly in that.

". . . So I think, yes, you could say I have a drug problem. And alcohol. I drink alcohol, too, but I have to get more information to be really convinced that alcohol is a problem for me."

That sounded good. That sounded real good.

"I'm aware I can tend to overdo drugs. Have overdone drugs. And I certainly would like to learn as much as I can about how to curb that appetite. I'm glad to be here—well, I'm not glad to be here, but I'm here, and I'm gonna take advantage of the situation."

That sounded so cool. She was looking right at me. I think she likes me. I think she sees that I'm open, that I'm a man and yet I'm sensitive and aware of my own feelings. She has to respect the process I'm going through. I seemed a little scattered at first, maybe, but overall I was succinct and I seemed to have a grasp of . . . Let's face it, there's something romantic about a fucked-up guy. Not that I'm fucked up, but I'm in a fucked-up place.

I think it would be great publicity for this clinic if it got out that Suzanne Vale met this great television writer here. It would be good for her reputation to be known as somebody who's going out with a writer. It would give her more credibility.

She's so funny, and she has great eyes. Who is this asshole therapist Stan busting her for using her humor as a weapon? An "affably hostile weapon." We're here for drugs, not to have our personalities dismantled. They better not try it with me, or I'm gonna punch that guy out. They're just jealous because they have to be in this clinic all the time, and she'll probably leave and make a TV movie about it. Maybe I'll write it. Oooh, this whole thing could really pay off.

I wonder if they let you fuck in the clinic . . .

DAY EIGHTEEN

Sid graduated today. There was a little ceremony to see him off and launch him back into the now, like a little detoxed boat. It was actually sort of moving, with all the junkies sitting in a circle of chairs in the television room. A coin was passed around, and everybody held the coin and said something encouraging and wise (or at least tried to) for Sid to carry with him. I couldn't think of anything to say, so I sang "I've Gotta Be Me." Carol cried.

I rarely cry. I save my feelings up inside me like I have something more specific in mind for them. I'm waiting for the exact perfect situation and then *Boom!* I'll explode in a light show of feeling and emotion—a piñata stuffed with tender nuances and pent-up passions. Until then, though, no sobbing for Sid.

I'll miss him holding my feet, though. I don't miss whole people usually. I mainly miss the things they do:

The way they wear their hats.
The way they squeeze my feet,
The memory of all that,
No, no. . . .

I wonder if I'll ever be able to cry, and what it could possibly be that would set me off. The image of Heathcliff looking over the moors, holding Cathy's newly dead body? The memory of my father forgetting my twelfth birthday? The sweetness of Sid holding my feet, recalled one day in traffic?

The new guy Alex may be good-looking, but he also seems like kind of an asshole.

. . . "I'm an alcoholic." "I'm an alcoholic." Why does everybody have to humiliate themselves by talking about it? I'm also a Leo, why don't they talk about that? They should have us stress the good parts about ourselves instead of dragging up all this bile. Why not a positive, uplifting approach?

I'm gonna go over and talk to Suzanne. Maybe we could even have dinner together. I want to talk to her . . .

So who are all these people? That Wanda, she's pretty, but that guy Sam told me she tried to kill herself. I don't like suicides. I think it shows a real weakness, to asphyxiate yourself and then overdose in a hospital. How do they know all this stuff about each other? Is your chart just available for scrutiny at any hour of the night? We might as well put out newsletters. God, there's no privacy here . . .

There's one thing I didn't try that I bet works: hypnosis. I think that might be the key. And I could join a gym. I mean, I could go to the gym I already belong to. But I don't like to go 'cause it's all gay people. But maybe I'll get a friend and start going to the gym. And do hypnosis. There's lots of things you can do before you end up in meetings. I'm not gonna become one of those AA Moonies for the rest of my life.

Unless Suzanne goes. She seems open to this meeting thing. I'd go to meetings with her. Then it wouldn't be so bad if my friends found out. I could say, "Hey, I went with my girlfriend, Suzanne Vale."

I hope nobody tells Joan I'm here. She'd just say, "I knew it. I knew it all along." That bitch! I was never loaded as many times as she thought I was. I'm just naturally very hyper.

Her other boyfriend before me was a druggie, too. I don't mean . . . *He* was a druggie. I liked drugs, but he was a *druggie*. It's like she just goes out with people who take drugs so she can pick on them. Joan of Narc, patron saint of the addict. And every time I would do something good for myself, she'd make fun of me. Like when I bought the exercise bike and she called me "Mr. Health" and said I'd never use it.

I couldn't tell her *anything*. I remember when I read that they found out aluminum cans could be a cause of Alzheimer's, and when I tried to warn her she said, "Oh, please. You dump poisons into your system and you're gonna get on me about my diet soda?"

She could never stand to see me have a good time. She always looked like she smelled something funny when she was with me, with her head back and her shoulders as close to her neck as they could get, like I'd done something *really sick*. I took drugs, that's all. She should look after her own stuff. God, I'm relieved that's over. I can finally breathe. Aaaaahhh! I hope she doesn't find out I'm in here. That's all I need. I can hear her now: "I told you so. I knew it. Nyah nyah nyah."

That's why it would be good with Suzanne. She could never point the finger at me because she ended up in a place like this, too. Joan will feel so bad when she hears I'm going out with Suzanne. But I want this thing to start very slow. I don't want it to be really obvious. I don't think she has any idea at all that I'm watching her. I don't sit near her in group and I don't sit at her table for lunch. I'm keeping my distance, playing it cool. I think that's a very good tactic. She's probably used to people flinging themselves at her. I'll just keep off to myself and look a little sad and sensitive, and eventually she'll come to me.

Maybe this was all for the best. I have a better idea of my life now. I'm gonna have a relationship with Suzanne, and I'll get my career back on track and pay my parents back all the money I've borrowed over the past couple of years. That'll be good. Then my dad won't look at me with that disdain he thinks is so funny, and my mom will stop picking on me. Maybe I'll get a bigger apartment and . . .

I feel good! This is a good time to sit back and reflect, and get a grip on my life. I think I'm taking a really realistic view of it all—probably for the first time, to be brutally honest about it. Maybe I'll even get involved in politics, who knows? . . .

DAY NINETEEN

Another new guy checked in tonight. He actually checked himself in, but not before he stopped at the bar in the building next door for a couple of drinks. He was in excellent spirits when he got here, and he was wearing a very festive Hawaiian shirt. His name is Ted.

When he leaned down to sign the admission contract, a cocaine bottle fell out of his pocket. "Oops," he said, and giggled sheepishly as he retrieved the vial. "My lucky cocaine bottle. Look, the spoon was handmade. It's *bronze*." Lucille, my favorite nurse, took it out of his hand and said, "It's beautiful. I've never seen one like it." He started explaining the history of this coke spoon, and Lucille listened to him as if it was the most fascinating story about a coke spoon she'd ever heard. He was still describing the workmanship as she steered him into his room.

Carl watched all this with me. When they were out of earshot, he said, "Shoot, *any* coke spoon was my lucky coke spoon, as long as there was coke on it." I love Carl. He's like a disc jockey from hell, and you can never change the station. His impact on people is undeniable. Alex literally perspires when Carl is around.

I could swear Alex is deliberately not looking at me. He still hasn't said a word to me. Somehow I don't think I'm missing anything.

. . . Look at Suzanne. She acts like she's really getting into this shit, but it's obvious she's just as bored as I am. She'll go through this whole thing, and then she and I'll be in a bar in about two months. I can tell.

No one could be seriously cooperating with this situation. At least nobody smart, nobody decent. There's no way I could seriously feel like this was a good thing. And I've gone to these meetings now, so it's not just what they call "contempt prior to investigation." I've *been*. Greg was right. They're boring and you can barely breathe in there because everyone is smoking. Smoking and drinking coffee. Aren't those drugs, tobacco and caffeine? And they're *really* not good for you.

If Julie says that thing about looking for the difference instead of the similarities one more time I'm going to scream. I'm not looking for the differences. I don't have to look. They're obvious. I'm very different from these people. My situation is *completely* different.

I mean, *Carl!* That story he told in the park about how he wound up in prison—what a *moron*. Even Suzanne seemed repelled by him. God, and this fucking Manson guy, he never talks to anybody. He's always mooning around. He looks like he's got glue in his eyes. Jesus, *he knows Manson*. What am I doing in here? It's safer out there taking drugs than being in here not taking drugs with these people.

If that guy Sam comes up to me and puts his arm around me and calls me "Buddy" one more time, I'm gonna have to complain. But to who? Julie? She wears so much perfume it makes me sneeze. My nose is still irritated from all the pollen and everything, I have an allergy condition. I can't be around people who use too much perfume. What a nightmare!

Carol's okay, though. I think she likes me, which couldn't hurt because her husband is a big agent or something. I hope she doesn't get a crush on me. I don't want to have to go to her husband on business and wind up explaining why I'm fucking his wife. That could be rough. She's okay, though. Redhead, but not a real redhead. I remember when I came in last week seeing her and thinking, "Not a real redhead."

It wouldn't be bad to do a little business in here. It *is* a part of life. I haven't been writing lately, but I'm gonna have to start working on something. If I'm gonna be with Suzanne, I'm gonna have to be able to keep up with her financially. I don't expect her to support me.

Shit, there's Sam. Don't come near me, man, don't even *think* about coming over here. That's right, go look out the window. A *scalper*, for Christ's sake. What am I supposed to have in common with him? He didn't even scalp tickets for concerts I would have gone to.

I wish I played an instrument . . .

DAY TWENTY

Carl told the greatest story in the park today about how he ended up in prison. He had gone to rob a movie theater, and he went to the office and pulled a gun on the secretary, who said that only the manager knew the combination to the safe, and he'd gone out for a while. Carl told her he'd wait. Pretty soon an usher came in to see the secretary, and Carl made him wait with them. Soon after, two kids from the concession stand came looking for the usher, whose mother was waiting outside to drive him home, and they became part of the group. Then the mother came up. Before long there were about fifteen people staring at Carl and his gun in this tiny office. Carl said it got pretty awkward and very hot.

When the manager finally did come, the alarm went off. The police came, but Carl sneaked out and started to drive off. The police shot at him, a bullet went straight through his Afro, and Carl shit in his pants. He had to sit in the back of the police car while they wrote up the report, with his pants full of shit. I said, "You're kidding," and Carl said, "Shoot, you have a bullet go through your hair, you'd crap yourself, too, I don't care *who* you are." Carl is a wonder.

I talked to my agent today. He thinks maybe I should do a television series. I would like to do something where I have to work all the time. Keep my mind off my mind, as it were. Get up real early in the morning, act like someone else all day, and fall asleep at night. A perfect job for me.

The fix that doesn't.

. . . So I go in to watch *The Outer Limits* and maybe see some *Star Trek* before bullshit group therapy—I know we're supposed to be writing our drug inventory, but they can just hold their breath before I'm gonna write *that*—and all the guys are sitting watching basketball. I *loathe* basketball. And they're all doing that macho yelling shit. I don't care if it *is* the play-offs. We *always* watch *The Outer Limits*. As far as this place can go, it's a tradition. I've gotta get out of here.

Suzanne is in Carol's room. Why are they always together? I'm starting to think Suzanne may be a little bit of a snob. What does she think, that she's too great to talk to me? I mean, all right, sure, maybe I haven't talked to her, but I've seen her talking to a lot of other people on the unit. I don't think I'm so unavailable and unappealing.

Julie sort of cornered me when she said I was isolating myself from the group. I'm not isolating myself, *they're* all ignoring *me*.

I'm not saying it's deliberate, but it's not going completely unnoticed, let's put it that way.

What do I care? I have plenty of friends out of here. But why won't she just come up and talk to me? I heard her on the phone yesterday talking to her agent. I wish I could make a business call so she could overhear how fabulous I was and how together my life was, and then she'd come up and ask me something about business.

That's it! That's what I'll do. I'll call . . . No, I won't call anybody. I'll *pretend* I'm calling my literary agent. Suzanne's in Carol's room right next to the phone so she'll be sure to overhear this. All right, I'm gonna do it. It's a great idea. So what do I say? I'll say I've got the idea for this drug rehab thing and I'm . . . Wait, I don't want to give away the whole plot. I'll just casually say I have a great idea. Be very vague. Don't give anything specific away. All right. All right, here I go.

Oh, fucking Christ! Carl is on the phone. This is unbelievable, this is truly, truly unbelievable. Jesus, I hate this place. He's probably talking to his dumb wife. He's always fighting with his wife. Why do *I* have to know all this stuff about *his* life?

"Hey, man, you gonna be long? I gotta make a business call."

That sounded real cool. I bet she overheard that.

"Thanks, man."

I'll just dial a fake number and I'll say . . . What name should I use? Jeff. Jeff . . . Markoff.

"Jeff Markoff, please. Alex Daniels. I'll hold . . . Jeff? Hi, it's Alex. Sorry I took so long to get back to you."

That sounded so great. Oh, here she comes, she's coming out of the room. Okay, okay, casually turn your back to her and throw your voice over your shoulder.

"So, Jeff, about the idea we pitched to Fox. I think I'm ready to do a first draft and . . . Oh, great, great. The deal went through? Great. Yeah, great. You tried to call here? Yeah, it's always busy. There's always, you know, people on the phone.

Well, I'll be waiting for you to send over the contracts. Oh, sure, well, I'll sign them when I get out of here, then. That'll be cool. All right, and how's everything? Great. I'll talk to you soon then. Bye-bye."

That's perfect, that was *perfect*. She looked at me. I know she's impressed. Well, maybe I'll go in and watch some basketball. I feel a little calmer now, I feel like I made a little headway here. Certainly she knows a little more about who I am, and that I'm not just some asshole in a drug unit. I've got a job. A deal, I've got a deal. I've got a job, a deal, and a future.

Is that her laughing? She's always laughing, always having a good time. Well, soon she'll be having a good time with me . . .

DAY TWENTY-ONE

Alex did the most amazing thing today. Carol and I were coming out of her room and he was on the pay phone talking real loud and weird, like a white version of Carl. He was saying something about Fox and first drafts, and as I passed him I could hear a busy signal through the receiver. I barely made it around the corner before I burst out laughing. He must have been trying to impress us. Carol thinks he has a crush on me. He probably does. He's exactly the type I *would* attract.

Carol and I have started exercising every afternoon. She tells me how perfect her husband is, how adorable he is and how happy they are. Finally I said, "But Carol, there must be *something* wrong with him." She sort of shrugged and said, "He works sixteen hours a day. I only see him late at night, and on Sundays he stays home with me and reads scripts."

Oh.

. . . This is an absurd film. *Hooked on a Line*, what a title. Jesus, that dancer being snorted up into someone's nose under

50

the opening credits, and these people in half-shadow talking about their cocaine problems—I could write better shit than this. Maybe I will when I get out of here. I'll write a really good drug movie. I'll help a lot of people. I'll become *known* for helping people.

Christ! Who cares about this girl with her family and their floral sofa? That sofa is enough to drive you crazy, watching people sitting on that floral sofa talking about cocaine. *I* never had these problems with cocaine. *I* never ran into people with guns. Well, that one time in Vegas there *were* some guns in the room, but nobody was chasing me with them.

I've never met *anybody* like the people in this movie. These are all older people, except for that really young girl. How am I supposed to relate to any of this? I mean, there's nobody my age. Maybe these are real people, but they're horrible real people. At least get interesting real people if you're gonna use real people.

Take me, for example. I have a better story than this. Not that I have an addiction problem like them, but some of my drug experiences are interesting enough to tell in front of groups. Sometimes I think maybe I should lead kind of a splinter group of Cocaine Anonymous. Make my own cocaine meetings, with really hip people at them. Where the hip people just naturally come, like Suzanne and maybe Carol and her husband.

Suzanne keeps talking to Carol. I should be sitting next to her. We could talk about how much we hate this film, and how much better ours is going to be. I wonder how much money there is in this . . .

DAY TWENTY-TWO

Sam and Julie got into a big fight tonight and Sam stormed off the unit. Julie said something typically condescending to Sam, whose face got all red and puffed up, like he was blowing up an invisible

51

balloon. The gist of what he said was, "How dare you talk to me like that? Don't you know who I am?" And Julie said, "Who are you? You're in a drug clinic. Who could you be?"

Sam charged back to his room and smashed some pictures against the wall. He got his wallet and a sack of Chee-tos and left the hospital. Julie called Sam's wife Amy and told her to expect him. I wonder if he'll get loaded.

Carol, Ted, and I watched *The Incredible Mr. Limpet* on the four-thirty movie. We all agreed that Knotts's work was superb, and were perplexed at the absence of a sequel. We decided to inquire about the availability of the rights when we get out of here.

Maybe I should have a baby.

What if I got into this? I doubt I would, but I know I'd be a better therapist than Stan. He's so unpleasant to everyone. I think he has something in particular against me, which isn't fair. They should get someone unbiased.

They should have a *real* doctor or something. I would like to be treated by someone in the medical profession rather than by these amateurs whose only qualification is that they took a lot of drugs eight years ago, and now they haven't taken drugs for eight years. I think they should be more qualified than that.

They keep telling me this is a serious situation. Well, if it's so fucking serious, there should be *doctors* here. We should be on medicine. I don't think I'm getting properly attended to. I don't know that any of this is that good for me. I keep hearing about all these other drugs I didn't even know about. It's like putting thieves in with murderers—they learn how to be murderers. Well, I'm learning how to be a drug addict. What if I wanted to walk right out of here and go find some lodes like that guy Sid took? I'd never even *heard* of lodes before I got here.

Fuck *them*! Telling me I'll never stay sober, I can't beat the odds. I'll show them! I'll do it. I'll do it without them. I can't do it without going to meetings? *Fuck them.* I'd rather go to a doctor than be judged by people who took a lot of dope. I mean, what is that? *What is that?* I have no intention of sitting in a room with a bunch of alcoholic personality types drinking caffeine and smoking cigarettes. That's not how I envision my life.

I know Stan has something personal against me. I think he's keeping Suzanne away from me. I think they've said something to her about me. Fucking *Stan.* And Julie, with that string of pearls. I just want to rip it off her neck and watch them go bouncing down the hallway. She wears enough perfume to knock out a horse. I just don't see the point of talking to these people, and watching these stupid films with the floral couch and these understanding parents and their whacked-out daughter and the group therapy . . .

Group therapy with my parents. I would sooner *die.* I would sooner swallow a handful of lodes and die than sit in a room with my father and mother and talk about my "drug problem." I just want them to keep paying the bills and stay away from me. Well, not paying the bills, but paying the bills until I can get back on my feet again. I think I'm owed that. They fucked up somewhere along the line and I ended up taking chemicals.

If they actually expect to get Stan and my parents and me in the same room, they've got another think coming . . .

DAY TWENTY-THREE

My inner world seems largely to consist of three rotating emotions: embarrassment, rage, and tension. Sometimes I feel excited, but I think that's just positive tension. Stan gave us a list of emotions today and told us to circle the ones we've felt recently. I lied and circled seven.

Mark refused to come to group today—he stayed in his room and listened to the Doors. He had his Walkman on so loud at breakfast we could hear the music through his nose.

Marvin announced at lunch that he thought he might be an alcoholic. We all sang "God Bless America."

Amy brought Sam back today. He seemed a little chagrined. I was embarrassed for him, and subsequently tense. Two out of a possible three.

. . . This is what I get for coming to her rescue. *This* is my reward. Everyone goes off to a shopping mall and I wind up stuck here alone in this stupid room. I hate Stan, I *hate* him.

I can't believe Suzanne went without me. How could she? I *defended* her. He was attacking her and I stuck up for her, and I wound up getting nailed to the wall. That's my thanks. Fucking Stan. Doesn't he know who I am? Doesn't he know who I'll be? I've got to get out of here.

I'll just leave, right? What are they gonna do? Call the police? I'm not breaking the law. I'll just leave. I'm not . . . What am I doing here anyway? I hate it here. I hate these nurses with their little name tags, and they won't give you any aspirin. They'll give you Tylenol. I've got a flaming headache. I've got a flaming headache and all I get is two little Tylenol. Well, that's *not enough.*

I'm just gonna check out of here and then she'll feel bad. She'll be sorry she didn't talk to me, even after I took her side. Stan was attacking her for being too nice or something—what is his point? I don't understand his point. *He* should have a problem like being too nice. It's like he thinks he's God, but God never took drugs.

How dare he come after me? He thinks I'm "nervous," does he? Well, I'm not nervous! I'm tense. I'm not nervous. "Nervous" is a ditsy kind of a . . . I'm . . . Sometimes I'm tense. I think to live in this world, everybody's tense. I'm not the only tense person. *Stan* is tense, with his jaw clenched so tight it twitches.

Fuck it, I don't care. I don't care about any of them. I don't care about how Wanda's father doesn't like her. I don't care about Carl and his scrawny legs. I don't care about Sam and his homemade tattoos. And Mark. Mark! Manson's buddy. These are my peers?

And this fancy fuckin' jargon. It's like being in est. Well, I didn't want to do est and I don't want to do this. I don't want to sit around and swap war stories about drugs and alcohol. I'm sick of it. It's *bullshit.*

And Suzanne! At least Carol came in and said, "Come to the mall with us." But Suzanne, who I defended and got slapped down for my trouble, did she come in? No. I might have gone if *she'd* asked me.

I'm sick of this place. I don't like the blanket on my bed, I don't like the noise of the toilet, I don't like the homo pubic hair in the Jacuzzi, I don't like Ping-Pong. I don't like the food *at all.* I can't stand the cute little desserts, those squares of pink and white cake, and I *loathe* Jell-O. And I don't want to watch *The Outer Limits* anymore. I've seen all the episodes. I have them on tape at home. I can watch *The Twilight Zone* and *The Outer Limits* anytime I want. I don't have to sit and do it in a drug clinic, and I don't have to have them ramming themselves up my nose about how nervous I am. I'm not nervous, I'm *pissed.* It's a waste of time to sit in this place. I'll just sneak past the nurses' station and . . .

Fuck it! Then Suzanne will think I'm a wimp and I can't take it. Well, I can. I can take anything they can dish out. I'll stay. But I'm not gonna like it. I have my own opinions, I have my own tastes, and they can't take that away from me. They're not gonna turn me out like something on a conveyor belt.

God, I want out of here . . .

DAY TWENTY-FOUR

Alex walked out of group today. Stan had been on my back about my "wonderful girl act." He said I didn't just want people to like me, but that I wanted to make an impact on their lives they'd never quite recover from. It wasn't a startling revelation. I've been in therapy since I was nineteen, so Stan is not likely to be giving me stunning insights into my being that I've never considered before, but he was trying. He said something about how I probably hoped people would mistake my nervousness for vivacity. I was about to make some glib comeback when Alex suddenly leapt to my defense.

Stan slapped him down by saying, "Oh, and I guess you're hoping people will confuse your nervousness with aloof cool." Stan can really be a bastard. An addict made good—now he's a marathon runner. The junkie of the seventies is the athlete of the eighties. Anyway, Alex bolted to his room and refused to come out for our excursion to the mall. Carol tried to persuade him, but Stan told us to leave him alone. I feel bad for him.

Shopping was hilarious. We went as a group of ten and crawled all over the mall like a giant junkie spider. We bought popcorn, cotton candy, cola, and chocolate. Stan said I eat just like a heroin addict (but I break just like a little girl). It was hard to keep the group together. Sam wanted sunglasses, Wanda needed styling gel, and Carl ate three hot dogs. I'm so glad I overdosed now. If I hadn't, I never would have been in a rehab and shopped with junkies.

I wish Alex had come shopping instead of hiding in his room. I've never really talked to him, and he's been here for over a week. He just seems so tense. He doesn't seem to get that this is a serious thing. I do think I'm lucky in a way. I had a frightening thing happen: I had my stomach pumped. It was a fairly graphic illustration that my way wasn't working. If I had to have my stomach pumped the last time I took drugs, why should I think the next time I could take a normal amount? And just what is a "normal amount" of Percodan? Alex probably still thinks he can take normal amounts of cocaine. There but for the grace of overdose go I.

• • •

"No, we *don't* need to talk about what happened yesterday! I've talked about as much as I'm gonna talk in this place. Yeah, I know my parents are coming in. Oh, you would? You'd like the four of us to sit down? You'd like that? Good, the three of you sit down and talk, 'cause I've fuckin' had it. I've *had it*! I've sat in rooms with my parents and I've sat in rooms with you, and I didn't like either one and I don't think I'd like both. I'm fucking *out of here*! I'm *gone*, so you can kiss my ass good-bye. I don't need this clinic, and I certainly don't need some asshole ex-junkie like *you*.

"Oh, really? I don't get it? I get it, mister. From the day I came in here I got it. I got that you were an asshole and this place sucks. I don't need this place to not do drugs. No, I don't. What happened to me was purely accidental, and you can tell me from here to tomorrow all this shit about me being an addict—you, with your shooting up. Carl told me you even murdered somebody once to get drugs, and *you're gonna tell me*? I grew up in this nice part of town and you, Mister Murderer Junkie, are gonna tell me how to stop doing drugs? I have nothing in common with you. Sayonara, you asshole, I'm outta here."

Ha! I told that fuckin' asshole, that murdering junkie son-of-a-bitch. I told him, I fuckin' *told* him. Christ, I'm so sick of the sterilized smell of this place.

"Hold the elevator!"

I bet they think I'm just gonna walk out of here and do drugs. Well, they've got another think coming. I'm not the cliché everyone else in here is. I'm differen. I know they told me everybody here thinks they're different, but what about the poor son-of-a-bitch like me who *really is* different? Why do I have to pay for everyone who came through the door and thought they were different and weren't?

Aaaahhh! I'm out. Aaaaaaahhhhh! What a relief to be outside and not in a fucking group going to the park to listen to Carl go on and on about that stupid wife of his. I don't want to know about anyone else's personal life. I don't even want a personal life of my own. I'm so sick of personal lives.

Whew! I'm never gonna end up in one of those places again. It's like I got out of jail. I could *sing* with relief. So, I guess I'll go home. Maybe I'll read. I'll have an old-fashioned Norman Rockwell kind of Sunday. I think I can really appreciate this kind of normalcy I'm gonna go for now after that prison camp experience in the clinic. That's behind me now. At least I got a little of that anger off my chest. How was that for dealing with my emotions, Stan?

Okay, how do I get home? How do I get home? I've got a little cash, I'll take a cab. First I'll stop in the Blum's and have a little cake and celebrate. I'll eat a little something, maybe have a couple of beers and go home . . .

Nah, I'm not gonna have any beers. Fuck it. Sure, and what if that asshead comes looking for me and finds me with some beers. "I told you so, Alex." Well, fuck you, you know? Suck this, you know what I'm saying? I'm no alcoholic. I'll have some cake, maybe a little chocolate ice cream and French fries, and I'll get home. And no red meat. I don't want to fuck up my arteries . . .

Aaahhh! My own apartment. Goddamn, it's good to be back. My car is back in the garage . . . I wonder how they got it back. Who cares, it's here. Let's see, did I get any messages? Two? Only two messages in *ten days*? Okay, who called? Jesus Christ! Joan. My mother must have told her. "I'm so glad you went into a clinic." God, that I-knew-it-all-along voice. Gloat, why don't you? Who else called? Shit. My mom. So they know I left the clinic. Great, now I'm not safe in my own house. This is a nightmare.

Wait, what's this? A lude. No. No. If I take this, they'll say it proves their point. Well, I'm not one of their traditional drug-gies. Here's the lude, I'm throwing it in the toilet, it's gone. Good-bye lude, hello no drugs.

I guess I'd better go out in case my parents show up. I'll go for a drive. I'll just go out and drive around and enjoy life like I've never enjoyed it before. I'm straight, and I threw away a lude. That proves I'm the master over this. I'm not what they thought I was. Hey, here's that Valium. Down the toilet with this, too. I'll show them. I'll throw all my drugs away. There goes the Valium, and there goes that little piece of hash. All right. *All right.* No real drug addict could throw away their drugs. They'd laugh out of the other side of their clinic if they could see me now. All right! No junkie I.

So it's drive time. Maybe I'll go to a movie by myself. That's kind of a mature thing to do. I've seen people do that. It looks desperate, but it's probably not desperate at all. I don't want to see any of my friends yet. I don't want to talk about this. I'm gonna have to re-evaluate a couple of things. I think I'm really getting a sense of what my life is about now. I'm feeling real strong after throwing away all those drugs. I'll show them . . .

Wait. Wait just one minute . . . My secret stash. My secret just-in-case-gram-hidden-in-the-holed-out-dictionary stash. I'll just throw . . . No. *No,* I *won't* throw away my coke. I'll leave it there and never do it. That'll show them. Yep, there it is. If I was really a junkie I wouldn't be staring at it right now, I'd be snorting it.

Well, I'm not. I can just imagine them laughing and saying, "Yeah, yeah, what a drug addict." Well, I'm *not.* I threw away all my Valium and my hash and that lude, and now I'm just looking at this cocaine. I'm not doing it. So there.

All right, all right, let's go for that drive. Should I take the gram with me, as kind of a willpower test? Nah, I'll just leave it right here, as a symbol of the new me.

A drug addict, am I? I'll show them . . .

DAY TWENTY-FIVE

Alex left today. He and Stan had a fight and he marched out. I was in my room with my mother, and suddenly, from down the hall and behind his closed door, we heard him yelling, "Fuck you!" and so forth. I guess it's not a tremendous shock. He was never totally here to begin with. It's as though he came to leave. But what a departure. It was almost operatic in its melodrama.

It's always frightening when someone bolts back into the blue. I guess he hasn't been scared enough. Just because everyone else thinks he's hit bottom doesn't necessarily mean he has.

Mom brought me some peanut butter cookies and a biography of Judy Garland. She told me she thought my problem was that I was too impatient, my fuse was too short, that I was only interested in instant gratification. I said, "Instant gratification takes too long."

The glib martyr.

... What a *stupid* film. *Doctor's Orders*. What could I have been thinking? There's a lesson here—just 'cause a movie is playing near your house doesn't mean it's not a piece of shit. Jesus, *I* could act better than that. I could certainly write a better script. I should write a script. I'm gonna start writing my script.

I wish I could do speed, though. I always wrote better on speed, the ideas would just *come*. I wrote my first pilot in two days on Dexedrine. I bet I could take that again. I don't see how they could say I'm a drug addict if it's for work ...

So, my script. My script about my experiences in the rehab and my insights into that whole world. Maybe it could be the story of somebody who is accidentally put into a clinic, like *Cuckoo's Nest*. The guy is just having an allergic reaction to some drugs, but they put him in a clinic with all these addicts and one's a celebrity, and they fall in love and get married. Maybe I could take a couple of Didrex and write it. I think that would be okay, if I only take speed to write. I think that's fair, because I've always had a lot of trouble writing without a drug. I don't even think speed is technically a drug. You can get it from doctors, and if doctors prescribe it, it's a medication. And I need a medication to write.

God, it's so good to be back in regular life and just be driving onto my street in Laurel Canyon. It's a nice night, I had a mature evening. I went to the movies in my car. I'm in *my* life. *Everything* is going my way. It's all uphill from here.

Oh, *fuck*. My fucking parents! I can't even have a normal night at the movies by myself. Almost thirty years old. I should be able to come out of a clinic and go back into my life unattended. I think I'm quite capable of doing that. I shouldn't have to come home from a movie and find *my parents' car in my driveway*. I can never grow up if they keep treating me like a baby. Well, if they think I'm a baby, I'll act like a baby. They can have it their way. If they think I'm such a junkie, I'll *be* a fucking junkie. I'll go out and get loaded. Fine. If they want to worry, I'll give them something to good and well worry about. Fuck 'em. I'm going to Brentwood. I'll fucking go back to Brentwood . . .

I would never have done this if they hadn't come over. I would *never* have done this if they hadn't driven their Cadillac up to my house, where I'm trying to relax and enjoy the rest of my youth, the twenty more minutes I have left. I go to the movies, I'm handling it beautifully until . . . Well, fuck them. I'm in Brentwood and it's their fault. They pushed me to this. If they would just let me grow up, maybe I *would*. Forget it, I'm gonna do what *I* want to do now, or what they think I want to do. I'll just do what they *think* I want to do now. I hope that guy's here. He's always here. They think I'm such a loser junkie, I'll *be* a—

"Hi, man. No, I'm fine. No, I know you had to call my parents. Yeah, yeah, it's cool. I was in a hospital, they detoxed me. I'm fine. I left today, I'm a little upset. They just . . . You know parents, they don't get off your back. They can't just blend into another relationship where they leave you alone. I can't even go back to my house now. They're there, probably going through my stuff.

"Do you have parents? They bug you? Yeah. You're lucky you don't have my parents. If you had my parents, they'd be *here* now. So, what kind of blow are we talking about? You know, I haven't done any in a while, I've been clean and . . . Fuck it, you know? Everybody thinks I'm a junkie. Hey, I'll bet you have this same problem. Yeah? Yeah, they think you have a problem 'cause you do drugs. Not everybody who does drugs has problems. There are a lot of people giving those of us who just do drugs socially a bad name, but I think . . .

"Aaah, it doesn't matter what I think. Let's get some blow. I stopped at my cash machine, I've got five hundred dollars here, and I've got this Rolex. Not that I need more than a couple of grams but, you know, I was thinking . . . I got this great idea. I can trust you, right? I've got this great idea for a movie. It's about a rehab. A guy who's . . . Maybe I could cut you in on a piece of the action as kind of a technical advisor if I . . . Well, anyway, I want to research this idea. I'm just talking off the top of my head now, but what I was thinking is I'll just go and write this thing. I'd just like to knock it off and get it done, and I want to research the part and maybe see what it really feels like to get strung out on cocaine.

"I don't know, maybe half an ounce? I'm good for the money, you know that. I've been coming here for years, right? I mean, we're fuckin' mates in this thing. Or maybe you could take my watch. It's worth a couple of thou, you could easily get eight or nine hundred for it. My parents gave it to me. Obviously you can take the inscription off. I don't know how they do that, but I think they just melt it off or something. What do you think? Great.

"Maybe you can act in the thing. Can you act at all? You look like you could. I mean, in all the time I've known you, I've always thought you had an interesting face. You could play the dealer, maybe. The guy who sells him the cocaine. Well, I don't know. I'm just thinking out loud again. You know, the creative process . . .

"I need some blow. Let's do some now, let's just do a hit so I can test the stuff. Yeah, I know half an ounce sounds like a lot but I'm not gonna do it all at once. I've got to write a script, and when you write a script that means you have to *rewrite* it . . .

"(*sniff*) Ooooh! (*sniff*) Oh, man! *Now* they're playing my song. Oooh, you *know* what I like! Oh, man. Whew. Wow, it's been a while, you know? And I have had a *stressful* couple of weeks. You can't imagine. I mean, you guys give me a little smack, you know, to take the edges off, and I end up in this fucking clinic with Suzanne Vale. Can you imagine? Yeah, I think she had quite a drug problem, which is amazing for someone that cute. And she's little, too, which is probably why it caught up with her so fast. Yeah, there were a lot of interesting people there. Actually there were *not* a lot of interesting people, *she* was the only interesting one, but it was an interesting experience. I think it would make a great TV movie about how this writer guy . . . Give me another hit.

"(*sniff*) Aahhh. Oooh. (*sniff*) Oh, I'll tell you, this reminds me of so many nights . . . God, I'm getting such déjà vu, I feel like . . . I was gonna say I feel like I've done this before. I mean, *obviously* I've done this before, but it just reminds me of something so great, you know?

"Fuck her? No, you don't fuck in the rehab, but I'm gonna be seeing her again. She'll probably star in this thing. So, can I have the blow? Oh, right. Here's the cash, and here's my watch. I really appreciate this. I'm sorry I was so nuts when I came in. Can I have one more . . . Here, let *me* give *you* a hit. I'm feeling very generous tonight.

"(*sniff*) Ooh, this is good. This is better than what you usually get, isn't it? (*sniff*) Oh, ooohhh! Maybe I could have a beer to take with me for the drive? I'm gonna drive out to the desert, unwind there, and just get away from everybody and write this thing. Thanks, man. Okay, great."

This beer is really good. A little beer, a little drive, I'm feeling fine. Glad to be away from that guy, though. He gives me the creeps. Where's my knife? There we go, *there* we go.

"(*sniff*) Ahh. (*sniff*) Aaahh."

What the hell, one more.

"(*sniff*) Mmmmhh! (*sniff*) Ahh! (*sniff*) (*sniff*)"

I'm glad no one can see me. They'd think I was quite the pig. Okay, the idea's forming in my mind. There's this guy who doesn't normally take that much drugs, and he's spending the evening with some friends from school or something and he gets in this really good mood and they tell him to try some Ecstasy and he does and he gets in this *great* mood and they talk him into trying heroin and he ends up in a rehab where he does not belong. But when he gets there he meets all these incredible people, like Carl—he'd make a good character for a movie. He was a bad one for real life, but a lot of those people I hated in the clinic were great movie characters. Oooh, *this* is the thing to write with. Hell, a lot of people write with drugs. I heard Lewis Carroll wrote all of *Through the Looking Glass* on mushrooms, and Edgar Allan Poe was a laudanum freak. Freud, Sherlock Holmes . . . It's so good to be out of the hospital, out of the movies, just *out*. I'm *out*.

"(*sniff*) (*sniff*)"

My ear squeaked. I wonder if . . . There's that drip in the back of my throat. Great . . . I'm feeling real edgy, though, I don't think it's the blow, this is good blow, but I don't want to drive anymore. I feel cooped up in this car. I should . . . I know. Why go to the desert? Fuck it. I'll check into the Ramada Inn. They probably have some writing paper and a pen, and I'll start to outline this idea. Ramada Inn. I pass this place a lot, and I've always wondered . . . Let me just do a couple of hits to get me to the room.

"(sniff) (sniff) (sniff) (sniff) Ooooww!"

Shit, I've gotta chop this when I get upstairs, it's really chunky.

"(sniff)"

Okay, I think I'm cool. All right. Go in . . .

"Yeah, uh, hi. I'd like a room for two or three nights. No, I . . . No luggage, just this . . . Some groceries. Yeah, I eat special foods."

None of your fuckin' business, man.

"Is there a pool here? Oh, great. Great."

That'll be nice, I'll get some color. This is perfect, this is perfect. I'll do some writing, I'll do some swimming, I'll lose some weight . . . I'm sweating. God, it's hot in this lobby.

"No, I don't need the bellboy. Just . . . What floor? Eight? Great."

Jesus, they do look at you weird if you don't have luggage. But I *do* have luggage. I have my beautiful blushing white bride here. Oooh, my hand is shaking, I wonder what that . . . I must be starved. I'm not hungry, but . . . I'll order something from room service when I get upstairs. *Christ*, where's the fucking elevator? Jesus . . .

"No, I'm fine. Here, let me sign for this. Let's see, six Long Island iced teas, two Smirnoffs, hamburger, French fries, and cake. Yeah, great. Thanks. No, don't come back. I'll put the tray in the hall. No, I'm fine, I'm fine, I'm just . . . I have a little flu. Thanks."

Who did that guy think he was, prying into my life? Get him *off* of me. Yeccch, look at that burger, it's *alive*. And that soggy bun, those greasy fries. This is an American hotel, you'd think they'd at least be able to . . .

I'm getting very jumpy. Very, very jumpy. This food made me very tense. I should write. I should chop a couple of lines and then really get down to work. Why can't there be a dimmer in this room? I feel like I'm in the dentist's office. Let me have some of this drink . . . That's what I needed. Obviously I needed to have a little drink. And now a nice fat line, and then down to work.

"(*sniff*) *Ouch!* (*sniff*) Owww!"

Fucking fuck! There's *cut* in this, I know it! I'll put some under my tongue. I wish someone was here to blow it into the back of my throat, but then I'd have to talk to them. Okay, where's that paper? Okay, here we go.

I wonder if they have . . . They do, they have cable. Let's just see what's on MTV. It's that blond bimbo so it must be pretty late. What time . . . Oh, right, I gave him my watch . . .

So, what's my idea? What's my idea? Let me just do one more line . . .

"(*sniff*) Oowwww! (*sniff*) Ooohh!"

I wonder if they have a pharmacy open. I could use some Vaseline for my right nostril . . . All right, all right. So, a guy has an allergic reaction to drugs, but they think he overdosed so they put him in a clinic. Such a great concept. I mean, it's practically *written*. Whew, we're rolling now.

"(*sniff*) (*sniff*)"

Oooh, my heart is racing . . . One of those vodkas. Okay, we're totally rolling now. The guy feels haunted by his parents, like in *Frances*, his parents are . . . Why would they put him in the clinic against his . . . They're crazy. *They're* drug addicts. No, they're not drug addicts, but they don't want to take care of him anymore. He's old, though . . . Have another hit.

"(*sniff*) (*sniff*) Aaah."

I wish I had some cigarettes. I don't smoke, though. So, the parents put him in because they're drug addicts. No, because . . . An inheritance. An inheritance is always good. But they're his parents, wouldn't *they* leave him his inheritance? No, because he was his grandfather's favorite grandson and he was left all the money, but the parents get to execute his estate if he's somehow proven to be disabled. Perfect! That's totally perfect! So, he's an heir to a fortune. The muse is upon me.

"(sniff) (sniff)"

Oooh, I think I'm gonna be sick. That hamburger. Get it out of here, put it in the hallway . . . That's better. Okay, he's in the clinic and he meets this actress—maybe he's a musician or a songwriter—and she falls in love with him and he helps nurse her back to health. Then they escape the clinic together, and there's this whole chase sequence where people like Stan—*lots* of people like Stan—come after them and try and keep her loaded. Why? Why would they try and keep her loaded?

"(sniff) (sniff)"

So that she'll do commercials about the clinic, and write articles about drug addiction and make them famous. I think I'm on to something . . . I gotta take off my clothes. Clothes are sticking to me . . . I . . . Really, I think this is great. How can they say drugs are bad? . . .

What if they don't like it? I feel so frightened all of a sudden. What if it's *not* a good idea? What if Suzanne *won't* be in it? Oooh, I don't feel good. Take a drink . . . Ice is melting . . . I wonder why they call this Long Island iced tea. Maybe I should call this movie *Long Island Iced Tea*.

"(sniff) (sniff)"

What's on MTV? I hate this song, I *hate* this song. Look at this band. Fucking look at this band. I'm not good-looking, am I? I never was good-looking. No wonder my parents don't like me. Maybe they do like me. Where are my parents? They're probably at my house rifling my drawers looking for the cocaine. Well, I'm not a drug addict. I've checked into a hotel and I'm working. What time is it? I don't want to know. I'll just call . . .

"Operator. What time is it? Thanks."

Fuck, it's 4:30. Maybe I should sleep. If I slept a little bit I could get up tomorrow afternoon and get back to work, really flesh this whole thing out. Maybe even call Barry Diller. Oh, man. All right, I'm lying down. I'm not wearing anything. I'm feeling good. I've got a great script idea, my first one in a while . . . Try to sleep. Just empty your mind. Fucking AM radio in there. Shut up! Shut my brain down. Just relax and go to sleep, wake up fresh.

Oooh, my heart's going so fast. I can't even keep my eyes closed. I better drink something. Shit, only one vodka left. God, I'm really sweating. I smell so bad. I shouldn't have done so much cocaine so fast. Maybe I should just stop, not do any for a while. I'll just do a couple more lines and then not do any for a while.

"(*sniff*) Ooowww!"

What am I doing? This is fucking stupid. I've got to be able to sleep. No more cocaine. Please, God, let me go to sleep or I'll never be able to write. I'll never be able to do anything. I'm exhausted. My eyes burn. I'll just lie here until it wears off a little bit, and then I'll be able to get some shut-eye. Christ, it's getting light out . . .

What is that noise? What is that? It can't be the air conditioner, it's boiling in here. Fuck it, I'll just do another line. I might as well stay up all night. Hell, I used to do it when I was young. "Hey, man, let's pull an all-nighter." It can't kill you. What am I getting so worked up about?

I should make myself eat something, absorb some of the alcohol. I wonder if that hamburger is still out in the hall . . . Here it is. All right, all right, just close your tastebuds and eat the hamburger. I should take a little blow to numb me to the taste.

"(*sniff*) (*sniff*) Aaah, oh yeah."

All right, so it's morning. I'll watch the sunrise. Like John Denver or something. Ooow, it's too bright. Never mind. I'll turn the air conditioning up . . .

All right, all right. I shouldn't beat myself up about this. So I did some blow. Anybody could . . . I think it's good research for the script. Certainly there should be a character who does a lot of blow at some point. Maybe the dealer . . .

Okay, so I'm up. So what do I do? I'll take a bath. I'll take a bath and then I'll do a little more writing in a couple of hours.

Maybe I'll watch an old movie and get some ideas from that. Look at this wallpaper. It's *yellow*. Who could think people could relax in yellow rooms? They're probably like this all over the country . . .

I wonder if Suzanne realizes . . . She must miss me. Well, we'll see each other again. Wait till I submit this script. She'll come in and read for it and say, "Have I met you somewhere?" Yeah, I'll surprise her. I'll surprise *everybody*.

I shouldn't have done so much blow. Why did I get this much? There's so much left . . . The script. 'Cause I'm writing a script. I can't write in a yellow room. Look at this *bedspread* . . . Just lie down, put your head down and breathe. That's right. Breathe, breathe. Everything's all right. You have friends, you had a girlfriend—she was a bitch but you had a relationship— you have a life, you're good-looking, you have a pretty good body . . . Breathe out, that's it . . . You have parents, you're a writer . . .

Aah, I feel a little bit better. Maybe I should get into an activity. I'll chop the rest of the cocaine. I don't want to do any more of these rocks. That's probably why I don't feel well . . . Maybe just one more hit . . .

"(*sniff*) (*sniff*)"

It's so light in here, it's too fucking light. There's no window in the bathroom. I'll chop it in there. But I can't sit in a dark bathroom. I'll seem insane. Well, who's gonna see me? I'll take a bath in the dark. I'll chop a couple of lines for right after my bath. I'll have a relaxing hot bath . . .

There, there, there. My bath is running, I've got it going. All right, this is good. This is good. I've got a good idea for a script, I'm young, my life is in front of me. Let's go. All right, we're chopping it up now, here we go. All right, yeah. Jesus, it's a lot of blow . . .

"What? Who is it? No, I don't want it! I don't want the bed changed! Don't! Don't come in here! Get out of my room!"

I *spilled* the cocaine! I spilled the cocaine in the tub! I spilled all the blow in the bath!

"Get out!!! Get out! I'm gonna sue this hotel! My watch! I gave away my two-thousand-dollar watch for . . . Get out! *Get the fuck out of my room!!!"*

What am I doing?! Get it out of the water! Oh my God, oh my God, the blow's in the water!! What do I do? . . . I'm hysterical. Calm down and shut up. Get a lamp! Dry out the rest that's in the bag. I've got to save it! Three thousand dollars or whatever it cost . . . Okay. God, turn off the water. What have I done? Okay, okay, be cool. Oh my God, oh my God. The maid! This isn't happening, this is not true. This could not happen to me . . . Put the wet coke on the towel, I can dry it under a light. Oh, oh, oh, I'm having a heart attack. Oh my God, I'm seeing stars. I'm dead . . . Put your head down . . .

"Uhhhh, uhhhhh . . ."

Oh my God, I've gotta call a doctor. . . . What do I do? They'll call the police, the maid'll call the police 'cause I yelled so much . . . I don't know what to do. I've gotta be a man . . .

I have that gram at home. If I had another couple of hits I could decide what to do . . . I can't focus on this, it's too unreal . . . They'll call the police . . . My parents wouldn't still be there. I'll go get that gram . . . This is a nightmare . . . Maybe I can get my money back because the cocaine spilled. It wasn't my fault. I wish they insured drugs . . . All right, all right, I'm leaving. I'm gonna be calm . . . Get your shirt on, here we go . . .

Okay, cool, no maids. Okay, here's the elevator. Fuck, there's people on it. Okay, keep your head down and breathe. They're laughing at me. Oh my God. How did this happen to me?

"What do you mean, 'How's the weather in Miami?' I don't know anything about Miami."

How could they talk to me? Look at them, all perfect and dressed and going to jobs. I'll never have a life. I'm an animal. I'm an animal. *I have a drug problem.* Maybe I . . . Oh, no. Oh, no. I can't get off the elevator. They're like the New Christy

Minstrels and I'm this devil from outer space. I'm nothing . . . Oh, Jesus, Jesus, I've got to go back to my room and think. I'm in trouble. This is big trouble now . . . I don't know what I'm doing. I don't have any kind of a grasp . . . What am I doing? It's like I'm killing myself . . .

I've gotta call someone. My nose is bleeding. I've gotta get someone . . . What am I doing here? What have I been doing? I got half an ounce of cocaine and checked into a hotel. What am I thinking? . . . My arm is numb . . . I have no taste in my mouth . . . I'm sick, I'm sick . . . I can't call Stan. I can't let him know . . . Know what? . . .

So maybe I can't . . . I can't do drugs. I did too many drugs, I hurt my face with drugs . . . I'll call Julie, she was always nice. She was *too* nice, but she was nice. Maybe I could talk her into not telling anyone about this. I'm so embarrassed . . . What do I say? Help me, I'm a . . . Oh, Jesus, it's hard. I don't feel well, though. I've gotta . . . I'll just disguise my voice and say I'm a friend of . . . No, no, I'll just . . . Oh, fuck, I'll just tell them to come and get me. This'll be what it's like if I don't. I'll be in rooms like this all my life, with drugs that go down the drain and yellow walls and hamburgers that move . . .

I've gotta go where somebody can take care of me. All right, just call. I can go back and they'll take care of me and then I'll be okay. Calm down, you'll be okay . . . I'm so scared . . . Just call . . .

"Uh, yeah, is Julie Marsden there? Uh, hi, Lucille. It's Alex. No, no, I'm all right. Could, um, could I talk to Julie? Oh. Well, do you have her number? It's important. Yeah, it's . . . Okay, thanks."

Four-seven-six-two-nine-four-five. Four-seven-six-two-nine-four-five. Four-seven-six-two-nine-four-five. Okay. Okay . . .

"Hello, is this Julie? This is Alex. No, I'm okay . . . No, I'm . . . I'm in a hotel. I . . . God, could you? Could you come and get . . . Yeah, I hate to be a . . . Okay. Yeah, it's the Ramada Inn in Burbank. Room 823. Okay, I'm here. Yeah. No, I'm here."

Okay, just sit, just hold your knees tight. Okay, rock . . . Oh, God, oh my God . . . Okay, okay, she's coming. Somebody's coming. It'll be okay . . . Just hold yourself, hold yourself . . . It's gonna be okay . . . Somebody's coming . . .

DAY TWENTY-SIX

Alex is back. The story is that he checked into a hotel in the valley with a pound of cocaine. He had done quite a bit of it when he thought he heard someone breaking into his room and he freaked out and spilled all the rest in a bathtub full of water. Something like that. Bart told me, and he tends to exaggerate a little. Anyway, then he got in the elevator to go get more coke (!?!) and there were these people who laughed at him and said something to him about Florida, so Alex freaked out and went back to his room and called Julie.

Of course, this being the top story of the day in rehab world, everyone is scrambling for details. Wanda was in the nurses' station when Julie brought Alex in. She said he looked frightening, nose bleeding and everything, gripping Julie's arm with his head down like someone on trial getting past the press. We all pumped Wanda for more, since she's the only one of us who saw him, but that's all she had.

This just in!

Carl overheard Julie telling Stan that when she got to Alex's room it was about 11 A.M. Alex let her in and embraced her like a long-lost relative. He was sweating and crying, totally panicked. "I'm so glad you're here, thank you for coming," he kept repeating. While he was talking, a huge rock of cocaine fell out of his nose and landed on the carpet. Without missing a beat Alex bent down, licked his finger, picked up the coke rock, and put it in his mouth. He then offered Julie a Long Island iced tea and asked her if she had to tell his parents about this.

If World War III broke out now we'd still talk about Alex.

• • •

... Christ, I feel dead ...

DAY TWENTY-SEVEN

They brought in three people to speak at the hospital tonight at our own AA meeting. The first guy told us he was known as the Blackout King. He used to come out of blackouts speeding down the freeway and not know if he was chasing someone or being chased. He once came to in the middle of a huge fight and didn't know whose side he was on. He said that in the end he could only get high by tying himself off and calling the paramedics and telling them there was an overdose at his address. Then he would hang up and wait until he heard the ambulance siren, and then he'd shoot up, knowing they would save his life. So almost dying became the biggest high of all.

The second guy told this long tale of cocaine dealing and prison. At one point he was talking about being at this party in San Francisco. There was this girl there and he said, "I wanted to go out with her and she didn't have the time of day for me. Then she went off to New York and became this big star, and today that girl is in this room. Now we're in the same club."

I got this cold feeling inside, because I suddenly realized he was talking about *me*. He was bragging that I once thought I was too good for him, but now I'm not so bloody fucking too good for him. They say around here that some are sicker than others. Well, I decided that somebody was sicker than somebody in this situation, and I didn't care if I had to be sicker than him, just as long as I wasn't in his category. I never heard the third speaker, because I walked out of the meeting.

On the way back to my room, I stopped to see how Alex was. He was in bed and Lucille was taking his blood pressure. He looked like those pictures of kidnap victims that they send to the families with the ransom notes. He was pretending to be asleep, so I didn't say anything.

. . . I'm so humiliated. What am I gonna say to everybody? What must they think? God, I'm *exhausted*. At least they didn't make me see my parents. *That* I'm not quite ready for . . .

I feel awful, *awful*. I'm just glad I didn't get arrested or anything. I hope everyone doesn't stare at me like I'm some kind of animal. Maybe I went a little out of control. I did, I went out of control. I'm somebody who went out of control, which means I'm somebody who could go out of control again. I don't know, maybe I haven't been completely realistic with myself.

I still think I should write this script, though. I still think that's a good idea. What if at the end the guy finally sees he's an addict? He leaves the clinic and goes out and does a bunch of drugs to write this script about himself, and in the process he realizes he's an addict. I don't want it to be a corny ending where the guy gets really gung ho and starts going to meetings and applauding the people who make the coffee. I mean, he doesn't become one of those Q-Tip heads who come up to you at airports and say, "I have a gift for you." This is a cool guy anybody can identify with. An Everyman. With a drug problem, though. I bet my agent could get me an actual meeting with Barry Diller for an idea like this. It's current, I haven't seen it done before . . .

Maybe I should take it easy for a while, and not write it right away. I feel like such a moron. I'm so ashamed. Here I am way out in the middle of my life and I feel like this. It's like I've got wind blowing through my chest or something . . .

Maybe if I talk to some of these people they can help with some of these feelings. I don't have to like them, I just have to learn how to not do drugs from them. Not Stan, certainly, but I could probably do all right working with Julie . . .

What the fuck? I'll try it their way for a while. I haven't got too much to lose, I guess. I'm still not gonna use that Jacuzzi, though . . .

DAY TWENTY-EIGHT

I can't quite believe I'm actually going home in two days. I'm not *completely* leaving, though. They said I could continue coming during the day for all of next week. I'll be an out-patient. Bart is going to do that, too. So now I'll get the best of both worlds. It's hard to imagine a day without Carl talking too much in it. I wonder if he'd do my answering machine message for me.

Today was Mark's twentieth birthday. His favorite gift was the Big Mac that Stan brought him.

. . . Okay, okay, I'm an alcoholic. I can't get loaded anymore. If I do, I could die. Or worse. I remember Stan saying once—I *loathe* that sucker—but he said the worst thing is not dying, it's *living* like that. That would be bad, to spend my whole life in Ramada Inns with pockmarked dealers. Certainly the cocaine never enhanced his looks for me. It doesn't ever really do a lot, but that first hit . . . Well, I shouldn't get off on a rant about dope.

I think what I can do now is throw myself into my work, my writing. And I'll go to these meetings—at least then my parents will stay off my back—but I'm never *ever* going to an AA dance. It seems so tragic to stand around with a lot of people who don't—no, not even don't—*can't* take dope anymore and do the twist or something, like twitching at the end of some pathetic line in the river without any fish. Oooh, that's a good analogy. I think this script is going to go well.

Julie said I can rejoin the group, so I'll start gathering data. And I heard Suzanne's leaving tomorrow. I've gotta talk to her, or else it's like I made all this shit up. I don't want to have to think I'm deluding myself that we have any kind of connection. She's the one person here I really feel a connection with.

I have to admit, though, that maybe my attitude was bad. I guess now these people have to be my friends or something. This is like a joke. If there is a God, he's like Shecky Greene, throwing me in a Ramada Inn with a bag of cocaine and then putting me back here again. Well, at least it's a very dramatic story, and I've got some good characters to work with here. And this is my version of a breakthrough, so I don't want the clouds to open and God to drop me a note. I don't want to be religious. Something in between what Julie is and what I usually am is probably the way to go.

I mean, I would like to have some friends, but I want to have the cool people in AA as my friends. No smiling jerks, no zealous, crazed Republicans. I don't want to be a Republican. It's so uncool to be what some of these people are, and I hope they don't expect ... Okay, I won't take dope again, but I'm not gonna become a Jesus freak. That's it. You have to draw the line somewhere. I won't do drugs, but that doesn't mean I'm gonna replace them with hearts and flowers. Forget it.

I've got to talk to Suzanne before she leaves. There's a park outing in the morning, and I'm gonna go up to her and ... It's no big deal. I shouldn't make a big deal or I'll get all pressured and freaked out. But if I don't talk to her I'll beat myself up for the rest of the time I'm here. I can't miss any more opportunities. And she'd talk to me. It's like the changing of the guard of the new drugless generation. She's going out and I'm staying in.

I'm sure there's a lot of things we have in common. We could talk about not liking Stan. We could talk about Carl. We can't talk *to* Carl because he never shuts up, but we could talk *about* Carl. I don't know, and Sid. I could ask her if she misses Sid. Hey, we know a lot of the same people ...

DAY TWENTY-NINE

At lunch Wanda said to me, "God, I really envy you being in all those movies. You really have it all." I liked the concept of being envied by someone in a drug clinic while actually in a drug clinic.

Sometimes I don't think I was made with reality in mind. And now I can look forward to an eternal, open-ended reality. A reality that dreams me without waking. Unrelieved reality. Some might call it a challenge, others a sentence. Whatever you call it, though, we here in the rehab—the newly clean and sober—belong to it as completely as slaves. Reality's puppies.

Nomads, yes-men, kings.

. . . All right, all right, it's park time. That *horrible* nurse is taking us to the park, the one with the shrill cartoon voice who clicks her keys on my door. On the other hand, maybe this is a good character: the Annoying Nurse. She could be a good antagonist for my protagonist.

How do I look? Shit, this sweater still smells. Well, I can't worry about it. This is my last chance. I'm gonna talk to Suzanne and today's the day. Here we go. God, this is so pathetic, with everyone waiting by the nurses' station to go . . .

There she is! Oh, God, and she's got her suitcase by her door. It's like the end of camp. Drug camp. We should be making drug lanyards. Okay, here we go. Who can I latch on to so I seem like a part of it? I'm so out of it. If I'd done this before, this would be more natural and . . . Wait, there's Carol.

"Hi, Carol. No, I feel better. I . . . I fucked up. Yeah. I've been on Inderal for a couple of days. They say my heartbeat is very accelerated. Anxiety? No, maybe it's from the cocaine leaving my system."

That sounded stupid.

"It's probably from anxiety."

Okay! Now!

"Hi. Hi, Suzanne."

God, I should have said more. What else can I . . . Don't look down at your feet. You don't smell, you don't smell. You look fine.

"Yeah, we haven't really officially met. Yeah. I heard you're going home today. You nervous at all? Yeah. Yeah, I was nervous when I went home. That's true, I didn't really go home like you're going home. So, do you think you'll come back and visit people?"

That's dumb. I sound so desperate. Just be cool.

"You have any work lined up? Do you think it hurt your career to be a drug addict? Yeah, I guess it would. I guess it would. So, the park. Going to the park."

Fuck, I can't think of anything to say. What do you say? Tell her she looks good. I can't. What will she think I'm trying to do, date her?

"So, you're coming back to your group meetings next week. That's smart, that's very smart. Maybe I should do that. I mean, after I leave. You think I should? I'd like to know what you think I should do, because . . ."

I'm sounding like such a putz. Like Jim Nabors or something. Jesus! Just keep forging ahead.

". . . I mean, you being the senior here at drug college and me for all intents and purposes a freshman . . ."

That sounded good. Okay, get on that roll.

". . . Um, you know, I feel like you're graduating, and I'm sort of new blood, you know, I don't know all the rules. Is there anything you'd suggest? I mean, obviously, other than not doing drugs? Uh-huh, yeah. Let me ask you, what do you think of Stan? Really? I don't know, I find him . . . Can I be frank about this? I think he's very unpleasant. There was that one day we almost did have a conversation . . . Yeah, and I felt he was out of line. I mean, not that there *are* any lines in the clinic. I don't mean that like a coke pun . . ."

Aauugh, she's gonna think I'm a real moron.

78

". . . You know, it doesn't seem like there are any rules here other than not taking drugs, but I do think courtesy and decency could . . . I mean, as bad as I ever got on dope, I think I was always very cordial to everybody. Certainly, my dealers liked me. I mean, that sounds like a joke, but it's true. My dealers did like me. So, um . . ."

Say something. Don't let the air go dead. If you don't keep talking she'll walk away. She's an actress, they like to talk and . . .

"What are you going to do about your career? You know, I wanted to talk to you about that. I mean, I know this sounds like I'm a moron in a drug clinic, right? But I don't know if you know that I'm a writer and, um, I've just been chasing around this idea about maybe writing something about this and maybe you could take a look at it. Yeah, a script, and maybe you'd want to be in it. I mean, I don't want to bother you . . ."

Don't say stuff like that. Learn how to sell yourself.

"You would? You'd read it? That would be great. Well, I haven't written it yet. I mean, you know, I like to get a lot of it in my mind first, and then when I think I've got the whole thing I put it down on paper. It just comes out. At least, I hope so. I haven't tried to write without drugs yet. A journal? Really? You keep a journal? Was it your idea or . . . ? Uh-huh. And we don't have to turn it in or anything at the end? That's a good idea. So, do you write about . . . ? You write about people? You mean like Sid and Carl and everyone? Yeah, that sounds good."

Look at her, she's bored out of her mind. I'm gonna fucking kill myself.

"The swings? Sure. I mean, aren't we too large? Won't our legs go down in the sand and . . . ?"

Go! She asked you to go to the swings with her. *Go!*

"You want me to push you? I would be *honored* to push you in the swing. Should we ask that little boy to get off or . . . ? Do

79

you see his mother anywhere? Oh, there's one free, those little girls are leaving. Okay, I'll push you. That'll be great. It'll be how I see you off. I'll sort of push you off."

Another bad pun. She'll never read your script. Just stay with it, though, don't keep apologizing. She must hate me now. I sound like someone who wears Vitalis.

"Okay, here we go. Here we go."

I'll never forget this in my whole life. I'm making anecdotal history. I'm pushing Suzanne Vale on a swing. People will think we're in love. Maybe we can be in love.

"Is that high enough?"

Don't make any puns on the word *high*. Just let it go. Be quiet. Listen to the wind, the trees . . .

"This is nice, isn't it?"

Shhhh! Don't talk. Just enjoy the moment. Be totally in the moment. I hope no one else comes over. I want to burn this image into my brain. I'm pushing Suzanne Vale on a swing in the park next to the drug clinic . . .

DAY THIRTY

I spent the morning in the park with Alex. He's not a bad guy, really—but he's not a great guy, really, either. He did push me in the swing for a very long time, though. There are two things that I know for certain guys are good for: pushing swings and killing insects.

It's such a bizarre scene in my mind: the guy junkie pushing the girl junkie in this little kiddie swing with all these little kids squealing and running around, with their mothers sitting on the benches watching. All those little children and two huge ones.

Alex told me he's writing a script about the clinic. Being here is probably the most colorful thing that ever happened to him. He should call it *Rehab!* "Just when you thought it was safe to go back into your coke vial."

I can't wait to drive! Maybe I'll go to the movies tonight. I heard *Doctor's Orders* was pretty good. Anyway, I've enjoyed writing this journal. Maybe I should start keeping one at home. It would have to be good, though, in case they publish it after my death.

Sid and I are going to an AA dance in the valley on Thursday. Maybe I'm going overboard, but what the hell ...

I must be brainwashed, because it feels so clean when I think.

Notes on Rehab Movie

Suzanne left today. I feel really good about the connection we made in the park. It took a long time, but I think it was worth waiting for. I'm glad she didn't get to know me before, when I was such a creep. She's great. If she lost just five pounds, I'd marry her.

I think her suggestion that I keep a journal for my script was a good one. I wish I could see her journal. She's no writer or anything, but she is Suzanne Vale. I wonder if she'll publish it.

I wonder if there's anything in it about me ...

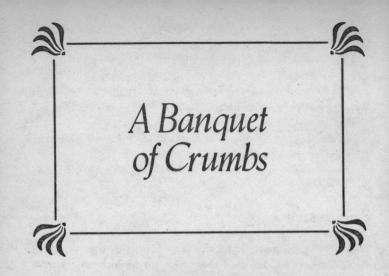

A Banquet
of Crumbs

"Sorry I'm late," he said. "I was in a production meeting. Did my secretary call you?"

"She did," she said. "It's all right, I brought my book."

"What are you reading?" he said. "Maybe I can option it. Oh, great. *Siddhartha*."

"Actually, I'm re-reading it," she said.

"A smart actress," he said. "I love it. What's your IQ? Mine's one forty-eight."

"A genius producer," she said.

"Yeah," he said. "For all the good it does me in *this* town."

"I love that they call it a 'town,' " she said. "I imagine there's like a dry goods store, and a clock tower, and a postman: 'Hey, good mornin', Mr. Phelps, how are ya? How's that rheumatism?' The 'town' of Hollywood. Tinseltown. 'Howdy, I'm the mayor of Tinseltown, and I'm here to welcome you to our fair city. How are ya?' "

"Funny, too," he said. "Andrea was right. I'm gonna like you."

"So," she said. "Do you remember your college board scores, too?"

"Six ninety six on the English," he said. "Seven sixty six on the math. I went out with this girl once who told me she wanted to stick her tongue in my mouth to get closer to my brain. She was a *bimbo*."

"How did you meet Andrea?" she said.

"Through Candy," he said.

"Oh, yeah, she's great," she said. "When I was little, I always wanted to look like her. You know, growing up in L.A., there's such an emphasis on looks. I mean, even in school, I decided what I was gonna wear the next day before I did my homework. There was this girl in my class, Beth Ann Finnerman, whose knee socks always stayed up, and mine seemed to sort of rumple toward the ankles. And I really thought my life would be better if I could do things like have my knee socks stay up."

"Well," he said. "You look fine to me."

"I've recently found," she said, "that to keep up my appearance, it has to be through health. I used to think this was corny, but I guess 'healthy' equals 'attractive' now, you know?"

"Should we order?" he said.

"Yes," she said. "I realize I'm talking a lot, but I don't want you to think I'm nervous. Maybe I *am*, but I don't want you to *think* I am. I skipped lunch today, and whenever I do that I get really wanged out. Also, I should tell you that I'm on Pritikin. My cholesterol is way up. I could have steamed vegetables or a little protein, like chicken. I mean, I'm not like a fanatic, I'm just trying out the Pritikin thing. Anyway, I don't go totally over the edge with this, but I do like to know. To be educated in these things, so when I do choose to eat a refined sugar or an oil or an animal fat product, I at least know what I'm doing. That I'm turning my arteries to pizza. And no eggs, *ever*."

"You don't—" he said.

"Oh, and I haven't had any caffeine since I started meditating a week ago," she said.

"You don't have any eating disorders, do you?" he said.

"Actually, I'm a failed anorexic," she said. "I have anorexic thinking, but I can't seem to muster the behavior."

"I dated a girl for a while," he said. "It turned out she was bulimic, which I didn't know at the time, but she had a great body. I guess that's how she did it."

"I could never be bulimic," she said. "I could *never* make myself throw up."

"You're so open," he said. "I like that."

"In a woman?" she said. "Listen, it's too complicated to order something special. We're at Pasta Hello, I'll just have the lasagna."

"You're sure?" he said. "Great. Waiter, two lasagnas, a Heineken, and . . . ?"

"Diet Coke," she said.

"And one Diet Coke," he said. "Thanks. You know, it's interesting, you mentioned meditating. A transcendental state on an intense person must be really interesting. I wouldn't think I'd be one to have a mild transcendental experience. I think I'd go straight for satori. I've done some reading on Zen. Certainly, if you could get it through reading, I would have it. Of course, if you go by Zen, it always comes down to, 'I could make the movie, *or not.*' That whole 'or not' thing. It's like, how many Buddhists does it take to screw in a light bulb? Fourteen—seven to do it, and seven not to."

"Did you hear about the Polish starlet who came to Hollywood?" she said. "She slept with all the writers."

"Yeah, I know that one," he said. "I love it. Before I forget, I've always thought you had a tremendous quality. I loved you in *Mist on the Lake*, particularly that scene when you're standing on the cliff in that diaphanous dress and all that hair, just staring. I gotta tell you, I got *hard*. And not from your cleavage, from your performance. I mean, you were even good in *Porky's Nerds*, and I would have said that was impossible. So, I mean, we're not talking

Pia Zadora here. You've got good chops. How did a smart girl like you wind up acting?"

"My shrink, Norma, says it has something to do with not getting enough affection as a child," she said. "So I'm trying to make up for it by getting as much attention as I can now. That's why I have a very seductive nature. Because, you know, you go off on a lot of calls, and you meet people for a brief period of time, and it's very important to cram your entire personality into that meeting so they'll really want you for the job. Even after you get successful it never gets any easier. You always have to please people. Fill their every possible fantasy about you. And you can never show that it's hard, so you're always looking like you're having the best time, and everybody thinks they're your soulmate. And you don't feel comfortable with *anybody*."

"Producers have to meet people and pretend we like them," he said. "Put them at ease. Everybody becomes more sensitive to other people's feelings and desensitized to their own."

"You can't find any true closeness in Hollywood," she said, "because everybody does the fake closeness so well. Your phone rings all the time and you have all these friends, and you feel like if you were a little less successful, they would never call you."

"I know just what you mean," he said. "For years I went to hookers, because, let's face it, I'm a very successful producer and writer, and I'm thinking of directing—Columbia really wants me to do a picture for them and direct it, and I feel it's the right time. I mean, I'm certainly developing films I feel I could direct. There's this one about high school that— Anyway, I've been doing this for a while now, and people might like me for my money. So I figured, if someone's gonna like me for my money, it might as well be a hooker, who's gonna like me for my money anyway. There was this girl, though. I don't know that we were in a committed relationship, but we went out for a while. But, you know, I saw other people. It's hard for me to . . . I don't know why, I think . . . When you grow up the way I did, maybe . . ."

"You have an intimacy problem," she said.

"It's not that I have an intimacy *problem*," he said. "I just don't *want* to be intimate. I don't see the point. I mean, I'm very involved in my career and . . . It's not *really* that I don't want to be intimate. I don't want to be *committed*. I don't know, I suppose that's finally just an excuse. My lawyer says I *am* afraid of any real involvement. He lives with a girl, and it just looks like, what's the point? I don't really know what the *point* is. I *love* sex, don't get me wrong. One could even go so far as to say I'm compulsive about sex. I mean, I hope you don't think I'm blunt—I'm sort of known for my bluntness—but, you know, I'd like to have sex with you. I mean, you seem like someone who'd be great to have sex with."

"How romantic," she said.

"You're right," he said. "I'm cold. I've recently noticed a coldness about myself that scares me. It scares me that I don't really care about much but my work. I guess you could say I'm a workaholic. If I wasn't a producer I'd be a football coach, 'cause it's so intense. I need intensity, I thrive on it, I *am* it. So I love environments that complement me. I can relax at a Bruce Springsteen concert. In the middle of that kind of energy, I can relax. I would have been *great* in the army, I think, as long as . . . Well, I wouldn't have liked being wounded, I don't like pain. Which I know doesn't make me unusual."

"But you thought you might mention it," she said, "in case I was thinking of stabbing you with my fork."

"Anyway, I'd *like* to want a relationship," he said, "because everybody else does, and it looks nice."

"Intimacy to me is two people sitting in front of a candle listening to important music nude," she said. "Thinking it means something that you both love the same video and neither of you could finish *The Sot-Weed Factor*. I was out with someone the other day and I said I didn't like sushi. I called it 'whale gums,' and he said, 'Really? You don't like it? I hate it, too.' And it was like he was saying, '*Finally!* Somebody who understands me!' "

"We live in America," he said. "Everyone who speaks English understands you. How they interpret you is something else."

"There's usually one thing that targets somebody for you," she said. "Like, he says something nasty about shrinks, and you say, 'Oh, you don't like shrinks? I think they're awful, too. You can do it yourself, everyone did for years. What did the pioneers do? I can't cut down that tree, I've got a noon appointment with my therapist? My shrink told me killing Indians was acting out aggression?'"

"I've noticed that people who admit they're lonely and angry tend to clump together," he said. "Like that's enough of a common denominator. A little club of dissatisfied people filled with angst. Phi Beta Rage."

"Phi Beta Rage," she said. "I'm stealing that."

"When you first meet someone on that first date, all the emergency adrenaline is there," he said. "You bring out your best material as though you do it all the time. As though this is just a natural environment for the great parts of your personality to come through. And it's not. It's totally forced."

"I went out with this senator," she said, "who kept saying, 'You are so terrific, what a great girl you are.' And I thought, 'Well, shut up about it!' He was telling me what he thought I needed to hear, rather than what he really felt to be true. And if he *really* felt it to be true, I would *know*. I would be able to *glean* that he thought that. Anyway, I *know* I'm a terrific girl. I don't *want* to be a terrific girl. That's what I am for auditions. I want to be something *else* to someone."

"When the actors come in on my pictures, my heart goes out to them," he said. "I started out as an actor. I went to acting college, Jeff Bridges was in my class. In fact, I've been in a couple of my movies. I think I'm a natural performer. My father was a preacher, so I got that kind of energy from him. A lot of preachers' sons are actors—Olivier, I mean, you could name a few of them. Anyway, I do all the readings with the actresses. I'm surprised you never came in to read with me."

"I read for you six years ago," she said. "You were very nice, but you seemed preoccupied. It was a huge call."

"Really?" he said. "I would have thought I'd have remembered someone like you. Wait, was that on *Why Is Ruth Dead?* I was doing a lot of cocaine then. I read that you were in a clinic recently, so I figure you know what I mean. I never got into freebase, but I was . . . I was taking a *lot* of cocaine. And I really, you know, I *like* cocaine. I had to stop 'cause I was having anxiety attacks. Still, I would think I would have remembered you, because you're very attractive and mainly because you're bright. It's this new thing I've been saying lately—I don't mean to quote myself, but if I don't, maybe no one else will. In India they say that the body is the envelope of the spirit, and the spirit, I guess, is essentially who you are. Well, we live in a city of envelopes. The thing that's terrific about you is that *you* are a *letter*. I mean, it takes a letter to know a letter, and I can see we're really two letters in a town of envelopes—"

" '*The envelope, please,*' " she said.

"—so when you find someone who actually has an interesting letter, you want to read it," he said. "The only problem is, you've gotten so conditioned to reading your own mail, so immersed in the letterness of it all, you just . . . Sometimes I think maybe I've met Her, and I just can't see her because I'm so busy looking at myself to see if I look all right in case she should arrive."

"I know what you mean," she said. "Sometimes I'm with a guy and I think, 'I *love* this person. This is *it*.' But who I love is who I am when I'm with him, and it has almost nothing to do with him. It's me having an excuse to just do myself one more time, proving once again I'm bright and I'm funny and I'm powerful and that I *can*. That I still know how to pour blood in their shark pools."

"I envy people meeting me for the first time," he said. "That first meeting is everything, because I can watch their eyes and see it all happen, and I want to *be* them. *I* want to meet somebody like me."

"What I do," she said, "is, as soon as I know they're devoted, I start to find fault with them. It's not that *I* find fault with them, really. It's the Sleeping Giant in my system who wakes up with a 'Fe Fi Fo Fum!' and says, 'Yecchh! Look at that *hair*.' Or, 'Oh my God, did you hear the *stupid* thing he said?' The Sleeping Giant who knows no pity is hungry for faults, he hunts them like Easter eggs. But the *Giant* does this. *I* like them. I feel *bad* that the Giant is gonna do it. There's something in me that wants to warn them, '*Please don't be stupid,*' like people can help it. And then the Giant says, 'He's not good enough.' And the thing is, I truly—the Sleeping Giant doesn't—but I *truly care* about people. Now, sometimes I don't show compassion but, I mean, I walk around with it. I'm devastated when teams lose in sports. I want to kill myself when they show the faces of the losing team. I *know* how it feels. I mean, I can barely squash bugs unless I feel directly threatened."

"My problem is, I only know how to need needy people," he said. "I wouldn't know how to recognize somebody who was all right. They could be wearing a sign, 'I have no problems, you can believe me,' and I wouldn't even *see* them."

"The only way to become intimate for me is repeated exposure," she said. "My route to intimacy is routine. I establish a pattern with somebody, and then I notice when they're not there. Once you get this routine thing going, you have to take a lot of vacations, so there's a constant renewal or harking back. When you see them, it's like your favorite song that was number one that you almost got sick of. It's been off the radio for a while, and then you hear it one day and it's like, 'Oh, greeaatt! How great to hear this again!' That's people for me."

"To me, it's finding yourself in everybody," he said. "But not enough of you to stay with any one person. There's so much of yourself, you're so many-sided. I had a guy in India come up to me on his skateboard and say, 'My brother, my brother.' It haunted me that he called me his brother, and then I thought,

'Yes. Yes! I see that, of *course*.' And so if I can find me in a *leper* . . . I'm looking for myself and I find me everywhere. Just not enough to make a difference."

"I don't know what I want to find anymore," she said. "I've gotten so involved in searching. I've done it for so long it does me. The genesis was truly to find someone, was truly to make an impact, to *bond*. The difference now is that since I've never found it, I proceed as if I never will. Now I'm just into looking, not finding. Winning, not the prize. And the prize *is* the winning, maybe just the three minutes when you've actually won. That's why the sweetness of the sexual contact is perfect, but it can only be a disappointment afterward. Because all you wanted to do was get there, not be there. All you wanted to do was want, but not have. As soon as you fuck, it's over. *As soon as you fuck*."

"You should see my house," he said. "I think of it as my bear cave. I like to keep it sort of damp and cool and dark. I'm a creature of habit, that's why I liked cocaine. There was such a heavy ritual attached to it. So without it, I've intensified my rituals in other areas. They're not all fun, either. I don't like brushing my teeth, for example—it seems to just hold up the whole process—but I do it anyway. If I waited to like everything I did, I don't know that I would ever do anything, except talk about what I wasn't gonna do. So now I've decided I don't have to like it, I just have to do it. I don't have to want to, I just have to go. So I show up. I do love to shave, though. I love to clip my beard and put after-shave on it. And I love the exercise guy to come over. I have a certain terry-cloth robe I wear in the morning after my shower—"

"The Robe Warrior," she said.

"—and," he said, "I have another one with another kind of material, I don't even know what it is, that I wear at night. I have certain sheets that I *adore*. Pratesi. Italian sheets, the softest, softest sheets. I used to think I would love to loan my sheets out to a clean Norwegian family for three years, and then they'd give them back all beaten in. But now I *buy* them like that. You know, and I have my alarm clock, and everything is just so. I know it sounds anal, but I take real pleasure in the details of my life, in just putting things where they belong. I guess I *am* anal. It just gives me a great deal of pleasure. You should see my house."

"You're not in a high-risk group, are you?" she said.

"That's very funny," he said.

"Remember at our last session when you said that maybe I shouldn't date for a while? Until we'd worked more on my awareness in this area? Well, how long do you think 'for a while' is?

"Not that I've been dating, but I just wondered, how long till you think it's okay? I mean, I know it's not okay yet, I haven't been dating, but I did go out with somebody. A couple of . . . three times. I tried to call you—well, I *wanted* to call you, but you were out of town. So I figured there wouldn't be any big harm in going on a little date.

"The thing is, he's another interesting guy, and that's what I'm drawn to. I know boring men are the ones to go for, but all I can see is the light glinting off the edges of the interesting ones. And, of course, 'interesting' means 'problems.' I don't even think, 'This time it's going to be different' anymore. I think, 'This time it'll be the same, in a different way.'

"Anyway, my friend Andrea set me up with him. He's a producer, very successful and attractive and all that. I met him for dinner and we had a nice time. He's very intense—between him and me there wasn't a whole lot of dead air. The thing about this guy is, I found him not dissimilar to me. We have a similar attack, similar appetites. Well, he's more into the sexual appetite thing. I've never been good in that area, as you know. I always feel I'm out of my element. I don't know what I'm doing there. Every time I'm in sex, I feel like, 'How did I end up *here*?' That's why I like to avoid it as much as possible.

"So I met him and we had dinner, and I really felt like he understood me, or at least like he might if he ever stopped talking. I mean, this guy was like the testosterone version of me, and *I'm* the testosterone version of me, so it was really weird. It was like being with more of myself. You'd think I'd have had enough of myself, but anyway, we had a nice time, and then he wanted me to see his house. I guess I should have known . . .

"And I didn't even have contraception. What was I going to do, wear my diaphragm to the restaurant? It's so embarrassing when they know you knew it was going to be sex. It's like, sometimes I try to be contemporary and modern, and on some level I just don't agree with anything I'm doing. So I told him I wasn't comfortable having sex with people I'd just met, and he seemed to get it. He said, 'Why don't you stay the night?'

"So I stayed over, and we necked for a while and it was nice. At one point we were kissing, and he said, 'This would be a great shot of you.' He told me that when he was in India he looked at the Himalayas and said, 'Great shot!' And he was *there*. It's like we don't know we're there anymore. We're so detached from our own experience, and so into how we can *use* that experience. As we're having it, we're putting it into another medium. Life is the largest medium we've got, and we want to put it in these smaller ones, to get it down to scale . . .

"Anyway, I stayed over, and then in the morning I felt like he was distant from me. He was still being nice, but he seemed . . . I don't know, I mean, it *was* the morning so a little distance is understandable, but I *thought* I felt him moving away, which instantly made him incredibly attractive, and we had sex. I made him breakfast, which I told him I never usually did, but I kept telling him I never usually did everything I was doing. It wasn't a brilliant breakfast—the eggs were brown and I burned the first two pieces of bacon. I can't seem to time food to end together.

"Then he went off to edit his new movie, *Ziz!*, and I went home. By the end of the day I'd talked to most of my friends . . . Sometimes I'm not sure I even have any friends. I may just have a large group of people that I tell everything to. It's like I've made intimacy a superficial gesture. Anyway, their consensus was, 'Watch out, he's a known sex addict, he fucks *everybody*.'

"And I acknowledged that, but deep down—and you don't get too far deep down with me, because I've thrust all the deep down right up to the surface—but somewhere in me, I just thought . . . It's like when I was younger and I used to fall in love with homosexuals, because they had rejected me before they even met me. Womanizers don't reject you, but they accept you in a rejecting way, so it's similar. And just like I used to think with gay men, I thought, '*I'll* be the one who makes a difference.' I don't mean that I'll have a relationship with him, necessarily. I don't allow myself to hope for that much, but I guess underneath my non-hoping is the hoping thing . . .

"I wish you'd been here last week, because maybe if I had talked to you, you might have helped me to not have sex with him. Because I couldn't seem to not have sex with him on my own. I need people to encourage me not to. Could we just work real hard in this area? Saturate ourselves with work on this, like when they stepped up the bombing and escalated the war in Vietnam? Let's escalate the war on this area of my life, and if we can't make me better, can we at least make me not *care* that I'm not better?

"Anyway, I knew I should probably cool it. I knew he was supposed to go to this Jackson Hole Film Festival on the weekend, and I didn't want him to catch me wanting to do something with him, so I made up some story about visiting friends in Napa. On Monday he called just before ten, and we went to lunch, and then we had sex at my house. He likes my house. He was very nice, and I kept thinking I had to try and look indifferent, which was weird, because on some level I *am* indifferent to him. I mean, he's cute and he's powerful and all that, but you have to take his reputation into account. He's a former *cocaine* addict and he fucks *whores*.

"But we have these great talks. It's like we talk about the real issues as if we're talking about the weather. And he said he couldn't see me that night because he was meeting with this rock group, Bad Hetero, about the title song for his film. And then you weren't back yet, so I went to Santa Barbara just to get away and not think about him. Or maybe just to get away and *only* think about him. I guess you could say I was obsessed with him.

"In the parking lot at the hotel a few days later, I ran into this film editor, Evelyn Ames, who I've known from parties for years. This is a real wild girl, and she enjoys her reputation, or at least she keeps up the pretense that she does. *Somebody* has to enjoy her reputation besides the guys.

"So we went to lunch, and in the course of talking to her, I mentioned I'd met this guy, Jack Burroughs—his name is Jack Burroughs—and I sort of asked if she'd ever slept with him. I don't know her well, but she's somebody you don't have to know that well in order to ask something like that.

"She said, 'Yeah, I slept with him.' She asked me, 'Did he make you do this?' and she drew her knees back over her head right there at the table, and I said, 'No.' And I thought, if that's the only way he demonstrated his respect for me, I guess that's something. She also said that while he was with her, he talked about another girl he was going to fly in from Boston who had really soft skin. He rubbed her skin and talked about this other girl's skin.

"Then she said that she had, in fact, seen him quite recently. It turned out she'd been with him Monday night, after he'd been with *me* Monday afternoon. I thought, God, this girl is a *lot* of girl, and to need *two* lots of girls in one day is . . . The phrase 'out of control' did cross my mind. And she felt bad that she'd told me all this stuff, so she said, 'He probably really likes *you*. We just fuck, and he talks about other girls while he's inside me.'

"So I thought, I should just stop this. I mean, it's humiliating to run into someone who's been with a guy you've been with on the *same day* you were with him. I was *furious*. When I was driving home I made this hard right turn and the wheels sort of lifted off the road, and I imagined having an accident and being taken to the hospital, and him coming to visit and me having him thrown out of my room. And I thought, I'm really out of the box now.

"Then, when I got home, I got a call from my business manager, Charlie, who wanted to know if it was true that I was dating this guy. I said, 'Well, I would hardly call it *dating*. Why do you ask?' And he said a friend of his had gone out with this guy Tuesday night, and that he'd told her he was seeing me. So that was three in two days or something—and those are just the ones I heard about. Imagine what I could pick up about him if I got one of those satellite dishes.

"I wanted to call him and tell him never to call me again, but there was still part of me that cherished the hope that *this* would make him sorry, and make him realize how much he loves me and what he'll be missing if he doesn't marry me. I felt like a total jerk for thinking this, but it's like I've been genetically tampered with. I was born imagining myself with an apron on, with pies cooling on the window sill and babies crying upstairs. I thought that all that stuff would somehow anchor me to the planet, that it was the weight I needed to keep from just flying off into space.

"So I called him up and tried to make a little joke about the situation, and he *jumped* on me. He said, 'Well, this is like the pot calling the kettle black.' Implying that just because I've slept with these two other people he knows—over a period of *five years*—and because I slept with him on the morning after our first date, I'm some kind of slut. I guess anybody who slept with him would have to be a slut. So we had this huge fight, and he accused me of having initiated the whole sex thing with him in the first place, and I said, 'Well, if I initiated it, then I'm stopping it right now. I make a great memory.' And I hung up.

"When he didn't call me back, I decided to call him and tell him not to even *think* about ever calling me again. His machine was on, and he had a one-word message that said, 'Slut!' And I freaked out. I mean, I knew it wasn't just about me, it was about every woman he's ever been with, and I was lumped in there somewhere. I was so shaken I can't describe it to you. I imagined him dead, and I left him a message in a very cold voice. But then he called the next morning, and he said that his message didn't say, 'Slut!' It said, 'What!' And then I thought, maybe I made this whole thing up. He was being so charming, and maybe he . . . I mean, he *did* say the thing about the pot calling the kettle black, but maybe he meant it in some other way.

"I was so confused that I could have made a 'slut' out of a 'what,' and I knew he'd said some pretty reprehensible things, but now I was thinking, maybe I did, too. And the night before I'd sworn I'd never speak to him again unless he apologized, and he didn't apologize and yet there we were having this conversation. And I thought, 'I love this guy,' and then I thought, 'No, I don't, I've got a crush on him.'

"He asked me out to lunch, and I said I couldn't come. I told him I had low self-esteem, not no self-esteem. Then he called me that night and joked about how we'd broken up. He asked what I was wearing, and I told him I had on a huge ball gown with bowling shoes and a scuba mask and a red wig, and no underwear. We were very funny, and it was like it was new again, only it hadn't had that much time to get old. But it *had* gotten old. We had taken it to its illogical conclusion, but it wasn't finished.

"On Sunday afternoon he called to ask if he could come over that night and watch this awards show with me, and I said okay. I was still keeping a little bit cool, which I'm sure attracted him. He can't resist people who can resist him. So he came over and we heated up food badly together, and he said he'd missed me and it was great. So he slept over again, and we had some sex.

"This time, though, he got away with a shatteringly low amount of foreplay. In fact, he told me this joke: What is Irish foreplay? It's when the guy says, 'Brace yourself, Bridget.' Then he wanted us to stay in bed all morning, but I had to come here.

"The thing is, I hope I'm not pregnant, because I have a feeling I could get pregnant easily. I mentioned this to him and he said he wouldn't mind going to the abortion with me if I was. I guess that's how guys are thoughtful in the eighties—they accompany girls to their abortions. That's the new manners. It seems so awkward, though, to see each other for a week and then you go and have an abortion together. Maybe I should just have a child . . .

"What worries me is, what if this guy is really the one for me, and I just haven't had enough therapy yet for me to be comfortable with having found him? How long do you think this whole process is going to take? Do you think we should have double-length sessions? It's like, not only am I changing cabins on the *Titanic*, I'm dating the crew.

"Maybe I should be coming every day . . ."

"There's a lot of pressure to get this new film done in time for Christmas. And what I do when I have a lot of work pressure is, I try to relax, and how I like to relax is . . . Well, I used to like to get loaded, but now I like to go out with women. Certainly this comes as no shock to you after all these years. I'm not looking for a girlfriend, but I'm going out with girls and keeping my mind open to the right girl if I could meet one.

"It really pisses me off, I met this one girl last week, this actress, Suzanne Vale, and . . . You know, I'm very up-front about not wanting to get into a committed thing. And girls always go along with this at first, and then suddenly they're into this relationship thing. Right away it's 'Who else are you seeing?' And if you're seeing anyone else they call you promiscuous, or a womanizer. I hardly think that sleeping with two or three, maybe four girls a week—rarely more than four—makes me a 'womanizer.'

"I'm very selective. I only go out with certain types of girls: beautiful or voluptuous. And it's not that I go out with them just to have sex, but I don't think you should get into a serious relationship without testing out the sex area. I mean, if *that* doesn't work . . . So, I say this to this girl and she says, 'What do you mean? Is this like a litmus test, and if your dick comes out of her blue then you know you've found a girlfriend?' I mean, that's absurd! The point I was trying to make is that if the sexual area doesn't work, then you shouldn't really pursue any of the other ones, because you can't really repair it.

"It's starting to get on my nerves that I have this reputation for being sexually compulsive. I like sex a lot, I admit it. But, you know, I like food a lot, too, and nobody calls me a foodaholic. I just don't like that people are always putting a label on you. Women *expect* you to come on to them. It's like, if I didn't, they'd think I was a fag or something. Impotent. Well, it's not like I couldn't handle it if somebody thought I was impotent, but I don't *like* the idea of people thinking that.

"I'm not defensive, I'm *angry*. I don't think I'm defensive. That's what *she* said. I don't know ... Everything goes so fast, you know? And I always wait for them to slow it down, and they never do. I thought maybe this girl was going to be different, 'cause she did say she wouldn't sleep with me right away. She came back to my house, and then she said she wouldn't sleep with me, and I thought, 'Well, good. Maybe somebody is finally going to slow the whole proceeding down.' I could see she was a very intense girl, and everything seemed like it could get very sped up, so I was relieved she was going to be the one to put some brakes on. I don't know how to do that myself. It's a skill I'd like to develop, but as of yet I don't have it, so I usually look to the girls to slow it down. Possibly *I* should be the one who says, 'No, no, never mind my boner, let's not have sex,' but it's against my nature. My dick wants what it wants, and then *I* want what it wants.

"You may be a shrink, but you're also a guy. You know what I'm talking about. I see a woman mailing a letter, and I see from the way her breast is curved under her sweater that there's no bra and I want to bend her over a car and have her. You know, you see these movies of prehistoric people who just bend people over and, *Bam!* I wish it was like that. It's an appetite men have as mammals, damn it. I've always meant to do some more reading on it.

"I don't know, maybe I'll be able to have a relationship one day. Or maybe I'm not made for relationships. There are probably some people who aren't. But, you know, I'm thirty-five now and I'm slowing down ... Well, actually I'm not slowing down, I'm just ... I'm *not* slowing down. But I think I should just let my process continue and ...

"The thing is, it's all so interesting. Every part of the sex act is interesting. How they undress, how they look during it, their reaction to it, *all* of it. And I think I'm really sensitive. It would be hard for me to believe a woman could fake an orgasm with me. I'm that in tune with what's happening with them, like a safecracker.

"I could write a travel brochure about women's bodies. I like when a woman is backlit and you can see what's under her clothes. I like it if she moves a certain way and something is revealed. I like something to suddenly appear that didn't seem to be there. I like to be surprised in the area of flesh. I don't necessarily like to be surprised in the area of brain, although I must say this girl did interest me that way. At one point she said something like that I should fuck bimbos and have the cigarette with her, which was a funny line. She says some very funny stuff.

"In another sense, though, she's the same as all the others. When she said she wouldn't have sex that first night, I asked her to stay over anyway, thinking that maybe in the morning if I acted a little distant ... And sure enough, *Bam!* Girls just can't handle that distance business. Even smart girls aren't so smart about that. And she's *very* possessive. I mean, this girl is a little nuts. She called me up one day and I had this very abrupt message—'What!?!'—on my machine, 'cause I was in a bad mood that day, and she thought it said, 'Slut!' She thought I was calling her a slut. I mean, talk about projection.

"I don't know, I think it's the wrong time for me to get into a relationship, but maybe something will happen from this. I *do* like her. Of course, I like to think I'm in love. That's what gets me through the whole process, so it doesn't seem cheap. I can't act like I'm in love unless I *am* in love, so I become in love each time.

"Sometimes I think I should marry one of them and just fuck

around. There are times when I wish I had kids. I just don't want a *wife*. I think I need the kind of relationship where if I want to see other women every now and again, the woman I was with would understand it was just a physical thing, and not about loving somebody else. I would certainly be discreet, like I was very discreet when I was with Jill, my last girlfriend. True, she did find out, but not for a long time. And she didn't leave me because of it. She left me because I gave her crabs—remember? That was the final thing, that I gave her crabs . . .

"Maybe I'm kidding myself. Maybe that isn't the right way to have a relationship. It's just that I get very claustrophobic and . . .

"Here's what I think. I think my areas of expertise are areas of expertise because I do them to excess. I'm expert at my work because I do it to excess. And I think that if I'm finally able to have a relationship, it will be because I do *it* to excess. It's almost as if I'm working at it, but it's a pleasure doing that kind of business. The trouble is, this girl leveled a couple of accusations that really . . . I don't think they hit home, but they hit near home. They certainly hit my neighborhood, and I don't like that.

"I don't know if I should see her anymore. I mean, we're talking about someone who's smart and funny and has great skin and great tits—you *know* how I love tits—and a great ass and a *perfect* pussy, but you never know. I mean, she's great, but there could be a better one. Maybe somebody like me dies looking for the perfect one. I wish I could look and see it all in one girl. I wish I could stay with that one girl and not feel suffocated, not feel frightened of my need, or repelled by it, or whatever.

"It's like there are so many different facets to each of them, and it's always interesting, but it's never interesting for *long*. This girl's flaw is that she's a woman, one woman. She's only one woman, not all of them. And she's gonna act like one woman. She's gonna do all that stuff where she needs me, or she yells at me, or she wants me to be something I'm not. Not that I would respect a woman who accepted me like this. She said something funny, she said, 'If I could make a man, I'd make him just like you and then I'd try to change him.' I thought that was pretty self-aware.

"I just don't like all that nosing around, you know? Where they count the days since you called, and they know exactly what you said you'd be doing, and they remind you of it when you say you did something else? I mean, I think I'm a sensitive guy, but I can't watch everything I say all the time. I can't just take care of them all the time. It's too much responsibility, I'm not ready for that. I don't know if I'll ever be.

"At this point, I'd rather make good films than a good home. I'm not saying this is an ideal outlook, I'm just saying it's how I see things right now. I do think this new picture's gonna be really good, which will be a drag in a way. Because then, you know, I won't be able to tell whether women like me for myself or for Ziz! . . .

"I was at Helena's Friday night and I saw George there," he said. "He was so cold to me I couldn't believe it."

"Who were you at Helena's with?" she said.

"I don't think . . . I'm just telling you about George," he said. "I don't think that that matters."

"It's not that it matters," she said. "Look, we've known each other for three months. I know you don't see me exclusively, we've gone over that. Who were you with?"

"Well, you'll probably hear about it anyway," he said. "Charlene Hasselhof."

"The girl from television?" she said. "The television actress?"

"Yeah," he said.

"Really?" she said. "I wouldn't have thought you'd go out with somebody from television."

"Actually, I normally wouldn't," he said. "I find it a very limited medium, as you know. But it turns out she's very . . . She's bright. She's almost as . . . No, I would just have to say she's *as bright* as you are."

"She's as bright as I am," she said.

"Uh-huh," he said.

"Is she funny?" she said.

"Well," he said, "she's not as funny as you, but she is funny. Yeah, she's funny. I mean, I was very surprised."

"Why would you tell me this?" she said. "*Why* would you tell me this?"

"What do you mean?" he said. "You *asked* me. I thought you'd want to know that there was another smart girl out there."

"Why?" she said. "Why would you think I would want to know that? What is it about me that looks like I would want to know there are other smart pretty girls? Because I'll fix it. I'll change it. Is it something I'm wearing? Is my lip curled in a certain way that says, 'Got to tell her there's another bright woman around'? Why would you think I would want to know that a beautiful, gorgeous, supermarket-famous face from television is as bright and funny as I am?"

"I didn't say she was as bright and funny," he said. "She's not as bright. She's not bright like you. She's bright in a totally different way."

"How can she be bright in a different way?" she said. "What is her area of expertise? Is she bright about cooking? Literature? She knows languages?"

"Oh, Jesus," he said. "I really—"

"It's just so interesting to me," she said, "that you thought I would want to hear that this beautiful girl is also brilliantly smart and you love her."

"I *don't* love her," he said. "I don't know why we're having this conversation."

"I'm jealous, okay?" she said. "I admit I am jealous. Look, we don't have a commitment, but we certainly have an area of commitment, which is that we talk to each other. I mean, we don't understand each other, but we don't pretend to understand each other like other people do, and I feel betrayed here. I suppose you talk to her like you talk to me?"

"No, I don't talk to her," he said. "In fact—"

"Well, what is she?" she said. "A great fuck?"

"No," he said. "In fact, we haven't even fucked yet."

"Oh, great," she said. "Great. You respect this one too much to fuck her. You didn't do that little distance thing in the morning? Or she's too bright to fall for it?"

"Look, I—" he said.

"You like to have smart girls get stupid over you, don't you?" she said. "Well, watch out. If they get too stupid, you might as well go back to just boffing bimbos."

"Look," he said, "I don't think we should continue this discussion. I don't like this side of you."

"I'm not a box," she said. "I don't have sides. This is it. One side fits all. This is it."

"How did we get on to this?" he said. "Do we need to have this fight? We have an understanding that we don't have an understanding, and we enjoy it very much. Now I think we should just order some food and have a pleasant evening, if that's possible."

"All right, yeah," she said. "I let myself in for it. I should never have asked you."

"What do you want to eat?" he said.

"Something bad for me," she said. "Caffeine and sugar and salt things. French fries, probably some Coke. You know, just stuff that jolts your system. You order."

"Okay," he said. "Two cheeseburgers well done, a large order of fries, two Cokes, and whatever other carcinogens you have. Thanks."

"Oh," she said, "that guy Gary was going to set me up with called."

"What guy?" he said.

"I told you," she said. "Gary was gonna get me a blind date with this friend of his."

"Really?" he said. "I don't remember you telling me that. What does he do?"

"He's a screenwriter," she said.

"Oh, a screenwriter," he said.

"Yeah," she said, "he just did a script for Spielberg."

"Really?" he said. "So you talked to him and . . ."

"Well," she said, "he has a huge vocabulary."

"It sounds like maybe it's a little *too* huge," he said. "I mean, normally you don't notice people's vocabularies, do you? It's like with your teeth. You don't want people to say, 'Good caps.' You want them to think you have a nice smile. A *huge* vocabulary."

"No, no, not too huge," she said. "But he did use two words I didn't know."

"Really?" he said. "What words?"

"I don't know," she said. "I mean, I understood the sense of the sentence, but I didn't know the words."

"Really?" he said. "So he's trying to impress you with the way he talks. So, when are you going out with him?"

"I don't know," she said. "He said he'd call me back. He was at his agent's office and he had to go. I don't know what he looks like or anything, but he was funny. I told him about the Oedipal thing, about my father leaving when I was very young so I knew how to pine for men, but not how to love them. So he said, 'You probably would have been perfect for somebody in World War Two. You'd meet him and then he would get shipped overseas.' And I said, 'Maybe on our date I could drop you off and you could enlist,' and he said he would just go out and rent a uniform. So he was very funny."

"Really?" he said. "That's funny? I guess that's funny. You told him that, though? You told him the thing about the pining? Why would you tell him that?"

"Well, he was a very smart guy," she said. "It was interesting. Gary says this is a great guy. He's very young."

"Really?" he said. "How old is he?"

"He's younger than . . . he's thirty-two," she said. "Gary says he's real good-looking and he has a great car, like I give a shit about that, but you know . . . I wonder, you know, what could be the matter with him if he's available. He's thirty-two, he's got all this money, and he's smart . . . Why is he alone?"

"Yeah, exactly," he said. "*Why* is he alone?"

"Well, I don't know," she said. "Maybe he . . . Why am *I* alone? Well, I'm not alone, I'm with you, but really I'm not with you, so, in effect, I'm alone."

"So, you told this guy a voluminous amount of shit about yourself?" he said. "All this intimate stuff ? I thought we reserved that area for this."

"Honey, we don't know what this relationship is," she said. "What is your relationship with the actress?"

"Well, I don't know what's happening there, either," he said.

"You don't know what's happening there," she said. "You don't know what's happening here. None of us knows where we stand, so we're sitting all over the place. Maybe we could all double-date. You've got your cutie from TV with the IQ. She's got TVQ and IQ, this is an extraordinary date for you. And who knows, maybe this guy has more IQ points than you. Oooooo."

"Don't make fun of me," he said. "Don't make fun of me about the IQ thing. I didn't make fun of your reaction to my thing with Charlene. So, what's this guy's name, by the way? Have I ever heard of him? *Spielberg*. Spielberg has so many projects . . ."

"His name is Arthur," she said. "Arthur Soames."

"Really?" he said. "Oh."

"Have you heard of him?" she said.

"Yeah, I read a couple of treatments he did," he said. "They were all right. I mean, he has some raw talent, I suppose. I don't know."

"Have you ever met him?" she said. "Is he good-looking?"

"I believe I did meet him," he said. "I can't remember that he was that remarkable-looking. I can't . . . I don't want to say, because I feel like I might be prejudiced in this area. I have certain odd feelings of jealousy in this area myself. Not that I . . . Well, I feel attached to you, let's say. I feel an attachment to you. I've grown accustomed to whatever this is, and I like the ambiguity of it, and yet . . . Where's the food? I'm really hungry. Aren't you hungry? I'm famished. I could eat a—"

"Television star?" she said.

"That's not funny," he said. "I don't think we should talk about this anymore."

"Eddie Samuels said the other day that you sounded just like me in a meeting," she said.

"Well, we spend a lot of time on the phone," he said, "but I doubt I sound just like you. We sound like each other a little bit. We talk a lot. I mean, Eddie Samuels is a putz, okay? That's why he's a production secretary. He doesn't know dick about shit."

"Dick about shit," she said. "That's so beautiful. There's that IQ rearing its ugly head. Hey, my shrink said this great thing this week—"

"Norma the Insight Queen?" he said.

"She said you were my fantasy playmate," she said.

"Really?" he said. "It sounds like a *Playboy* title or something. What else does your shrink say?"

"She calls us the Mind-Fuck Twins," she said. "She says I'm feasting on a banquet of crumbs."

"Sounds like *she* should be writing scripts," he said. "You really think you're going to a good shrink? Those don't sound like such enormous insights. I mean, forgive the pun, but I don't think I'm so crummy to you. I think we have a very modern relationship. I think it's a reaction to the times. You know, we have no real rules, and we're both very independent, but certainly we kind of respect one another. In a certain way, I admire you."

"Thank you," she said. "I admire you, too. I love your work and your eyes. No, I think she was just saying . . . She actually doesn't like the idea of me seeing you. She thinks it's not good for me. She thinks I sort of use you because I would have a lot of difficulty having another kind of relationship."

"What's wrong with this relationship?" he said. "I mean, it's not a relationship, but what's wrong with this? We both have similar feelings, we feel cut off from other people, we share a certain disdain for the Hollywood lifestyle we love, and I think we have a camaraderie that's very—"

"Come on," she said. "We have a camaraderie, but this is kind of a weird thing we're doing. I mean, it's weird. We have an oddness . . . What does your therapist think?"

"I don't let my therapist run my life," he said. "You know, I go in, I talk to him . . . I think of him as a good bounce. Mainly I go to hear myself think, and sometimes I'll discover something through what I say. I've been seeing him for a lot of years, and we did most of the main thrust of the work on my early family stuff in the beginning. Now it's just . . . It's like going in for a brushup, like teeth-cleaning. Anyway, you're probably not describing this accurately to your shrink, or she wouldn't object to it. I mean, she doesn't know me, so she's not basing her objections on an experience of me but on something you're telling her. And I think you must have misrepresented this situation, because I don't think there's that much wrong with it."

"Well," she said. "So the screening is what, Thursday?"

"The Ziz! screening?" he said. "It's Thursday. You know that. Which one are you coming to, the seven or the nine?"

"Which one are you going to?" she said.

"I'm going to both," he said. "I'm the producer. Obviously I'm gonna go to both."

"Well, I'll go to the late one," she said. "Are you nervous?"

"I think it's a fabulous film," he said.

"I know," she said, "but what if everybody else doesn't think so?"

"Well, fuck 'em," he said. "I think it's a fabulous film."

"Remember that line from The Philadelphia Story?" she said. " 'To hardly know him is to know him well'? I feel like that's us, like we'll just go on and on and on like this, but we'll never quite get past the incandescence of that first meeting. There's this sort of dull phosphorousness we maintain now, but . . . I mean, on a certain level, you're the closest thing to love I have in my life right now, but it's still far away. The closest thing I have to a relationship is very far away. I think that's interesting."

"I'd like to meet someone like you," he said. "But there's no one more like you than you."

"Maybe we can get somebody to introduce us," she said.

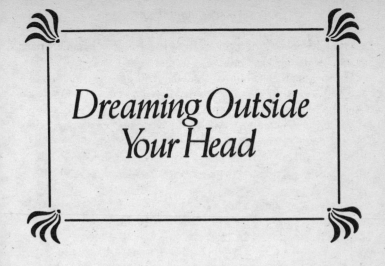

Dreaming Outside
Your Head

Suzanne was desperate to do something she felt would legitimize her, or that would be perceived as legitimizing her. Something that would cause her to seem desirable. Ideally, she would accept the marriage proposal of a member of the Royal Family who would renounce his throne for her. Since this was hardly likely, she concentrated on an alternate plan: getting work.

She plagued her agents for months, until they finally got her an offer for a low-budget film called *The Kitchen Sink*, starring Robert Munch, who was best known for the series *Mr. Blue*, in which he played the janitor in a women-only apartment building. More recently, he had portrayed a bishop in the miniseries *Read My Lips*.

The Kitchen Sink was a mistaken-identity comedy about a pair of undercover cops—Munch and Suzanne—who endure a series of mishaps while investigating a prostitute ring, end up in jail, and then get married. Since the film was shooting just outside of Palm Springs, Suzanne decided to stay with her grandparents, who lived in a two-bedroom house in the desert. The house had a flag in the front and a pool in the back, both of which lent it a kind of protection, a strange bracket.

Her grandfather, whom she adored, had gotten pretty senile. Suzanne was never sure if he quite knew who she was, but, whoever she was, he was always glad to see her. He spent most of his time sleeping or watching Mexican TV, though he spoke almost no Spanish. Her grandmother, though, was as Right There as she could be without making people wish she was somewhere else. She had three Yorkies—Jigger, Peanut, and Howdie—and when she wasn't doing her mosaics or microwaving Franco-American food, she was talking to her dogs. "Didn't she, Jigger?" she would croon. "Wouldn't I, Peanut?" "Isn't that right, Howdie?"

On the morning of her first day of shooting, Suzanne's alarm rang at five. She went into the bathroom and, without turning on the light, started her bath. Then she climbed back into bed for a brief reprieve, trying to be grateful she was finally working again.

She lay there, half awake, thinking about the wrap party of her first movie. She had hugged her dresser, Rosie, a forty-five-year-old woman with a thick Cockney accent, and said, "I'll miss you so much. Give me your address and phone number." Rosie had replied, "Luv, what's more'n likely's we'll never see each other again." Ten years had passed since then, and so far Rosie was right.

It was always like that, Suzanne thought, as she stepped into her bath. You did a film for a few months and you got a family. An intimate family with its own dynamic, its own in-jokes, its own likes, dislikes, and romances. The intensity of it was heightened by the knowledge that it was all temporary. Not only did you know *that* it would end but, give or take a week or two, you knew *when*. What you didn't know was how the whole thing would turn out. It could be good entertainment, it could be bad. It could succeed, it could fail. It was mining for celluloid gold. Suzanne dressed quickly, not bothering to dry her hair, and crept out of the dark house, past the dogs, the microwave, and the Stars and

Stripes, and into the station wagon that waited in the driveway to take her to work.

They arrived at the set at five thirty, just as the sun was coming up over the Joshua trees. Suzanne watched the frantic activity of the set against the otherwise serene backdrop of the desert. It was as if this movie set was some inane act of nature. "And the Lord said, 'Let there be entertainment,'" thought Suzanne as she got out of the car. Then, remembering the script, she added, "'Of sorts.'"

A man with a beard—Suzanne guessed he was an assistant director—came toward her, speaking into a walkie-talkie. "Yep, she just got here," he said. "I'll show her to her trailer." He smiled at her. "I'm Ted," he said, "designed to make your life a more annoying place to be."

Suzanne smiled back, bowed her wet head, and said, "Suzanne, designed to be annoyed."

Ted laughed. "Then we ought to get along great." He led her to a long trailer consisting of a row of doors, each of which had a name on it. "And this, of course, is your—"

"My hamster cage," Suzanne interrupted cheerfully as she surveyed her allotted space.

"I was going to say 'resting place,'" Ted said.

"My resting place," Suzanne repeated. "My final resting place. I always suspected it would end like this—alone in a tiny room with an air conditioner, a toilet, and an AM radio, in the middle of nowhere."

"Hopefully, it won't end like this," said Ted. "It'll just middle."

"Yeah, it'll probably end alone in a *large* air-conditioned room with an *AM-FM* radio."

"Well, this is a grim way to start the day," said Ted. "I know!" he said brightly. "Let's get you into some makeup. That'll cheer you right up."

"Oh, yeah," said Suzanne, following him to another trailer.

"Put a little base and lipstick on me and I'm just a giggling fool."

They walked up some steps into a fat one-room trailer where a man stood toying with a red wig while a woman sat reading a magazine. "I bring you the head of Suzanne Vale," Ted announced. "Suzanne, this is Marilyn, our makeup artist, and this is Roger, our hair stylist." Everyone exchanged hellos.

"Ooh, your hair is still wet," Roger fretted. "You'd better come to me first."

"I'll leave you folks and check on how the caterers are coming with breakfast," said Ted. He opened the door, letting in some beautiful dawn desert air, then slammed it behind him.

Suzanne sat in Roger's chair, staring at the reflection of her dread morning face. Roger browsed his cassette rack. "Do you want calming or stimulating?" he asked her.

Suzanne mulled it over for a few moments. It was a question she had asked herself about men. She had finally decided she wanted stimulating that very subtly became calming—a holocaust that became a haven. She had hoped Jack Burroughs might make this improbable leap, but he had merely made the transition from stimulating to stressful. "Calming," she finally replied.

"Calming it is," said Roger, popping a Windham Hill tape into his player and starting it. He looked at Suzanne. "Early, isn't it?" he said maternally.

"It's so early it's late," she said somberly.

"That's cute," Roger laughed. "Did you just make that up?"

"I don't know," said Suzanne. "I should know later."

"Listen to her!" Roger called over to Marilyn. "We're going to have a ball!" Suzanne smiled.

Marilyn lit a cigarette and walked to the door. "Can I get either of you anything from Craft Services?"

Suzanne looked at her. She was blond, somewhere in her forties, with blue eyes in a tan, weatherbeaten face. She was tall and thin, and she wore blue jeans and a T-shirt that said, "Some of us are becoming the men we wanted to marry." Suzanne smiled—

she had the same T-shirt at home. "If there are any doughnuts or pancakes . . . ," she said shyly, suddenly convinced that food—particularly *fun* food—would wake her up.

"Not really a health nut, are you?" said Marilyn, through her just-inhaled cigarette smoke. "I'll see what I can do."

"She's a trip," said Roger, shaking his long, tinted, curly blond head as the door closed behind Marilyn. He plugged in the hair dryer. "We've worked on . . ." He rolled his eyes upward, as if the number of films they had done together was hidden high in his head. "Fifth," he said. "This will be our fifth picture together." With that he raised the dryer like a friendly gun, pointed it at Suzanne's head, and said, "Bang bang, you're dry."

Suzanne searched her mind for an appropriate rejoinder. When none turned up, she simply sat grinning inanely at Roger in the mirror, the silence burning through her.

"I'm so glad to have a chance to work with you," Roger enthused. "I've always been a fan."

"Thank you."

"But more of you than your hair," he went on. "I've never actually seen a flattering hairstyle on you in any of your films. Not that you didn't look good, I just thought your hair could look better." He turned on the dryer and continued the conversation, shouting over the loud whine of hot air. "Except for *Mist on the Lake*. That's the best I ever saw you look." He ran his fingers through her hair as he spoke. Suzanne frowned at her reflection.

"But my hair was wet for most of *Mist on the Lake*," she screamed.

"Exactly!" Roger shouted back with satisfaction. "And that's close to what I want to try with you on this picture. Slicked back. The wet look. Dramatic but casual."

"Great!" she shouted.

Show business, Suzanne thought, as this man she had just met—this man she would probably know fairly intimately by the end of the week—played with her hair. It's all about distraction, a way of being transported out of your life, of having someone else's life for a while. Identifying with them. Feeling relief that their predicament isn't yours, or feeling relief that it is. A way of dreaming outside your head. Tilting your head with the actors when they kiss, thinking, "It's *so* real." The New Real.

The New Real was not *being* real, it was *acting* real. Suzanne was in the business of seeming—of entertaining people with her ways of seeming real. Portraying reality had become her way of experiencing it. She knew how to act like a regular person. She was self-consciously unself-conscious. She didn't mind being watched, but on some level she minded being recorded. It was as if she became an African native the moment the cameras started rolling, and felt her soul being robbed. If the natives were right about this, Suzanne figured her soul level was unacceptably low by now. It occurred to her that after she noticed her soul was completely gone, she would quickly lose her all-important ability to seem okay.

The door opened and Marilyn came in. "Lucky you," she said, placing several chocolate doughnuts in front of Suzanne. "I got to the doughnut tray before the camera crew, so there were plenty of the icing ones left."

"How can I ever repay you?" asked Suzanne, looking at the doughnuts as if her medicine had arrived.

"Just hold still while I'm doing your eyes." Marilyn moved to her area and took the lid off her Styrofoam coffee cup.

"She's all yours!" Roger announced to Marilyn, gesturing grandly. Suzanne thanked him through a mouthful of cake, then made her way across the room into Marilyn's chair. She squinted into the glare of the lights around the mirror, trying to adjust to their fluorescent horror.

"Loud, aren't they?" Marilyn said.

"Deafening," Suzanne agreed.

"Well," Marilyn said, placing Kleenex in Suzanne's collar to protect it from the makeup. "Is there anything you'd like to tell me about preferences or allergies or pet peeves? We might as well cover it before we get in too deep." She sipped her coffee, watching Suzanne over the rim of her cup.

"Just make me look like my face is thinner than it is and my lips aren't as thin as they are, and I can survive anything," Suzanne said. "Also, I have a particular horror of blemishes."

"Thin lips, fat face, and zits," Marilyn mused, as she examined the source of Suzanne's complaints. "Well, that won't be too much of a problem. We'll use lip line, shadow, and concealer. I frankly don't quite see what you're talking about, but if you ask me, most actresses look at their faces for too long and find too much wrong with themselves."

As she talked, she began applying base to Suzanne's face and throat. "I'll have you know that I'm *famous* for my zit cover," she went on. "I have a special little pencil I use, with almost a yellow tint to it, and over that I apply base and powder, and then, if more is necessary, I use a cover stick. Medium. You don't seem to have any spots at the moment. Were you referring to something specific, or were you just warning me for the future?" She stood with her sponge suspended over Suzanne's jawline, waiting for a reply, but Suzanne—lulled by the music, the makeup, and Marilyn—was asleep.

"Wake up, Sleeping Beauty. Your prince has arrived."

Ted shook Suzanne gently by the shoulders. "My mother thinks I'm a prince," he explained.

Marilyn watched Suzanne carefully as she surveyed her face in the mirror. "Pretty good for six thirty in the morning, huh?"

Suzanne smiled. "This has to be one of my favorite things. Going to sleep plain and waking up pretty." She eased out of the chair and walked with Ted to the door.

"I'll slick you down on the set," shouted Roger, who was blow-drying the pin curls on a wig.

"She's on her way to wardrobe," said Ted gravely into his walkie-talkie. "We're literally out the door," he continued, as they stepped out into the cool desert morning. "The producer is coming to see you," he said to her. "I mean, one of the producers."

"How many producers are there?"

"Three," he said. "The Father, the Son, and the Holy Ghost." He opened her trailer door for her.

"And which am I endearing myself to this morning?" she asked, climbing into her hamster cage.

"The Holy Ghost. Joe Pierce, our alleged line producer. Can I get you anything before he comes?"

"Coca-Cola," she said, as a red-haired woman appeared behind Ted with an armful of clothes.

"Rita, my darling," Ted said, "this is our artiste, Suzanne. Suzanne, our wardrobe mistress, Rita. Ladies, I leave you temporarily to yourselves." He bowed and wandered off, soothing someone on the other end of his walkie-talkie.

"I brought your clothes," said Rita, a voluptuous woman verging on heavy, with the kindest watery blue eyes Suzanne had seen on a movie set. "We should probably get them on you." Suzanne saw that Rita also had dimples and freckles—all the friendly features. Rita helped Suzanne get into her undercover cop outfit, which consisted of jeans, a sweatshirt, and sneakers. Just as she was tying her last sneaker, Ted came in brandishing a Diet Coke.

"Your caffeine ration," he said, handing Suzanne the cold can.

"Thanks," she said. "Where can I get more of these, should the need arise?"

"Prop truck," said Ted. "Ask Raider, the prop guy. Or I can get you one, if you're nice to me."

"Oh, I'm nice," she said. "I think these will be remembered as my nice years, quickly to be followed by the sullen months, and then, of course, the obscure decades. I only recently finished those wacky fuckup years, so you're the first to benefit from my reform."

Rita was about to say something when there was a knock on the door. "Who is it?" called Suzanne.

"Joe Pierce. Just came to welcome you aboard."

Suzanne opened the door and Ted went out, squeezing past Joe

Pierce. "Morning, sir," he said to Joe, then, to Suzanne, "So, can I tell them you're ready?"

"I guess," she said.

Joe Pierce walked into the trailer, a nondescript man wearing a white polo shirt and jeans that, on him, looked like slacks. He looked like somebody's stepfather. "Any more people in here," he said, "and we'd need a lubricant."

Suzanne laughed uneasily, and Rita excused herself. "See you later, Rita," Joe called jovially, then fixed what passed for his attention on Suzanne. "I just came by to say hello and make sure everything was up to snuff," he said.

"Everything's great," Suzanne assured him, forcing a smile.

"I want you to know we really appreciate your doing a drug screen," said Joe, who, with his tiny dark eyes in his big white head, reminded Suzanne of a sand dab.

She put her soda can down. "Sure," she said. "Did I pass?"

"Did you *pass*?" Joe echoed, laughing. "Of course you passed. *We* knew you would. It was the insurance company that was worried, not us. You apparently had some problems on your last film, but . . ." Joe slapped his knee and stood up. "I just want you to know we're right behind you one hundred percent. Well, I'll leave you to get ready." He opened the door. "See you out there," he said, disappearing with a wave.

For the first time since she'd arrived at the set, Suzanne was alone. She sat nursing her soda and thinking about her visit with Joe. She hadn't minded taking the drug screen. She understood that these truly had to be the nice, cooperative years for her. She didn't think of it as a punishment, not even the part about her salary being held in escrow until she finished the picture, just in case she got loaded and cost the producers money. She just figured she had to do all this until she didn't have to anymore. It was a repair process that could go on for as long as it liked. She only wished it was for a better film—a big-budget picture, for example, or even a small, interesting art film. A high-action, low-budget film, though, was harder to reconcile.

Suzanne heard the static of a walkie-talkie transmission outside. She swallowed the last of her Diet Coke, opened the door, and followed Ted to the set.

The director, Simon Markham, was English. A nice guy. She'd met him the week before, when they'd interviewed her for the job. For all her desperation, she hadn't cared that much if she got the part or not. She simply assumed she would never work again. Whenever she wasn't working, Suzanne knew she'd never work again, and when, inevitably, she did work, she knew it was the last time. It was a relationship with her profession that was based on trust.

Simon was standing near the camera. He was wearing a big straw hat, linen pants, a white T-shirt, and a jacket tossed cavalierly over his shoulders. "You look like you're dressed for a yacht," Suzanne said.

"Oh, good morning, darling," Simon said, almost kissing her on both cheeks. "You're looking well." The cinematographer asked him to look through the lens at the shot they were lining up: the scene where Suzanne and her co-star Robert Munch have been tied to a cactus by a bunch of pimps and left to die. It was a long scene with a lot of dialogue, especially Suzanne's speech about her fear of the dark.

She watched Simon Markham deal with the crew. It was his first feature film and he was nervous, although he seemed to be assimilating his nervousness into his naturally high spirits. Now he was listening to the director of photography explain why the shot wasn't going to work the way he wanted.

Suddenly Ted appeared at her elbow. "We're ready for a line-up," he said. Suzanne nodded and followed him to the cactus, where she was introduced to Robert Munch, was tied up with him, and talked to him about her fear of the dark, all before nine A.M.

• • •

Suzanne smiled as she rode back to her grandparents' house that evening. It had been a good day, she thought. She'd met at least five people who were in AA, including Bobby Munch and his wife, who was down here with him. She had found someone who would give her some water pills before her bathing suit scene. She'd remembered most of her dialogue, and Simon had seemed pleased with her work. She'd met the two executive producers—the Father and the Son—toward the end of the day, and even though they'd been nicer to Bobby than to her, she chalked it up to the overall sexism prevailing in show business and let it go at that.

Suzanne felt that her acceptance of her reality verged on the adult, and was almost proud of herself. Yes, all in all, a pretty good first day.

The next morning, while the cameras were being repositioned for close-ups, Simon came over and sat down next to Suzanne. He was friendly, but there was something else. He seemed almost embarrassed.

"What's happening?" said Suzanne cheerfully. "Did you have to take a drug test, too?"

Simon looked confused. "Oh, no, no," he said. "It's nothing, really. They just . . . The producers saw rushes last night and had some rather interesting notes."

Suzanne instantly tensed up. She began wringing out her hair, which had been soaked for the chase-in-the-rain sequence they were filming. "Well, what?" she said, as calmly as she could manage it.

"Now, don't take it the wrong way," Simon said. "I saw them this morning and you were fine."

"It was my first day," Suzanne said, staring at the ground.

"It was your first day, absolutely," he said emphatically. "I couldn't agree with you more. The producers simply felt you should have fun with it." He stopped and smiled at her. "Just," he shrugged, "have more fun with it, that's all."

Suzanne stared at him. "Simon, if I knew how to have fun with stuff, I wouldn't be in therapy. I wouldn't need to have drug tests."

"Now, now," Simon said, tilting his head and looking at her as if she wouldn't finish her vegetables. "I think they had some very interesting comments. Maybe I'm not saying it properly. What I think they mean is that you could own your performance. Make it more your own. Just sort of *have fun.*"

Suzanne stared at an anthill at her feet. "Really?" she said sarcastically to the ants. "And here I thought everything I did had to be fraught with torment. This is incredible. Why didn't one of my shrinks tell me this?"

"Now, Suzanne," Simon said patiently. "You shouldn't be in this business if you can't take criticism."

It was true that Suzanne couldn't take criticism. Even when directors gave her direction, she often took it as criticism. "But Simon, please," she said, not looking at him. " 'Have *fun* with it.' Don't you think I would do that with everything I did, if it was at all possible?"

Simon put his arm around her. "I know you can do this part. Just relax into it. Be yourself and you'll be wonderful." He kissed the top of her head and went off to talk to his D.P., as Ted walked up to her with a can of Diet Coke.

"NutraSweets for the sweet," he said, handing it to her.

"You know what I think?" she said. "Actors are the lowest of the low. Unless they have box office, in which case they're treated with respect without being respected." She took a swig of soda. "At least with me, there's an honest level of contempt. They don't respect me and they don't treat me with respect."

Ted nodded sympathetically. "You ought to be an assistant director if you want to sample the mother lode of contempt. And preferably a *second* assistant director," he said, taking her arm. "We need to get you touched up. You're in the next shot."

After the scene, Suzanne went over to the prop truck to check on the cookie and candy possibilities. The truck was on the far end of the location, and she normally wouldn't have gone, but it was a cool fall day and everything looked crisp to her. She had heard somewhere that the light in the desert changed all the time, so she decided to walk to the prop truck and see it change.

She moved through the warm hum of the crew as they checked lights, changed lenses, positioned extras. Suzanne loved crews. There was something reassuring about a crew, someting that said maybe it was all worth it after all. She loved the different baseball caps they wore, and their jackets and shirts from films and shows they'd worked on before. And their little stories about things that happened on other sets, the anecdotes about bad food, hangovers, and girlfriends. All the stuff of real life. Suzanne felt good when she thought of being a part of it.

She was humming "There's No Business like Show Business" as she arrived at the truck. She headed for the metal steps at the back, and as she rounded the corner she almost collided with Neil Bleene, the younger of the executive producers. "Well," said Neil, stepping aside, "fancy meeting you here."

Suzanne smiled a startled smile and went up the steps. Neil Bleene held a maroon leather-bound script under his arm. He wore beige leather pants and a plain white shirt open at the collar, with the sleeves rolled up. He had dark hair, a beard, dark eyes, pale skin, and he never seemed entirely to close his mouth. He looked as if he were pleasantly dumbfounded. Or dumb.

Finding no doughnuts or other treats, Suzanne got a Diet Coke and peered down at Neil from the truck. "I understand my enjoyment levels are down."

Neil looked down at his crocodile shoes and cleared his throat. "Well, no," he began in an amused tone. "We felt the performance was fine, but . . ." He scanned the horizon for the right phrase. "You're holding something back."

Suzanne realized she was older than Neil Bleene, who couldn't be much more than twenty-six. "Holding something back," she repeated solemnly.

"It felt like you weren't . . . that you didn't really make a choice. You made a nonchoice. Like you were concentrating more on *not* doing something than on doing something."

"I see," Suzanne said.

"I've acted in theater," Neil explained. "I've also directed theater. I'm doing this to make money, but basically I'm a theater director. From what I was told, you spontaneously hit Bobby during a rehearsal and Simon stopped you. Well, I don't think he should stop your impulses."

Neil was really wailing now. "The other thing is that sometimes certain line readings are appropriate. Like in comedy, it's a rule that inflections go up at the end."

Suzanne knelt down to look in his eyes, without giving up the separation and protection of the truck. "There's a comedy *rule?*" she asked.

Neil ran his hands through his hair. "Well, there's not necessarily rules so much as guidelines. Comedy guidelines." He paused for a moment, then came at her from another angle. "You were very good in *Public Domain.* What did you do there?" he asked patiently.

"I had Magna Valnepov as my acting coach and Benjamin Keller as my director," she almost shouted. "I didn't have *fun* with it. We had a month of rehearsals. We worked very hard. We hardly *ever* relaxed."

Suzanne noticed that Neil was watching her steadily now, holding his leather script to his chest like a shield. She realized she was getting pretty defensive. "Look," she said, "I may not take criticism well, but that doesn't mean I'm not hearing it. I'll hear it later. Right now I'm storing it in my delayed response area, because it's hard for me. I wish I was someone who welcomed criticism and immediately understood its value, but I'm not, and if I look unhappy about this, I am. I've had one day of work on this thing, and this is my second conversation about what's missing in my performance."

Neil shook his head benignly. "We're talking about two minutes of film. Two minutes of screen time out of ninety."

"Is it correctable?" she asked.

Neil laughed. "Come on," he said reassuringly. "It's not as though you farted during all your dialogue and we all sat in rushes and said, 'What's that noise all over her lines?' "

"I'm so relieved," Suzanne said. "That analogy has bathed me in relief." She jumped off the prop truck, careful not to spill her soda. "Thanks for the acting tips and pep talk," she said over her shoulder as she headed back to the set. "I'm feeling *much* more relaxed now."

On the ride home, Suzanne asked her driver, Les, if he liked show business.

"Sometimes, sometimes not," Les said. "It's a sissy job. Never steady." He shrugged. "Seems all right on the outside, then there's nothing behind it."

"Why did you go into it in the first place?"

Les grinned sheepishly. "Wanted to meet Jean Arthur," he admitted.

"Did you?"

"Sure did," Les replied proudly. "Drove her for three pictures she did at Columbia. She asked for me special the last time."

She hadn't been at her grandparents' house for ten minutes when the phone rang. "It's for you, of course," her grandmother said to her. "George something."

"George Lazan," Suzanne whispered, holding her hand over the mouthpiece. "One of my producers."

"Oh," said her grandmother, "Miss Snooty Britches." She went into the kitchen to open a can of something for dinner. "Miss Snooty Britches," she repeated. "Isn't she, Howdie?"

Suzanne put the receiver to her ear. "Hello," she said.

"Have I caught you at a bad time?" asked George Lazan.

"No, not at all," she said politely. "How are you?"

"Well, look," George said. "I saw the rushes and, frankly, you're holding back. See, I think of this piece as a light, fluffy piece, a kind of *What's Up, Doc?* for cops. So you gotta relax. You gotta just enjoy yourself and trust the process."

Suzanne watched her grandfather's incredibly long cigarette ash grow while he stared at the ball game on the living room TV. "Well," she said, "I can't really promise you I'm going to turn in a Barbra Streisand performance."

"No, no, no, no," George said. "You see, I think of Bob Munch as a kind of Ryan O'Neal type. He's a reactive actor. What we need is for you to be the one who governs the pace of the piece. If you dictate the pace, then Bob will follow you."

Suzanne sat down and pulled Jigger into her lap, and said nothing.

"So, we need you to establish the pace, and Bob will follow you," he restated brusquely.

Suzanne stroked Jigger. "I hardly think I'm responsible for the pace of the piece."

"Well, look," said George impatiently, "it's a *Happened One Night* kind of thing. You know what I mean." He cleared his throat. "Look, do you think you can do this part?"

Suzanne went cold. Jigger jumped out of her lap. The ash fell off her grandfather's cigarette. "Yeah," she said in a small voice. "Why?" This is surreal, she thought. I'm going to be fired from a bad movie for not relaxing.

"I always ask my actors that," he explained. "Look, just because we imagined Goldie Hawn or a Marilyn Monroe kind of thing in this part . . . Now we've got to deal with what you have to bring to it. We hired you, now we've got to go with what you have."

Suzanne sighed. This is a lot, she thought. This is as hard as I was hit for taking drugs. "I appreciate your comments, Mr. Lazan," she said finally. "I'll certainly give relaxing my best shot. If I'm not enjoying myself, though, it's not because I'm deliberately trying to sabotage your film."

George cleared his throat again. "I realize that," he said. "Just do the best you can."

"I'll try," she replied, in her most relaxed voice.

"Well," he said, "nice to . . . I'll see you on the set."

"You sure will," Suzanne offered, and hung up. "You sure will," she repeated to the air in front of her.

"And the farmer hauled another load away!" sang her grandfather. Suzanne looked at him and saw that he was smiling. "Yap, yap, yap, yap, yap, yap," he said. She walked to his chair, sat on the arm, and kissed his head.

"Soup's on," her grandmother called from the kitchen.

Her grandfather shook his head and said, "Don't that beat all?"

After dinner, Suzanne decided to go to sleep early and put this day behind her. She took off her makeup, brushed her teeth, and put on her nightgown. Before going to bed, though, she decided to call her therapist.

Before she lifted the receiver to dial Norma, the phone rang. "Suzanne?" a man's voice said. "It's me, Rob." Her agent.

"What's happening?" she said.

"Well, George Lazan called me today and he's very upset. He says you're not enjoying your work." Suzanne felt what she had been holding together all day quickly begin to come apart.

"If George Lazan is upset about that, he should see a shrink," Suzanne said tightly. "If he's upset about me not enjoying my work, he should fucking go into therapy."

"Well," said Rob, "but, I mean, what are you doing?" He sounded concerned. "What are you doing?"

"I'm on Quaaludes," shouted Suzanne childishly. "I'm on lodes and base and smack."

"There's no need to shout," he said.

"Rob, it's *me*, Suzanne," she said. "I've been working *one day*."

"Two days," he corrected her.

"Well, I usually don't go into my deep REM relaxation until about my fourth or fifth day on the set."

"But George Lazan told me you seemed to be holding something back."

"Don't do this to me," said Suzanne ominously. "Do *not* do this to me! I don't want to be in this business anymore anyway." She started to cry. "I will not be treated like I'm deliberately withholding something. I went into this on Monday, and it's Tuesday, and I'm doing the best I can. I got the job Friday night. It's *Tuesday*!" She sniffled loudly, and felt silly.

"Well," said Rob, sounding worried, "there's no need to get so upset. I simply wanted to pass on what Lazan said to me—"

"Are they going to fire me?" Suzanne demanded.

"No, of course not," he assured her.

"What *is* this, then? This is *not* going to achieve what they want. This is going to make me defensive. If they want me to relax and enjoy myself, this is not the way to get me to do it. I've been in this business twelve years, and they're treating me like I just got out of drama school."

"Suzanne, take it easy," Rob said. "George Lazan is on *your side*. He wants you to be as good as you can be in this part. So calm down and just go in there tomorrow and be great."

Suzanne sighed. "All right," she said finally. "All right. But I don't want any more of these conversations. If they call after tomorrow and don't like it, I want you to fucking get me out of it, and . . . I'm sorry. I'm tired. I got four hours' sleep and I worked all day, and I got a lot of acting lectures, and now . . ." She trailed off dramatically. "Let me talk to you tomorrow. I'll be more philosophical by then."

"All right, sweetheart. Take it easy."

"Thanks," Suzanne said, and hung up.

"Honey, you shouldn't get so worked up," her grandmother said from the doorway.

"They're treating me like I'm a jerk," Suzanne said.

"Just 'cause they treat you like a jerk doesn't mean you have to act like one. How they treat you is not necessarily who you are. My mother always told me that. She'd say, 'Honey, just 'cause they treat you like shit, you could still act like pie.' "

"This was a big recurring theme with Great-grandma Pearl," said Suzanne. "I remember her saying that a fly is as likely to land on shit as on pie. So she thought everything could be divided into two categories. Either shit or pie."

"Well, yeah, but she was a smart woman. Very smart woman. But I guess we were never rich enough to have your problems. Not so much time to get ourselves so worked up. Your grandpa worked on the railroad." She paused for a moment and sat down next to Suzanne on the bed. "You know what you should do? You should do something with your writing, with those poems you used to write. Some of your poems are better than anything I've ever read in those cards over at the Palm Desert Mall. Why don't you find out how you get into that?"

"I don't know if I want to," Suzanne said dubiously.

"Well, then, why don't you find a nice guy and marry him and settle down?"

"It's the 'nice' part I have trouble with," she said. "Don't you think that if it was going to happen, it would have happened already?"

"No," said her grandmother. "You're a good age for it. Find a nice guy to take care of you."

"Yeah, but Gran, I'm a lot to take care of."

"Oh, you talk big," her grandmother said. "You talk big and you think fancy, but you're just like other people. You act all rough and tough, but you're a pushover. You just think too much and you talk too loud."

"Don't you think my life is weird, Gran?"

"Weird, weird, you call everything weird. It's not so weird. But you've got to do something sooner or later to get your life together, girl. You don't take those drugs anymore, and I'm real proud of you for that, but now that you can see it clearly, you've got to figure out what you want to do with it all."

"What was that thing you always used to say? 'It ain't what you eat that makes you fat, it's what you get'?" Suzanne asked.

"Yup."

"What does that mean? I always thought it was specifically designed to confuse people out of their panic."

"No," said her grandmother, "it's like 'Your eyes are bigger than your stomach.' It ain't what you eat that makes you fat, it's what you get. It's like what you eat is what you get—even if it's a plate of cold beans."

"I see."

"What's happening?" said Suzanne's grandfather, who was standing in the doorway. "Look what the cat drug in."

"Hi, Granpaw."

"Hi, honey," said her grandmother. "What are you doing up?"

"Well, I heard everybody yap, yap, yappin' in here and I thought I'd come in," he said.

"You want some more beef jerky, Granpaw?" Suzanne asked.

"Did I have some already?"

"He doesn't remember," her grandmother whispered.

"Oh, I sure do," he said. "I remember. I heard that. Don't talk behind my back. You women, I tell you . . ."

"Honey, don't get all worked up now," said Suzanne's grandmother. "Do you want some—"

"I just want some coffee and one of my doughnuts," he said. "I just heard you so loud in here. I'm all right." He wandered back to his room.

"He gets worse every day," her grandmother said. "It reminds me of you, when you used to get all bleary from those painkillers."

Suzanne sighed. "All I want is to feel like I've got a regular life. Do you think I could make it if I moved here and wrote the insides of cards, and—"

"I don't think you could do it, quite frankly," said her grandmother. "But I think it's your way of having a nice dream. Most people dream big, you dream small. It's just whatever you haven't got is what you want. It isn't the life, it's what you do with it. So, do something regular with your irregular life, rather than trying to get a regular one, 'cause you'd just do something irregular with that."

"But do you think I could hold down a job? A regular job?"

"I'm one of those people who believe you can do whatever you set your mind to," her grandmother said. "But, that being said, I think some people have an easier time setting their minds down than others do, and your mind seems to hover. Your brother seems to have his head out of the clouds, but yours is right up there in them. You always read too much, always had your nose in a book. A bookworm. You just don't seem to have a level look on things, and I don't know if you can get that or not. Maybe you could just live with it. I don't think it's such a bad thing. Certainly there's worse."

"Was Mommy like this?"

"You're a little like your mother. She never was booky like you, but she had that big kind of personality. When you were a little girl you were very quiet. Your mother was more of a tomboy, but you . . . One time when we were driving somewhere I had you in the car seat, and we were taking these bumps really hard, and you took this big bump—you were less than two years old, *way* less— and you looked over at me and you said, 'Damn it!' And I don't know where you got that word."

Suzanne smiled. "What else do you remember?"

"You were very serious," her grandmother continued. "You had these big brown eyes and you were always going, 'What's that? What's that?' You wondered what everything was. You would frown and point a lot, like a conductor looking for your orchestra. You always seemed very busy, like you were between appointments all the time, but you were just a little child."

"You know what I remember, Gran? I don't know where I was, but I was little enough to be under doorknobs, and I wanted to say a word so bad, and the word was 'interesting.' And I tried to say it, but it always came out 'insterting.' And that was my first big, big frustration."

"You take things pretty hard," her grandmother said. "I always tried to get you not to, but I don't know, you can't get children to be other than they are, and your nature is you take things rough. You work them over too much. Let things be, I always figure, but you always mull around and check everything out. Oh, you were a nosy little thing."

"I like to hear stories about me," Suzanne said. "It's like I expect to hear some clue one day, like 'Rosebud,' where I'll think, '*That* was the moment.' See, I don't really remember feeling like a child, or like I imagine children are supposed to feel—that kind of *Yippee!* thing like running down a green pasture or something. That's why I love hearing stories about myself as a child, so it seems like maybe I didn't just land here."

"No, you didn't land here," her grandmother said. "You were a child. There's plenty of children in the world that are serious children. You had to grow up fast because of the divorce. That was hard, but it happens to lots of people nowadays. Of course, it's easier on children when it doesn't, but there's no use going over that. I don't know, you did things children do. You wore big hats and put on your mother's makeup and wore her big high heels. You directed little shows in the closet. You were a child, and you can still be a child if you want. If you want we can go down to the market and I can get you some baby food. You're not missing that much."

"I always feel like I'm missing something."

"Well, you always did feel that way. You never could even nap. Never."

"I've always had this sense of foreboding," Suzanne explained, "that something could go wrong and . . ."

"And what? You think that if you could be there you could prevent it? A little person like yourself? If it's gonna go wrong, it'll do it all by itself."

"I know, but I feel like if I were there, I might be able to make it go right."

"Well, that feeling is wrong," her grandmother said. "So maybe the foreboding one is, too. You can't stop things from doing what they're going to do, unless you're doing the things. And if you really want to get married and have children and cook, well, you better get a move on, little sister. You're not doing any of that stuff now. You should shit or get off the pot, pardon my French."

"Beautiful French," said Suzanne. "Is that some Berlitz thing I'm not aware of?"

"Don't you be fresh."

"Is there a cutoff age for fresh?" asked Suzanne. "Or does it just go on indefinitely as long as you have older relatives?"

"Don't make fun of me," said her grandmother. "You know what I'm saying is right. Just pick someone and make it work, rather than using all the make-it-work energy saying, 'He's too short, he's too tall, he's no good . . .' Just pick somebody. I've stayed with your grandfather now for fifty-odd years. I don't like him, but I picked him. I'm proud of the fact that we've had this long marriage. I can't say it's all happy, it's not always a good life, but we have a life together, and it's as God intended. You're there with your partner, and you don't always like them but you don't leave just 'cause you don't like it. You're spoiled. Your generation thinks that if you don't like something, you can do this or do that, take a drug or whatever, but that's not my generation. We make a choice and we stick with it, and I think you could learn something from that."

"Yeah," said Suzanne, "but you and Granpaw hate each other."

"Where did you get *that* idea? We don't hate each other. He just mostly stays in the back of the house and I stay in the front, but we see each other. We have our history together. We are each other's lives, and I don't hate my life."

"So I should just . . . pick somebody?" asked Suzanne.

"I'm not saying I just went out and *picked* him, but I stuck by him," she went on. "I can't say we've had the happiest marriage, but we don't just get up and walk out when we have a fight. We've been faithful to each other, and that counts for something. I love your grandfather. I don't like him all the time, I think he's an ornery old grunt, but he's my husband and I will stay with him."

"So, what qualities should I look for in a guy?"

"Well, you can't afford to be so choosy. You know, you've got twenty-year-olds also looking around, with their tits way up high and the best years of their lives to throw away on somebody. You've already thrown yours away, so you can't be all that choosy. If you find somebody who likes you and respects you, and if you like each other, then, you know, you can work on the rest of it."

"That sounds reasonable," said Suzanne, nodding.

"Don't think you're not going to argue with them," her grandmother said. "You can't spend a lot of time with somebody and not have them get on your nerves, or vice versa. If you expect to not argue, don't have a relationship."

"Well, I haven't," said Suzanne.

"Oh, you have," her grandmother said. "You've had a couple. I met Jonathan, I met that fellow Albert . . ."

"Yeah," said Suzanne.

"Well, what happened with those? You split up with them."

"We didn't get along anymore."

"See, I don't understand that," said her grandmother. "This is what I don't understand about your generation. You just stop getting along? You've got to work at getting along. It has to be something you care about, a priority."

"Gran, you should put out a relationship video. There's Doctor Ruth for sex, and then, once they've had the sex, *you* could tell people how to stay together."

"Go ahead, make fun of me," her grandmother said, getting up from the bed. "And don't take this movie thing so seriously. Don't they always say, 'It's only a movie'?"

"Yeah, Gran, that's what they say."

"Now, how do you want your eggs in the morning?"

"You don't have to get up," Suzanne said. "I've got a very early call."

"I'm up anyway," she said. "Your grandfather has to have his heart medicine."

"Poached," said Suzanne.

"All right. Good night, darling. Sweet dreams. Don't let the bedbugs bite."

"You were right there when they handed out clichés, weren't you?" said Suzanne. "Good night, Gran. I love you."

She was calmer when she arrived on the set the next morning. The first scene was being shot in a car, which was placed on a platform with the crew and all the equipment on it, all of which would be dragged along by a pickup truck. Rita had just finished connecting Suzanne's body mike when Simon walked by with Rocky, the first A.D., who was explaining how many extras they needed to do drive-bys in the car scene.

Suzanne followed behind them until Simon and Rocky were through. Then she said, "Excuse me, Simon. Could I talk to you?"

"Certainly, love," he said. "What's the problem?"

"The problem," she said sternly, "is that four people, including my agent, had conversations with me yesterday concerning my low enjoyment level, and it bothered me. I would prefer to receive direction solely from you."

Simon looked concerned, and the wind almost blew off his hat.

"Really?" he said, in an affronted English tone. "That shouldn't be. I'll have to have a word with them. Your *agent* called you about this?"

"My agent," Suzanne repeated indignantly. "As if I were a *child*. As if I were difficult to *communicate* with," she said, rising to some inner occasion. "I mean, why don't I give them my mother's number! Or better yet, call my grandmother! She's down here, she can stand by and make *sure* I'm relaxed!"

"That's it!" Simon said excitedly, snapping his fingers. "This is her! *This* is the quality I want for your character. Right there, what you're doing *now*. See?"

"But Simon," Suzanne said, trying now *not* to give him the quality he wanted in her character, "this is not relaxed. This is incredibly upset. If this is the quality, then maybe—"

"Darling," he soothed her, putting his arm around her and walking her toward the car on the platform, where the crew was waiting to do a rehearsal. "Just be yourself and you'll be fine. I know it sounds trite, but trust me. I'll talk to the producers and make sure that what occurred yesterday is not repeated. Now, try to calm down." He kissed the top of her head.

Rocky came up to Simon. "They need you behind camera," he said.

"Oh, surely, surely," said Simon, going around to the other side of the truck. Suzanne made her way to the passenger side of the platform, where Ted helped her up into the car. Bobby Munch came in a few minutes later, and Suzanne filled him in on the entire enjoyment/relaxation saga as the platform was dragged out to a lonely stretch of desert highway where they would spend the next few hours.

When she finished her story, Bobby smiled gleefully. "Telephone call for Suzanne Vale," he said. "Brrring! 'Hello,' you say. 'Hello, sweetheart, this is your Aunt Lillian in Tucson,' " Bobby said in a high little voice. " 'Listen, honey, George Lazan called today and mentioned that you didn't seem to be enjoying yourself. Well, now, I know that it's harder nowadays to have fun than it was when I was a girl. You know what we used to do for enjoyment, we would go down to the swimming hole and swing in one by one from a tire tied to a rope. Anyway, seems to me that if you want to do this dang fool thing for a living, you might as well try to enjoy it while you're at it. Well, bye-bye, dear.' "

Suzanne was as happy as she'd been in months. "Brrring!" she intoned gaily. "Hello," she said as herself, then went on, 'Suzanne, it's me, Mary. Now, listen, girl, I been lookin' after you since you was tiny, and I'm worried about you. This Mr. George Lazan called me, uh huh, he shore did. Says you're not relaxin' enough. Suzanne? What are you eatin'? I bet you're gettin' too much sugar and not enough proteins and things like that. You know, my Pete, what he do to enjoy himself—now, I know he's not an actor but he has a lot of tension—often he will take a very hot bath and a cold shower right afterward, and then he'll . . . Well, you can't drink, so that might not work for you, uh-uh. All right now, honey, stay warm. Bye-bye.' "

"Brrring! Brrring!" Bobby said excitedly. " 'Hello?' 'Hi, Suzanne? You may not remember me, but I was in kindergarten with you. Louis Bodenfelden? We were in Mrs. Webber's class together. I threw up scrambled eggs out of my nose one day on the way to the library. On the stairs? Anyway, this guy George Lazan called me. He thought maybe I could talk to you about relaxing in your performance. I don't know why he called me. He said he tried to reach Mrs. Webber, but she was dead. Anyway, nice to talk to you again. I've enjoyed your work over the years. Good luck.' "

Suzanne noticed that Simon and Rocky and all the sound guys were laughing, and she remembered she and Bobby were body-miked. Anyone with a headset was in their audience. She tapped insistently on her window. " 'Miss Vale?' " she said in a low male voice. " 'Miss Vale! It's your pool man, Jeff. Sorry to wake you, but this dude George somethin' or other called and said you weren't owning your performance. I told him you always seem pretty relaxed to me, but then you're usually asleep when I get here. Maybe there's too much chlorine in the pool. Well, take it easy. I say, shine the old guy on. Later.' "

It went on for hours. Between every take there were new calls from people George Lazan had contacted. Suzanne's dry cleaner, her exercise coach, her gynecologist, an old water-skiing instructor, a camp counselor, both her parents and all of her stepparents, Jack Burroughs, and, finally, the New York critic who had once suggested that Suzanne leave show business, and who now restated his position more vehemently.

"You were wonderful all morning," said Simon enthusiastically on the way back to the set. "Just a delight, on camera and off."

Suzanne smiled and blushed. Her entire body ached from laughing. She had to admit she felt pretty relaxed.

A week later, on her thirtieth birthday, Suzanne sat in an unmarked police car, soaked to the skin and waiting for Simon to call, "Action!" She looked over at Bobby. "If this is any indication of how my thirties are going to go—" she began.

"Your *thirties?*" he shouted. "Let's talk about my *forties* for a few minutes, shall we? Let's discuss that I have a wife and two daughters and I'm still soaked to the skin with a big movie wound on my arm, playing cops and robbers."

"What about that I'm thirty and I don't have any children?" countered Suzanne. "Or a husband, for that matter."

Bobby started laughing. "This is a perfect actor conversation," he said. " 'What about me?' 'Oh, yeah? Well, what about *me?*' "

"An actress on her thirtieth birthday obsessing about herself," Suzanne said, also laughing. "I've become typical."

"Sweetheart, you became typical long ago, only you were too stoned to notice."

"Oh, thank you," she said. "I suppose you're *not* typical?"

"I *revel* in my typicalness," Bobby said. "Do you think they remember that we're out here waiting to do this shot?" He squinted down the highway at the crew, where Simon and Rocky were having what appeared to be an important conversation. Simon looked down the road toward their car and held up five fingers. "Five more minutes," Bobby sighed.

"Hey, babe," teased Suzanne, "*you* wanted to go into show business."

"Not *this* show business," he said. "I wanted to be in the glamorous, fun show business." A soft warm breeze moved steadily across the desert, carrying the voices of the crew. "You're awfully cheerful for someone who's just turned thirty," he said.

"I'd just hate to remember my thirtieth birthday as an ordeal," she explained. "Sometimes I'm afraid I'm happy and I just don't ..." She paused, looking for the right words. "Sometimes I'm afraid I'm happy, but because I expect it to be something else, I question the experience. So now, when in doubt," she shrugged with true bravado, "I'll assume I'm happy."

Suddenly they heard Rocky call them, and Simon made a thumbs-up sign. Roger ran up the hill with a water bottle to spray them.

"Action!" called Simon.

Bobby clutched his wound and started driving down the hill. Suzanne grabbed her movie gun. As they drove past the camera, Suzanne was exhilarated. She was still young, good-looking, funny, bright, her wet hair was blowing behind her, and she had a gun in her hand. As soon as they were out of camera range she began to sing "Oh, What a Beautiful Morning."

As they hit the main highway, Suzanne saw that the Desert Palm Drive-In was showing *False Start,* a movie she had read for and not gotten. Her spirits sank instantly. "We should go back," she said quietly. "They'll be mad."

Bobby noticed the sign and smirked sympathetically. "Were you up for that?"

Suzanne pretended to be interested in her gun. "I'll get over it," she said stoically.

"When?" Bobby asked, turning the car around and heading back.

"When I have my therapy breakthrough and nothing bothers me anymore."

"You know," he said, "there are people who feel bad because they didn't get *this* movie. What would you tell *them*?"

"To rethink their careers," she said. "I'm always rethinking mine. It keeps my skin soft."

"Do you think you'll stay in show business till the end of this picture?" he asked.

"Do you mean this show business, or the glamorous, fun show business?" Suzanne asked.

"*This* show business," he said dramatically, gesturing grandly and stopping the car. Suzanne looked around and saw that the entire crew was mooning her and singing "Happy Birthday." Marilyn stood at the car holding a chocolate cake with thirty-one candles.

"I had the worst ass, so I got to present the cake," she said, smiling.

"It'll be hard to forget this," said Suzanne, blushing like a desert rose.

"Still," Bobby said, "maybe with enough therapy . . ."

"There *isn't* enough therapy," said Suzanne.

Dysphoria

She was going to a party, but she was pregnant and she didn't want to bring the baby, so she took it out and left it home. While she was at the party, she realized that you can't do that with babies, so she went home. When she got there, the baby was blue, so she panicked and tried to get it back in. "How could I have done this?" she thought. "How could I have not known what would happen? I didn't even want to go to the party."

All of a sudden she was flying, soaring over great stretches of countryside, and it was wonderful. *Wonderful.* Then, in the middle of her flight, she thought, *"I can't fly!"* and she realized she wasn't flying at all but was actually falling from a great height. She was trying to get the wind under her arms to keep herself in the air when someone on the ground started shooting at her. She felt completely exposed. She couldn't hide, couldn't duck the bullets. She wanted to get farther inside her clothes. There was nowhere to go. She couldn't go down because they were shooting at her, but they were shooting at her so it wasn't safe to stay in the sky.

Then she was in the passenger seat of a car. The driver was in shadow, but she could tell it was a man. She wanted to get out of the car—it seemed to be out of control—but it was moving too fast, traveling great distances in a direction she'd never been. Suddenly they came to a house, and she opened the door and was in a tunnel, a long tunnel. From deep in the tunnel, she thought she heard a little baby crying, and then she heard the echoes of the crying and she got very frightened. She started to run, and then the man from the car was behind her, chasing her through deep snow with a gun . . .

The phone rang, jarring Suzanne from her dream and out of immediate danger. She lurched across her bed. "Hello," she gasped, clearing her sleep-filled throat. "Hello?" she repeated, hearing the overseas hiss.

"Hello?" she heard a male voice cry from deep inside the phone. "Is Suzanne Vale there, please?"

"Who's calling?" asked Suzanne, with her eyes shut tight to block out the morning sun experience.

"Sven Gahooden," the accented voice carefully said. "I met her at an est intensive several years ago, and she told me to call her if I should ever—"

"Suzanne is on a verbal fast retreat in New Mexico," interrupted Suzanne.

"The Insight Chaparral?" cried Sven.

"I think that's the one," said Suzanne patiently.

"Well, tell her I just wanted to share with her about a breakthrough I had watching a film of hers in Stockholm," Sven said.

"I'll tell her," said Suzanne in her best let's-wind-this-up voice.

"And that I've quit medical school to work full-time on the Hunger Project," Sven finished.

"Okay, I'll tell her," said Suzanne with some gusto. "Goodbye, Sven."

"Who is this?" asked Sven politely.

"A friend of Suzanne's. Ruth Buzzi," said Suzanne.

"Well, thank you, Ruth."

"Thank you, Sven. Good-bye." Suzanne replaced the receiver and shook her head. "Ruth Buzzi," she thought with disbelief. "Maybe I should go on a verbal fast."

The storm of sleep had blown her nightgown around her body in such a way that it was cutting off circulation in her left arm. She threw off her blanket as though it was a magic cloak and stood up, preparing to enter the dangerous arena of her day without its much-needed protection.

She untwisted her nightgown, walked into the bathroom, ran some bath water, and moved into the kitchen for some eye-opening orange juice. "A man with a gun," she thought. "How obtuse."

Suzanne went back to her bedroom and put a cassette in her stereo. She liked to listen to soundtracks in the morning. In the car she only liked rock 'n' roll, but soundtracks were house music. This morning she put on *Somewhere in Time*, which sounded like what she thought love was like. It sounded like longing. She listened to the music thoughtfully as she sipped her juice and walked back into the bathroom. Her thoughts seemed more like poetry to her, and less like idle chatter, with this music on. She turned off the water and sat in the tub.

The score started to gnaw at Suzanne a little as she bathed. It had been recommended to her by a musician she had gone out with once named Chester Pryce, whom she had liked but had never heard from again. She couldn't remember whether she had liked him before she never heard from him again or only afterward. In any case, he had told her about this music—he said he listened to it a lot—but he hadn't warned her that it sounded like feelings you had to be brave about. Suzanne imagined Chester listening to it in his car as he wistfully drove over a cliff.

She reached for her towel, stood up, and got out of the tub, surveying her reflection in the mirror. She had to get thin. In fact, she had to get *too* thin, so she could eat for a couple of days and not have to worry that much about it. "I won't eat today unless I absolutely have to," she thought.

Then she saw the looming largeness of a new blemish on her chin. It looked to her like a new feature. "I'm already worrying about wrinkles and I'm still getting pimples," she thought. "Life is a cruel, horrible joke and I am the punch line." She was especially dismayed because she had to go to her friend Wallis's party that night, which would have been difficult enough for her to attend with relatively clear skin.

She got into her gym outfit, which was a black bathing suit with little teddy bears on it that she had purchased in Hawaii a few years ago after losing her luggage. She wasn't what you would call enthusiastic about teddy bears, but it had been an emergency and the suit made her tits look good. She pulled on her turquoise-and-black-checked shorts. Her ensemble was less than stylish, but when Suzanne got used to an outfit, she stayed with it. She pulled on her black socks and turquoise sneakers, sprayed herself with perfume and deodorant, wiped some makeup under her eyes, got her purse, put on her sunglasses, and left for the gym.

She drove out to Venice behind a Kharmann Ghia with a license plate that read BURRRPP. She knew the route by heart so she didn't even have to concentrate. She thought she was a wonderful driver, and she wished she could build a healthy self-esteem from that foundation. When it got down to the larger issues, though, she didn't think believing in yourself as a driver meant that much.

With the sunroof open, the windows down, and the radio up full blast, Suzanne felt at peace. She had once decided that God was in her car radio, and He would play her songs she liked when He was happiest with her. The week before—when God was evidently not that happy with her—she had blown out her amplifier playing a Pretenders tape. The speakers had gone dead after she went over a speed bump during "Middle of the Road," and she'd driven around after that in a daze of silence. She'd had it repaired the next day, and now the music—Bob Seger's "Still the Same" as she headed west on Olympic—was so loud it made her legs vibrate. She was always a little sad when she turned onto Lincoln

Boulevard, because it meant she had only one complete song left before she got to Gold's Gym.

She liked going to the gym, or rather, she liked having been to the gym, and the only way to have been was to go. She liked that little blip that she got between her shoulder and her triceps from lifting weights. Still, she knew that no matter how much work you did, the only way to get your body to look really great was to eat right. Suzanne only knew how to eat wrong.

She had always eaten wrong. It was a tradition in her family. Dairy, red meat, salt, sugar, caffeine, and fried everything: American food. She knew what it did to you, but she couldn't do without it for too long. Her diets lasted until about four thirty in the afternoon, when she couldn't stand it anymore and ate something absurd like teriyaki beef jerky.

She didn't like preparing food or sitting down to a meal, maybe because when she was young her mother had the children sit and "visit" after the meals. Suzanne felt that eating was a private thing that should be done in corners or in cars. Food was simply fuel for the body. Her car didn't "visit" with the other cars when she filled its gas tank. She smiled as she drove past McDonald's and Jack in the Box and smelled their familiar sodium fumes.

She got to Gold's Gym fifteen minutes late and saw her trainer Michelle waiting in front. Michelle was a muscular blond girl from back east who had been a PCP junkie and who now used the gym to give her what drugs had.

"Sorry," said Suzanne.

Michelle shrugged. Suzanne was always fifteen minutes late. "What are we doing today? Legs?" Michelle asked.

Suzanne's face went into a fist. Legs were the hardest. "Chest and shoulders?" she pleaded wanly.

"Okay," Michelle laughed, "but you can't avoid those puppies forever. We'll do legs tomorrow." Suzanne was relieved. She had a day's reprieve. She looked around as she followed Michelle back to the machines, recognizing some of the regulars: the tall guy with the headband and the Egyptian hieroglyphics on his arms, the wiry dark-haired actor who was always drenched with sweat, and her favorite, the giant black guy who was there all day, every day, and never spoke to anyone. From the way he acted, Michelle guessed that he'd served a lot of time.

"There's your boyfriend," she said under her breath.

"I love him," Suzanne said moonily as Michelle positioned her correctly in the shoulder machine. "He's so great," she said, beginning to struggle with the weights. "He never talks . . . He's the epitome of mystery . . . the paint-by-numbers guy . . . You can totally . . . fill him in . . ." She was forced to stop talking as the exercise became more difficult.

"I wish I found him interesting," sighed Michelle. "I wish I found anyone that interesting. I'm on E."

"On what?" gasped Suzanne.

"E," repeated Michelle. "Empty. Nothing motivates me. I haven't had a good crush in weeks. Do five more. Five. Four. Three. Two. One more!"

"It's too heavy," Suzanne moaned.

"It's only *thirty pounds*," Michelle exclaimed. She let Suzanne rest for a few minutes between sets, then led her to the next machine.

Suzanne got quieter as she got farther into the exercises. She marveled that she did it at all, especially since Michelle was constantly reminding her that the whole thing was pointless without dieting. Because her dieting skills were so minimal, she ended up with muscles submerged in fat like islands under water. She watched a dark-haired girl with a giant back make her back even bigger and wondered, "What does it all mean?" But then, philosophers had been wrestling with that one since the dawn of man, so who was she to figure it out? She wondered if Kierkegaard had ever been to any place like Gold's.

Finally they got to the last machine, which Suzanne hated because she had to sit facing herself in a mirror with bad overhead lighting. "Any word about Sal?" she asked, in an effort to take her mind off her body. Sal was Michelle's ex-boyfriend, who had recently disappeared.

"Oh," said Michelle brightly. "Didn't I tell you? I can't *believe* I didn't tell you!"

"Well, tell me now," Suzanne demanded. "What?"

"He's in a rehab in New York," said Michelle, with some obvious satisfaction. "One of those year-long programs."

"A year," Suzanne said, shaking her head. "I'd go crazy."

"He already went crazy," Michelle said. "I don't know how much crazier you can go than shooting coke all day. Do two more. Two, one, okay! One more set, then some abs and you're through."

"Well," said Suzanne, "he had a lot of practice shooting steroids."

"And he even lied about that," said Michelle. "Like someone could get a neck like a ham with just good old-fashioned exercise. He had a neck like a *ham*. You need help to get a neck like that. Ready?"

Suzanne did her last set in silence, trying to concentrate on something high on the wall so she didn't have to look at herself in the mirror. She had done eight repetitions when she started to give up.

"Go!" cried Michelle. "You're almost there!"

"No!" screamed Suzanne, embarrassing herself and finishing anyway, then letting the weight fall with a clunk. She did several unenthusiastic sets of abs, after which Michelle walked her to her car.

At the door they met Chad Paley, the Rams linebacker. "Hey, Sunshine," he greeted Suzanne.

"Chad," she said, "I bet you know. Who is that big black guy over there on the shoulder machine?"

He stared into the gym in the direction she had pointed, and his face darkened. "Keep away from him," he said, glowering. "He's bad news."

"Why?" asked Michelle. "What did he—?"

"He served time for manslaughter, for one thing," Chad said. "And for another thing, he's gay. You can see him most nights on Hollywood Boulevard."

"Oh," said Suzanne meekly.

"You stay away from him," warned Chad paternally. He chucked Suzanne under the chin and strode back to the life cycles. The girls walked out without looking back at the silent man pumping iron for Hollywood Boulevard. "Stay away from him," Suzanne said. "What was I gonna do, date him?"

They walked up to Suzanne's BMW. "Tomorrow," she said, confidently. "Legs."

Michelle nodded. "And stick to your diet," she said.

"I will," said Suzanne, turning off the alarm and getting into her car.

"You will not," Michelle said.

"Probably a little of both," said Suzanne, starting her engine. "I will and I will not. The Zen diet."

"And you'll end up looking like a Buddha," shouted Michelle over Don Henley's "All She Wants to Do Is Dance" on the radio as Suzanne waved and drove off.

She went home to wash her hair and change clothes for her lunch with Al Hawkins, some manager who wanted to handle her career. Her friend Bob Becker had set up the lunch, and she was not looking forward to it.

She put on a little blue dress that both was comfortable and looked halfway decent. It fell exactly between her two clothing classifications: "dressing for me" and "dressing for them." It was very hard to find a miracle dress like this, but she had accumulated three. This one had a little burn hole on the lower left side, but she was pretty sure nobody would notice.

She applied her makeup, checking on the steady progress of her blemish, and blow-dried her hair. She turned the dryer off four times while she was using it because she kept thinking she heard the phone ringing, but it never was. Then she put on some black high heels—which she felt firmly planted her outfit in the "dressing for them" category—and left for the restaurant she had selected: the Hamburger Hamlet on Beverly Drive.

About a block from the Hamlet, she found herself driving behind an enormous Bentley, the driver of which appeared to be on the phone. Staring at the back of his barbered head, Suzanne suddenly knew with absolute certainty that he was her lunch date. She tried to keep alive the possibility that she was wrong, but when he signaled his turn into the parking lot, she was overcome with dread. Could she drive around the corner to the Safeway and call the restaurant and tell Al Hawkins she was sick?

No. She'd already canceled and rescheduled this lunch three times. She had to go. "Oh, well, maybe I'll learn something," she thought philosophically as she handed her keys to the valet. She imagined herself smoking serenely on a pipe and gazing off to sea and saying, "Well, yeah, sure, he was an asshole, but he wasn't your typical asshole. I really *learned* something that day at the Hamlet."

The instant she walked into the restaurant she heard a loud New York voice bark, "Suzanne?" Sure enough, it was the skipper of the SS *Bentley*.

"Al Hawkins?" she asked meekly.

"The same," bellowed Al, shaking her hand. "Why don't we go to the table? Miss?" he called to a waitress. "Is our table ready? Thanks."

Al Hawkins steered Suzanne to a table against the wall, under a mirror. He was under six feet, with a short, almost military haircut, brown eyes, a deep tan, and very good teeth—his, Suzanne guessed. He was wearing weird sunglasses on the top of his head, long thick black glasses, the kind Ferrari would make if they went into the sunglass business. He was wearing a blue button-down T-shirt, tight faded blue jeans, and neat little brown shoes. He was like a sergeant in the Show Business Corps, and Suzanne felt like some lowly private with AWOL leanings. He handed the waitress a couple of singles to get him some cigarettes and steered Suzanne like an invalid into her seat. "You sit facing out, okay? Okay," he said. He was completely self-contained—he asked questions *and* he answered them. Suzanne felt superfluous.

"You're not blond," Al Hawkins said, fixing her with his intense glare.

"No, I never was," said Suzanne.

"Well, you've never been blond in any of your films, but . . ." Al shrugged. "I know a lot of girls who, after a while, just . . . go blond."

"Spontaneously?" asked Suzanne.

"No, they decide to do it after . . . Oh, I see. A joke." Al smiled. "Shall we order?"

The waitress appeared with a pad and pencil. Suzanne ordered cottage cheese and fruit. Al ordered a number eleven, a cheeseburger with bacon and Russian dressing and French fries, and a Diet Coke. Suzanne hesitated, craving caffeine, then mustered all her willpower and asked for mineral water. The waitress left them sitting across from each other in silence. Suzanne watched Al light a Vantage as though she'd never seen it done before. She wondered if she was in the midst of an anecdote that, for reasons of proximity, she was not yet able to perceive. "You have a nice car," she said.

"Isn't she a beaut?" said Al, beaming as he blew out a lungful of smoke. "I had her shipped here from New York. Do you have any idea what a pain in the butt it is to ship a car?"

"I once had someone drive mine out," Suzanne offered.

"Well," said Al, "I would hardly trust my Bentley with a *person*."

"I've never driven one," she responded lamely. "They must drive smoothly or something to have become such a status symbol. I mean, a cliché doesn't become a cliché for nothing." She no longer knew what she was talking about, so she stopped, plunging them back into silence. Their table was becoming a cemetery for dead air.

Al gave her a thumbs-up gesture and said, "It rides like a *dream*."

"Really?" said Suzanne. "That's great."

Suddenly, Al got to the point. "What I'd like to say right up front is how much I dislike your choice of agents."

"Pardon me?" Suzanne didn't quite know where she was.

"When Bob gave me your number, I hadn't known you had gotten a new agent," Al said. "I couldn't possibly work with Mark Auerbach. I think he's full of shit."

"Really?" said Suzanne, without expression. She could just as well have said "hunchback" or "toaster" for all the impact it had on Al. He was on a roll now, and she was truly incidental.

"None of my people are with the Empire Agency," Al was saying. "I moved all my people, even Zita Farina. *She's* going to be a *huge* star."

Suzanne nodded and wondered how much his watch cost as the waitress mercifully arrived with their food. She stuffed a banana into her mouth and made a mental note to kill Bob Becker.

"You know what I'd do with you?" said Al, salting his fries. Suzanne shook her head, even though Al wasn't looking at her. "I'd put the word out that you were a client of mine and we were interested in projects, and see what kind of reaction we'd get. See where you stand." He took a big bite of his hamburger and kept talking as he chewed. "You're perfect for a series, 'cause you can play intelligent, and people like intelligent. We have a series in development right now that you might be perfect for."

"Well, send it to me," Suzanne said, more to her cottage cheese than to him. "I'll read it."

"I'll send it to you when we have a script," Al said. "It's a show for a guy and three women. You'd be great for the younger woman, the magazine editor. Very bright, funny, down to earth."

"I'd like to do a series," Suzanne said seriously. "I mean, I'd be stupid not to. But I keep thinking that movies are more—"

"You're being naive," interrupted Al, waving a French fry dismissively. "If you can get a good part in a pilot, you should go for it."

"Who *is* this guy?" Suzanne wondered. "Whether I'm being naive or not," she said testily, "I would like to explore it a little bit before jumping into television world."

"It's a potentially enormous career-maker," Al said, chewing another big bite of burger. "Remember *Happy Days*? Henry Winkler got sixth billing. Remember *Welcome Back, Kotter*? Travolta was way down on the cast list, *tiny* speaking part."

Suzanne decided she didn't want a personal manager, and she certainly didn't want one that got *this* personal. People she had known for years didn't call her "naive." She felt defeated. She didn't seem to want to be anything badly enough to do what was required. She knew a lot of the right people, but she didn't know them in the right way. Something about pushing your way to the front seemed so undignified.

She liked acting, all right. She just didn't like a lot of what you had to do in order to be *allowed* to act: the readings, the videotapings, the meetings, the criticism, the rejections. She was too old, too young, too pretty, too short, not funny enough, *too* funny . . . It could wear you down after a while. After a while, it became a job in itself not to take those pronouncements personally.

"I'd like to see you do a guest shot on a *Miami Vice* or a *Cosby*," Al was saying. "Do some really good episodic. They could build a whole show around you, and then, *snap*," he snapped his fingers, "forty million people see you in one night. But even more important," he said, gesturing with his thumb behind his back, "*they* see you."

"Who?" asked Suzanne, looking over his shoulder.

"The industry," he answered, exasperated.

"Oh," Suzanne said. She felt nauseous. Al continued extolling the virtues of episodic, and when he paused momentarily, she interjected, "But not that many women go on to movies from TV. Except Shelley Long."

"You don't count Sally Field?" leered Al. "*The Flying Nun* made her."

"What about *Norma Rae*?" asked Suzanne hopefully.

"*The Flying Nun* did it," said Al confidently. "It *made* her."

Suzanne didn't want to argue *Norma Rae/Flying Nun* statistics for the rest of the lunch, so she got up and said with a smile, "I'm just going to the men's room."

"Quite the kidder, aren't you?" said Al. "I like that."

On her way to the bathroom she passed two women in their late twenties, who were standing by the phones and talking about how they could never live in L.A. because the nice weather all the time would annoy them. "I like seasons," one of them said. When Suzanne came out they were still there, talking now about a mutual acquaintance of theirs. "I heard she blew Don Johnson," said the woman who liked seasons.

When she got back to the table, Al had paid the bill. "I'm gonna keep up with you," he said, rising to greet her.

"Okay," said Suzanne, her chest tight. "Good."

"I'm going to South Carolina tomorrow to visit a client," he said as they walked to the parking lot. "But I'm going to keep pestering you about my pilot."

"Great," said Suzanne, desperate for her car. "I want to read it."

"I wish you weren't with that putz Auerbach."

"Well," Suzanne shrugged as her car arrived. "Thank you for lunch."

"What lunch?" bellowed Al. "You ate like a bird."

"I ate like a blonde," corrected Suzanne, sliding into her seat and closing the door while Al tipped the parking attendant for her. "Thanks, Al." She waved. "Talk to you soon."

"Bye, sweetheart," shouted Al. She watched him in her rearview mirror, working on his teeth and adjusting Al Junior, and imagined him nude except for a leather maid's outfit and some nipple clamps. She waved again, then drove into the post-luncheon traffic.

She arrived for her facial ten minutes late, apologizing as she ran past the desk to the back for her pink facial robe. As she threw it on, a small dark-haired woman turned to her and said, "Susie?"

"Suzanne," corrected Suzanne. "Yes, I'm . . . me."

"This way, please," said the woman, in a heavy Eastern European accent. Suzanne followed her into a small room. The woman turned on the light and motioned for Suzanne to lie down on the table.

"I am Marina, your skin consultant," she said. "Will you be having collagen or a vegetable peel today?"

"Uh, vegetable peel, I guess," answered Suzanne. She wished she had her regular facial lady, Jean, but she had rescheduled this appointment so many times in the past few days that Jean wasn't available. Marina put a terry-cloth headband on Suzanne's head to protect her hair, then moved some cleansing cream around on her face. She removed the cream with cotton and moved a big light over to examine her skin.

"When was your last facial?" asked Marina.

"Last month," lied Suzanne. She had had two last week.

"You need a cleaning very badly."

Suzanne thought she detected a note of contempt in Marina's voice. "I know," she said dejectedly.

"And," said Marina, "you have one very big—"

"I *know*!" interrupted Suzanne loudly. "I know," she repeated, more softly this time. "If it gets any bigger, I'll have to set up charge accounts for it."

"I don't know if I can get rid of that for you," said Marina doubtfully. "I don't think it's ready yet."

"Just do what you can," Suzanne said. "I'll understand."

"Okay, then we start," said Marina, suddenly brusque, as she moved the hateful light away. She began mixing something behind Suzanne's head, in a little porcelain dish. "Now," she said gravely, as she spread something creamy and strange over Suzanne's face, "you are going to feel a very big smell."

It was true. Suzanne felt the biggest smell of her life. Marina passed a paper fan in front of Suzanne's face to move the horrible vegetable peel fumes as they rose from the muck. After about fifteen minutes the stench died down, presumably taking with it a layer of Suzanne's skin, so Marina removed the peel and began steaming Suzanne's face for the deep pore work.

Suzanne hated the deep pore cleansing, but when you got down to it, that was really what facials were all about. She wondered what her skin would look like if she'd never had all these facials. Probably better. She'd probably ruined her skin's ability to clean itself by getting it addicted to this whole process.

"Am I hurting you?" asked Marina disinterestedly.

"No, not really," lied Suzanne.

"The nose and the chin are the worst part. We are almost done with the nose. It was very clogged. Are you using our cleanser?"

"Yes," lied Suzanne.

"Well, you should use it three times a day," said Marina sternly. "And use our scrub."

"Okay," said Suzanne. "Owwww!"

"Sorry," said Marina without remorse. "The chin, you know, very sensitive." She started to move under Suzanne's chin onto her neck.

"No, no," Suzanne said earnestly. "Leave that."

"But it is a very big—"

"Just leave it," she said adamantly. "Just do the part of my face the world sees, and leave the underbelly to me."

"But—"

"It hurts too much and I don't care enough, okay?" snapped Suzanne. "Leave it!"

"Okay," sniffed Marina.

They finished the facial in silence, then Suzanne slipped off the little pink robe and paid the bill. She left Marina, whom she loathed and felt guilty for loathing, a big tip.

She decided to have the car washed. She always felt good when she got the car washed, like she was truly participating in her life. While she waited, she called her machine to check her messages. Mark Auerbach's secretary had called about setting up a meeting for her on the new Spencer Matheisen picture, *A Total Bust*. Her dentist Dr. Gibbon's assistant had called asking if she had forgotten she had an eleven-fifteen appointment for a cleaning. (She had.) She'd also had calls from Kate Rosenman, a producer friend of hers in AA, and her brother Thomas, who'd called from Turkey, where he was filming a documentary on the unearthing of Noah's Ark. And, from New York, her friend Lucy Copeland had called from underneath a sleeping Scott Hastings—her newest married lover—"just to say hi."

When she got back in her car, she noticed how clean the windshield was. She was going to feel good now, Suzanne thought. She was going to enjoy her life as though she was someone else living it, someone who had won living her life as a prize. Her house, her friends, her family, her clothes, her car . . . She was going to appreciate them as though she had had this whole other life before, and now she had won this one. She drove through the heart of Beverly Hills, down the palm-lined streets, listening to Steely Dan sing "Don't Take Me Alive."

By the time she got home, her determination to enjoy her life had been crushed under the weight of pre-party tension. She opened a Diet Coke, ate a miniature Tootsie Roll, called and left a message for Lucy—she knew she'd be out, but she wanted to go on record as having called—then went in to run her bath.

"Why can't I look like Nastassia Kinski?" Suzanne thought, an hour and a half later, as she put the finishing touches on her makeup. She had read in *Vogue* that there was an operation that made your lips big like Nastassia Kinski's. Unfortunately, it involved taking skin from your vagina and moving it to your mouth. Suzanne couldn't quite bring herself to do this, fearing that it would ruin kissing for her. Still, it rolled around in her head for weeks as a vague possibility. She scrutinized her work and saw that she had disguised her blemish so well that it was now a highly conspicuous white spot, a headlight on her face.

She had a tendency to keep her chin down in her chest when her skin broke out. Even if people seemed to be looking in her eyes, she knew they were thinking, "Poor thing, she's got a zit. Her life must not work."

Sometimes when she looked in the mirror she thought, "Sure, *that* girl is attractive. *She* looks good." As soon as she walked away from her reflection, though, she added, "But *I'm* not." Her whole personality was designed to distract people from her looks. The fact that she was quite pretty—and that, on some level, she even knew it—made it all the more bizarre when she opened her mouth and Phyllis Diller came out.

She checked her outfit in her full-length mirror. With her tight blue skirt, with her top that snapped between her legs so that it looked tight, and especially with her stockings, she was definitely "dressed for them." She stepped into her treacherous black heels, put on her black jacket, grabbed her blue bag, and took one last look at herself.

She sighed. "I look like a basketball with lips," she thought. "An angry grape. A two-day-old balloon."

"You look fine," said her sane part, that tiny section of her brain that sat in the back and cheered.

"I look ready," she thought, then said aloud, "Let's party," and strode off to her car. She switched on the ignition and "Burning Down the House" came blasting out of her speakers as she backed down the driveway.

She took the long way to Wallis's house so she could have a nice, calming, deafening drive. She found she was now changing stations even when she found a song she liked. She had come to enjoy the quest for a good song more than the songs themselves.

Interesting. She checked herself repeatedly in the rearview mirror as she drove.

When she was a block away she saw the parking attendants, dark men in red jackets and black pants. Suzanne saw the cars they'd already parked—the Porsches, the Jaguars, the Rollses—and suddenly panicked. She should have brought a date, she realized. Should have had her hair done. Should have worn a different dress, other earrings, less perfume. She got out of her car looking as casual as possible and turned it over to a total stranger. Looking at the lights on the lawn, she thought, "I could still leave. I could still turn around screaming and sobbing and grab my keys back from the man with strange sideburns and . . ."

Suzanne walked stoically up the imposing driveway, like a condemned man about to face a firing squad without cigarette or blindfold, to the huge, secluded stone mansion. A butler opened the door. She stood in the entrance for a moment experiencing waves of HPT—Hollywood Party Terror—then went in.

Under a large mirror was a silver tray containing tiny envelopes with the names of the guests on them. Suzanne smiled wanly at the butler and headed dutifully for the tray. After some graceful rummaging, she found her envelope. Her name was misspelled. The butler asked if she wanted anything to drink. "Does it show?" she replied, and ordered a stiff Diet Coke.

The wall next to the stairs was lined with art, *lots* of art. The house was clearly a showcase for this collection, and all the furniture was in bland, don't-look-at-me colors so that guests could fully appreciate Wallis's fabulous art. Actually, it was Wallis's husband's art collection, but whenever anyone thought about Wallis and Milton Klein, they mostly thought about Wallis. Wallis had the personality, Milton had the money. Wallis had the style, Milton had the hit television shows. Wallis had Milton.

In the ten years she had known the two of them, Suzanne had never actually had a conversation with Milton. She talked to Wallis a lot on the phone, but then Wallis talked to everyone she knew a lot on the phone. Wallis had once pointed out to Suzanne that one of her ears was "smushed in" tighter against her head, and had said it was from talking on the phone so much. She had speaker phones now, but she still preferred the old-fashioned method of cradling the receiver between her shoulder and head. Wallis liked to say that she wasn't a gossip, she was *the* gossip, figuring that if you were going to be something you should be it completely. Wallis and Milton had had one daughter together and an assortment of children from other marriages. None of their offspring were in evidence tonight.

On the wall next to the guest bathroom was a painting that always looked very familiar to Suzanne. She assumed it was a famous painting, a Picasso or a Matisse. She thought it was awful. Maybe if she took an art class, she thought, she could appreciate some of the art that everyone around her seemed to appreciate. She wondered why she had ever quit smoking. Maybe she should just smoke at parties.

She walked down the two steps into the living room, with its unobtrusive furniture, its obtrusive art, and its view of the backyard that was set up to look like another painting: a painting of a backyard with a Henry Moore sculpture of a nude fat woman in it. She heard a squeal and spotted Wallis coming toward her, a smiling vision in red and blond. "If it isn't the brain trust herself!" cried Wallis, embracing Suzanne. "You look adorable!" Suzanne knew then, with absolute certainty, that she must look even worse than she thought.

"You mean my huge rubber head?" she mumbled into Wallis's perfect long hair that almost didn't smell of hair spray.

"Your rubber what?" Wallis said, holding her at arm's length. "What are you talking about? Come over here and say hello to Toni and Harlon."

Suzanne knew Toni and Harlon from other parties. Toni Barnes had just won an Academy Award for playing the murderous florist in *A Bunch of Violets*, and Harlon DeVore was her boyfriend and business manager. Suzanne thought she should probably smoke. *She* would never win an Academy Award, and even if she did, she would probably always be as tormented as she was now, so what could a cigarette matter? She congratulated Toni on her Oscar and asked Harlon if he'd missed her, just to see how good a job he'd do of pretending to remember who she was. Then she moved over to a bowl of nuts to breathe privately and plan her strategy. She was in a full-tilt panic, but she tried to look like she couldn't imagine doing anything more relaxing than standing alone at a table next to something that looked like pink whipped cream but was probably salmon mousse and picking cashews out of a bowl of nuts in a room full of celebrities in Bel Air.

Standing with her back to Suzanne was Rachel Sarnoff, an attractive studio executive who, Suzanne had heard from Wallis, had just broken off a three-month affair with Todd Zane, an English rock star and a legendary cocaine addict. Rachel had gotten Todd to promise he'd quit cocaine—Todd promised everyone he went out with that he'd quit cocaine for them—and then she'd caught him doing cocaine again, so she'd broken up with him. Suzanne wondered how Rachel was handling the breakup. She looked fine, but then, except for her, everyone in Hollywood looked fine all the time. That had nothing to do with anything.

Rachel was talking to a guy Suzanne vaguely knew from New York, a playwright named Tom Sarafian. From the conversation that Suzanne was desperately trying to overhear, she thought this was probably their first meeting.

"What does that *mean, A Night Full of Shoes?*" Rachel demanded. "It sounds so pretentious."

"Of course it's pretentious," Tom said, trying to soothe her. "In New York, pretentious is commercial."

"How can you *stand* it?" Rachel snapped. "How can you *live* there, with everyone so pale and intellectual and *sweating* from drugs?" Suzanne guessed the breakup with Todd Zane had been painful.

Just then, Wallis walked up to them with a "new girl." Milton collected art and Wallis collected artists, and this was her latest find, a dark-haired dark-eyed beauty whom she was presenting to

Rachel and Tom. "This is April Lanning, an artist from Manhattan. Milton bought a piece from her last week." April smiled politely and said hello.

"Don't you remember me?" asked Tom.

"No," said April blankly. "Should I?"

"We dated in the Hamptons a few summers ago," Tom said, then waited expectantly for her flash of recognition.

April looked quite embarrassed. "I'm afraid I don't," she said.

"Did you have sex?" Rachel asked Tom.

"I believe we tried, but I was . . ." He searched for the right word, then snapped his fingers as he found it. "Impotent!" he said brightly, as if it was a good word, like "tan." April looked very flustered.

"Really?" said Rachel. "From alcohol and drugs, or do you have some kind of psychological disorder?"

"Well," said Tom, "probably the latter. Let's put it this way, it wasn't the first time."

"I don't really . . . ," April stammered. "The Hamptons?"

"Maybe it'll come back to you over dinner," offered Wallis. "Come say hello to Suzanne." She steered April away from Rachel and Tom, who noticed Suzanne and waved at her. She smiled back, trying not to look at his sad crotch.

"Have you two met?" Wallis asked Suzanne as she practically carried April toward her. "Suzanne Vale, April Lanning."

"No," said Suzanne. Then, shaking April's hand, she said to her, "But you once almost had sex with an impotent acquaintance of mine." April looked ashen. "I'm kidding," Suzanne said. "Nice to meet you."

"You should see her pieces," Wallis enthused, squeezing April's arm. "I never knew I liked photorealism before."

"Have you been in L.A. long?" Suzanne asked.

"Huh?" said April.

"I think April could use a drink," said Wallis. "Come, dear." She led April past the painting made of broken teacup pieces, toward the bar in the corner.

Suzanne saw her skin doctor, Walter Marks, enter the room and felt reassured. She made her way over to his beaming bearded face. "You're disappointed in my hair, aren't you?" she greeted him. "I have too much makeup on, don't I? Be honest with me. Do I look orange?"

"You're not drinking, are you?" said Walter. "No, of course not, you don't drink."

"You don't drink either, do you?" asked Suzanne, kissing his cheek.

"Hardly ever," he said. "I like to feel like I could perform surgery at any given moment."

"That's interesting," said Suzanne. "My goal was to feel I could go *into* surgery at any given moment."

"Who are you here with?" Walter asked.

"No one. You think I'm desperate, don't you?"

"Impaired, yes," Walter said. "Desperate, no. Why do you keep coming to these things when they cause you such torment?"

"I don't know," she said, "but I'm working on it in therapy."

"How is Norma?" Walter asked. "What a terrific lady."

"She's great," Suzanne said. "She said a great thing last week. I told her I thought people confused fame with success, and she said they confused fame with acceptance and— Who cares, right? You don't care. Who's that?" she asked with a nod of her head toward the door, where a fortyish blonde was standing in a dress that looked like it had something long and stringy sticking out from the bottom.

"Portia Lamm," said Walter. "The agent. What do you suppose that thing is hanging out of her dress?"

"Probably the tie of the last guy who was up there," said Suzanne, wondering what Portia Lamm had been on when she bought the dress. "Who's the guy with her? He looks familiar."

"That's that European actor, Vittorio something."

"Vittorio Amati," breathed Suzanne. "Wasn't he in *Death Wore a Dress?*"

"No," said Walter, "You're thinking of *The Head of the Pin.*"

"Was he in that?" asked Suzanne, watching the handsome actor talk to Wallis and Milton while Portia Lamm got their little envelopes. Walter reminded Suzanne of who Vittorio Amati played in *The Head of the Pin*, then started telling her about his visit to the psoriasis center at the Dead Sea.

While she was listening to Walter, her eyes scanned the bookshelves behind him, coming to rest on a copy of *The Guinness Book of Sexual World Records*. She reached over for it and browsed through it while Walter enlightened her on the history of scalp ailments. Suddenly, she interrupted him.

"Listen," she announced. " 'Most Sexual Organs in an Insect.' The tapeworm has thousands of penises." Suzanne was the happiest she'd been all evening. " 'Most Perishable Sexual Organs,' " she read ominously. "Did you know that the bee penis breaks off in the other bee and he dies?"

Walter stared at her with a combination of amusement and what could have been concern. "This is weird of me, to be doing this, isn't it?" said Suzanne, but before Walter had a chance to agree, Wallis breezed by and announced that dinner was ready. Suzanne reluctantly decided against bringing the book to the table and walked slowly with Walter to the dining room, hoping Wallis had seated her with someone good, or at least with no one bad.

She found herself sitting to the left of a short, swarthy man she recognized as the Czech director Gustav Bozena, and to the right of the guest of honor, a businessman named Fred Weaver, whose autobiography was moving up the best-seller lists fast enough to have attracted Hollywood's attention. Fred was a thin, sixtyish man with even thinner white hair, blue eyes, a slight sunburn, and a small, almost feminine mouth. His face gave the appearance of having been sharpened especially for this party.

On Fred's left sat Selena Warner, the aging British starlet who played Dorothea Pierce, the red-haired evil head nurse on *Chestnut Lodge*, a night-time soap set in an insane asylum. Suzanne had been at several parties with Selena Warner—the most recent had been only three nights earlier—but, since it had never been a particular goal of hers, had never actually met her. Now, though, Selena smiled at her—or, more correctly, turned her face with the smile on it toward Suzanne—and said, "I saw you the other night, didn't I?" Suzanne mumbled an affirmative response, but Selena's attention had already shifted to Fred Weaver, who asked her something about acting. She answered as if she had all the important insights about the profession.

"Sir John once said to me," she said, and Suzanne smiled and thought, I've waited my whole life to hear a sentence begin that way. She stared at Selena as if she was watching her on television and listened as she went on, "He said that he was sort of limited in a way himself. He showed me his hands and said he'd never done a day's work in his life, so he couldn't play a laborer. And he said to me that, in the same way, I could never play anything other than a beautiful woman. I don't know if I quite believe that, but . . . Such a sweet man, Sir John."

Suzanne felt she couldn't really top the Sir John story, so she concentrated on avoiding the oysters in her oyster soup. She thought they looked like gray elephant boogers. Horrible food! Fred said something about business and Selena tilted her head and leaned in knowingly. Her lips moved over her teeth like bubbling water, and when she understood particularly well, she batted her eyelashes at him. Her face was a Richter scale registering her comprehension.

When he'd finished, Selena said, "Well, you know how actors are," and turned her smile on Suzanne, who felt oddly flattered that Selena assumed she knew how they were. The conversation shifted, with no discernible segue, to how demeaning it was to have to depend on acting to express your creativity. Fred said that yes, he could see Selena's point that actors had to wait to act until there was a camera or an audience, while painters—even bad ones—could just paint whenever they wanted to. Selena took out a stick of lip gloss and glooped some on her lips.

Suzanne shifted her attention to her right and, to her dismay, found herself in a conversation about film with Gustav Bozena, whose English was only marginally better than Suzanne's Czech. She tried to ask smart questions, but she thought they just sounded pretentious. Gustav said he liked John Ford, he liked King Vidor, he liked Fellini. I can't believe this, she thought. I'm an asshole at a party talking to a famous director about film. When she heard herself ask, "Do you believe that film is a more visual medium and that things should be described instead of dialogued?" she wanted to cut her head open and drip brains on the table. It was all she could do to keep from choking on her own social vomit.

"You do not look so American," Gustav said. "You look European."

"Really?" Suzanne said. "You're crazed."

Gustav said he came from Prague and lived in Paris, and that Suzanne didn't look American because she looked right into people's faces. "This Americans do not do," Gustav said. "It is very European."

"Really?" she said, and kept looking right into his face, as if to make sure he didn't go back on what he'd said. She heard herself telling friends, "Gustav Bozena said I was very European."

Across the table a rock promoter named Chris Hunt, who Suzanne thought looked like a losing Senate candidate—he reminded her of John Tunney—was telling a story about Noel Coward going backstage to meet the Beatles. According to the legend, which Suzanne recognized from Noel Coward's memoirs, the Beatles had already left, so Coward went back to their hotel to tell them how much he'd liked the show, and then none of them came out to see him except Paul, who was very awkward. Coward had noted their rudeness in his diary.

When he finished this story, the girl next to him, Joan Lilly, a former top British model, declared, "Well, Noel Coward hardly stands the test of time." She said it with total authority, as if she was stating an accepted political position and that anyone who thought otherwise was simply outmoded.

"In the final analysis," said Chris Hunt, with the cavalier nonchalance you might overhear wafting out of a car as it drives slowly by, "the Beatles were just more interesting. Noel Coward," he added dismissively, "was a wit."

Suzanne stared at him, her eyes demanding, "Be serious. How can you make this an issue? How did we *get* here?" She guessed that he and Joan Lilly had never met before this evening, and now they were bonded for life in their rigid stance on Noel Coward's pathetic inferiority to the Beatles. She wanted to say something to somebody about the absurdity of the moment they were all sharing, but conversation was now over for her. These two had given taking a position a bad name.

Somehow the topic shifted to Winston Churchill, whose wit was also belittled. An American television producer whose name Suzanne didn't catch theorized that his reputation was based on the fact that every joke at that time was attributed to Churchill because they sounded better when told that way. "You know," the producer said. "It's like if you say, 'I haven't eaten in a week, so he bit me.' It's funnier if you say, 'Churchill said it.' "

It turned out Chris Hunt was something of an expert on Churchill as well, and he rattled off several Churchill classics. Suzanne leaned over to Gustav Bozena and whispered, "It looks like one of our guests has done some reading." Then she turned her attention back to her left.

"I honestly don't know why people don't like my character," Selena was saying. "I haven't killed anyone. My husband Charles has killed *three people* on the show."

"Well," Fred said, "I think the reason they don't like Dorothea, or rather, why Dorothea *fascinates* them, is because she's deceptive."

"Oh?" said Selena. "That's very interesting. I've never thought of that. That's very intriguing."

"Let me get totally into my now," Suzanne thought. "We are in a fabulous house in Bel Air sitting under Picassos and discussing the character of Dorothea *with* Dorothea over bad oyster soup."

She had embraced the values of the room and found she had nothing. She promised herself to remember this sensation the next time she was invited to a party.

She looked across at Joan, who seemed to be listening to a faraway concert of weird classical music, then looked at Chris. She thought he looked like an old boy—someone who should wear a backpack instead of carrying a briefcase, but a very high-style backpack.

She realized with dismay that this was her type of guy. She always ended up with guys like this, in relationships she likened to being partners on a school science fair project. She always felt like calling them up afterward and saying, "You left your beaker and your petri dish here. Do you want me to bring it to class tomorrow?" Now the old boy was telling a joke.

"How many surrealists does it take to screw in a light bulb?" he asked, then looked around with his eyebrows raised and his mouth open. After a moment's pause, he said, "Fish."

There was another short pause, and then laughter. Selena Warner said, "How clever," several times. Suzanne said, "Funny," to Gustav Bozena, who nodded with reserved enthusiasm. She considered explaining it to him, then realized the enormity of the job and thought better of it. Then Fred asked if anyone had heard any WASP jokes. Suzanne had, but she said nothing.

Fred Weaver was radiant with joke hope. "Two WASPs run into each other on the street," he said, "and one WASP says, 'How are you?' and the other WASP says, 'Fine.' " He glowed and waited.

"Oh, I get it," Selena said. "That's the joke." Everyone had a hearty delayed laugh. Gustav looked confused.

"What is a WASP?" he asked Suzanne.

She hesitated. "A kind of insect," she whispered earnestly.

"Like a bee." He nodded and stared in front of him vacantly, using this news to try to unlock the puzzle of the joke. By now, though, Fred was telling another one.

"A WASP is trying on a suit in a clothing store and he turns to the salesman and says, 'How much is this?' and the salesman says, 'Four hundred seventy-five dollars,' and the WASP says, 'I'll take it.'"

Everyone at the table roared, even Gustav, who said to Suzanne, laughing, "A bee buying a suit!"

The desserts arrived, little cakes in raspberry sauce. Everyone made "Mmmmm" noises as they chewed and swallowed and clinked their forks against the china. Suzanne ate all her raspberry sauce, then broke apart the cake to find the filling, some kind of nut paste. Suddenly, there was a burst of laughter at the next table. Suzanne saw Wallis standing with Brian Whitlock, a New York director whom she now whisked over to Suzanne's happy group. Wallis was radiant. "I'm sure all of you know Brian," she said.

"Certainly," said Selena Warner, nodding enthusiastically. The others mumbled vaguely in the affirmative, though in fact no one at the table had ever met him.

"Well, I'm forcing Brian to tell this fabulous story of his to everyone," Wallis said. "It's just the most fabulous story."

Brian looked embarrassed. "Wallis, just let me tell it, okay?" he said. He pulled over a chair and sat between Selena and Fred.

"I was invited to this concert in London last week," he began. "Some benefit thing where everyone played—Bowie, Sting, Elton John, *everyone*. And the Prince and Princess of Wales were there. Well, I wanted to meet her so bad I was quite mad.

"Afterward," he continued, "there was a reception, and I found myself standing a few feet away from her. I knew she could hear me, so I started saying all this funny stuff, and I could see that she was listening and laughing, and I thought, 'She gets me. She literally gets me.' So I got myself introduced, and the guy who introduced us said, 'This is Brian Whitlock, he directed *The Punishing*

Blow.' And she said, 'Really?' It turned out she'd seen *The Punishing Blow*.

"So I'm in heaven, she's asking questions about my movie, and I'm making her laugh—she was very cute—and all of a sudden I hear someone say, 'Brian!' Well, I'm talking to the Princess of Wales so I try to ignore it, and I hear again, '*Brian!*' And I look, and it's an Oriental girl in sunglasses. I have no idea who she is, but she knows my name and she comes and stands between the Princess and me and says, 'I'm Yashimoto, I work in the office across the hall from yours. How long are you in London for?'

"So I lean behind her and I silently say to the Princess, 'I don't know who this is,' and Yashimoto says, 'I'm here doing publicity on this show and then I'm going to Lisbon tomorrow. Have you ever been to Portugal?' And the Princess drifts away, and Yashimoto says, 'I can't believe you're here, this is so great.' And I say, 'Do you realize who I was talking to?' and she says, 'Oh, I'm just one of those people who's not impressed by anybody.' "

Everyone laughed uproariously, even Suzanne. "That's actually true?" asked Chris Hunt.

"It has to be," answered Selena on Brian's behalf. "No one could make up something that absurd."

"But did you know the girl?" asked Joan Lilly.

"She worked across the hall from me in New York, I guess," shrugged Brian. "In the Brill Building."

Everyone at the table seemed to be entertained, so Suzanne figured she'd take a bathroom break and kill some time. Soon, she thought, she could go home. Soon the bell would ring dismissing her from party class, and she would run up the street with her hair flying behind her, free . . .

She excused herself to Gustav, and to anyone else who felt particularly close to her, and ventured forth into the huge house. There was no one in the little waiting room, so she went into the bathroom, closed the door, and locked it. The walls were all soft rose-colored cloth, and the sink was rose marble. Suzanne put the toilet seat down and began some real party breathing.

She heard someone enter the tiny room just outside. Two voices. Two women. They seemed to be reviewing the evening. "Did you see Selena Warner?" one of them said. "She looks *ancient.*"

"And what about that burp of a husband she's got," said the other.

"Well, you know what they say," said the first voice. "TV stars can't be choosers."

Suzanne was not breathing as comfortably now. Their voices suddenly became more muffled. Why couldn't she hear them? She put her ear against the door.

"I feel sorry for her," one was saying.

Who? thought Suzanne. Me?

"She hasn't worked in a while, and she lives alone," said the other.

It *is* me! she thought. Oh my God, they're talking about me. How will I ever get out of here?

"Why can't she get work? She's a pretty good actress, and she certainly has connections."

Suzanne was humiliated. I can never leave this powder room, she thought. She was breathing like a sick baby.

"Haven't you heard?" said one of the voices. "She's put on a lot of weight."

Everyone knows! Everyone's talking about me!

"Really?" said the other.

"Oh, yes, about thirty or forty pounds."

"*Really?*" said the other.

Oh, thought Suzanne. Who? Thirty or forty. Oh.

She was devastated now. It hardly mattered that they hadn't been talking about her. The way she felt now, they might as well have been. She had to get home, that much was clear. She flushed the toilet and walked out into the little room. The voices belonged to two attractive women in their forties, neither of whom Suzanne knew. She smiled and nodded at them as she passed, trying to look hopeful and thrilled.

She considered leaving without saying good night, but ruled that out when she considered how it would look. She went back into the dining room, where Wallis was presenting Brian to yet another table. Many of the guests were moving to the living room with their coffee and after-dinner drinks. Suzanne waited on the edge of the party, on the outskirts of the in crowd. When Brian began his story again, she caught her hostess's eye.

Wallis came over. "I just can't get over Brian's story," she said. "*Imagine* interrupting a conversation with royalty."

"I was on acid when I met Princess Margaret," said Suzanne. "Listen, Wallis, I gotta go. It was great. Great cake."

"So soon?" Wallis pouted. "Phil Esterbrook might play one of his songs. Are you sure you can't stay?"

"No, really," said Suzanne, letting Wallis kiss her as she moved toward the door. "I'm retaining water for a couple of people, and I've got to return it by midnight."

When she put her nightgown on and went to bed, she didn't know that she intended to stay there. By Sunday afternoon, though, she was fairly dug in, with empty soft drink cans piling up on her night table and the slow burn of television branding her cowlike brown eyes.

"Hemingway needed his rest," her mother assured her over the phone. "So did Paul Muni. Alfred Lunt would just retreat to his garden and let his wife answer the phone.

It always relaxed Suzanne to hear her mother compare her favorably to someone like Paul Muni or Alfred Lunt. She settled down under her covers. "You're just like me, Suzanne," her mother said. "You just get overwhelmed sometimes. I don't think you should feel bad about going to bed for a few days. You're a sensitive, questioning personality."

Suzanne wondered when she had begun to be more of a personality than a person. When her shrink had pointed it out to her, she'd felt as though she'd actually known it for a long time. When she was twenty-one she had written in her journal, "I narrate a life I'm reluctant to live." Soothed by her mother's voice, she found herself recalling the maternal voice of her therapist at her last session.

"I think that basically you are a very frightened, shy person," Norma had said, her eyebrows slightly raised with the effort of insight. "You seem very open about yourself, but it's really just part of your need to control. You want people to know that you're well aware of the truth about yourself. It's like a fat girl walking into a room and announcing that she's fat."

Suzanne had sat there glowing with a deep, happy blush. "That's wonderful," she exclaimed, gazing at Norma in admiration.

"You're just excited because now you have another truth to entertain people with," Norma had said. "Part of your little honesty show, which exists to make people think you're not trying to stay as far away from them as you actually are."

Suzanne had been thrilled. She'd been caught. Even as she had been hearing these new truths, she was storing them where she stored all the pertinent information she used when describing herself to new people, or when describing herself to old people in a new way. Describing herself was Suzanne's way of being herself. It was as close as she got, and it was way off the mark. She had shaken her head with wonder and asked, "So, now what do I do?"

"Nothing," Norma had said, as though this should have been obvious. "What could you do? This is simply how you operate."

"So this is it? I'm sentenced to a life of lifelike behavior?"

"We obviously have a lot of work to do," Norma had said. "You will, of course, always be like this to some degree. You have fashioned yourself a personality of highly intricate design. It would be almost impossible to dismantle, and that is not our purpose. I just want you to *feel* something, in between all this talking and thinking that you do. I want you to lead a life instead of following one around."

Now, in bed, Suzanne heard her mother mention Jane Powell.

". . . and Shirley MacLaine took several *years* off," her mother said. "Listen, dear, do you want me to send Mary up to fix you something? She has nothing to do when I'm out of town. She's just sitting in my house watching TV and eating Fritos. She could come to your house and fix you a bacon sandwich, or chicken crepes. It always makes me feel better when I've eaten something . . ."

It was decided that Mary would come up and fix her a meal and straighten up her house. Suzanne hung up, sighed, and rolled over in bed to face the TV. Someone exploded. She searched her bedding for the remote control clicker, found it under several pillows, and scanned the stations for solace.

When Mary arrived she removed all the empty cans from the bedroom. Suzanne loved Mary, who had taken care of her since she was six. "What was I like when I was little, Mare?"

"You were a good li'l child," said Mary, straightening the pillows behind Suzanne's head. "You were always a good li'l girl. Now, what can I fix you for lunch?"

Suzanne asked for a bacon sandwich and German chocolate cake. Mary went off to the kitchen, and Suzanne rolled over on her side. She wondered how long she was going to stay in bed. She wondered if she would awaken one morning—maybe *tomorrow* morning—and feel like bounding back into her life, refreshed and unafraid. Just now, though, she felt stale and paralyzed.

She wanted so to be tranquil, to be someone who took walks in the late-afternoon sun, listening to the birds and crickets and feeling the whole world breathe. Instead, she lived in her head like a madwoman locked in a tower, hearing the wind howling through her hair and waiting for someone to come and rescue her from feeling things so deeply that her bones burned. She had plenty of evidence that she had a good life. She just couldn't feel the life she saw she had. It was as though she had cancer of the perspective.

She was having trouble sleeping again, lying still with her thoughts tossing and turning. As far back as she could remember, she had had trouble sleeping. As a child she would wait out her naptime like a prison sentence. She would lie in bed and stare at the wallpaper pattern and wonder what would happen if there were no heaven. She thought the universe would probably go on and on, spilling all over everything. Heaven was kind of a hat on the universe, a lid that kept everything underneath it where it belonged.

Suzanne lay in bed staring at the television, waiting for her bacon sandwich, thinking about infinity.

By Wednesday, she felt kind of dingy. She accidentally caught a glimpse of herself in the bathroom mirror and thought there was a giant shell on her neck. "Is that anorexia?" she wondered. "Is it anorexia when you look in the mirror and your head looks like the top of a squid without all the arms?"

She felt bloated. She'd been going to the gym for a while, and had really started noticing a difference in her body, but now she was getting soft and shapeless again. "Caspar the squid," she said aloud.

Suzanne identified herself in her voice. She was as close as she ever got to being whoever she was when she was talking. She existed through sound. It startled her to see her reflection, because she didn't identify with her appearance. She wasn't what she looked like, she was what she sounded like. That was why she always got confused in the closet. What should she wear? It was hard to dress a voice.

She walked into her closet, Pandora's Closet, bursting with options, and experienced the automatic reaction: "I have nothing to wear." That wasn't it, though. Obviously, she had plenty of clothes, but they were the wrong kind of clothes. They were clothes she had already bought. Suzanne only liked clothes she was about to buy. She knew someday she would find the exact right outfit that would make her life work. Maybe not her whole life, she thought, as she got back in bed, but at least the parts she had to dress for.

Around noon, her friend Lucy called from New York, where she'd gone two weeks earlier to be with the married guy she'd gotten involved with. Lucy liked affairs with married men because, as she'd explained to Suzanne many times, "You don't have to have entire relationships with them."

"I met him on that TV movie I did," Lucy said. "*Blood on the Snow,* that ski resort murder thing. He played the murderer and he stalked me, and it was very romantic. I mean, he played a good murderer. He didn't play a regular murderer, he played it like a charming guy. And we were on location in Idaho, and being on location is kind of a permission zone, anyway."

"You're a star fucker," Suzanne said matter-of-factly.

"I like celebrities, I've got to admit it," Lucy said, "but I'm not a star fucker. I'm a *talent* fucker, and this guy is very talented. Well, actually he's limited, but the area he's limited in is more interesting than most people's entire range."

"Scott Hastings," Suzanne said. "He made that name up, didn't he?"

"No," said Lucy. "Actually, his first name is Bob. Robert Scott Hastings."

"Bob Hastings," said Suzanne, "*Colonel* Bob Hastings. No wonder he changed it. So, is his wife there?"

"Holster Hips?" said Lucy. "Yeah, they rented a house in Connecticut, but he's in the city a lot rehearsing for his play."

"Another married guy," Suzanne sighed. "I have to say, I never did like that last one."

"Earl?" said Lucy, with some surprise. "Really? You didn't like him? I thought you liked him."

"Well, I *told* you I liked him," said Suzanne. "I had to tell you I liked him, because you liked him so much. In fact, you liked him enough for both of us. What happened with him again?"

"He started to get sort of removed," Lucy said. "I mean, more removed than I like. I need a guy to be a little unreliable so I can stay interested. I don't know any women who don't feel that way, but then maybe if *I* didn't feel that way, I would know other kinds of women. Anyway, he got so removed he started having an affair with Isabel Hasbar."

"The English actress?" asked Suzanne. "Reginald Fleemer Hasbar's sister?"

"Yes, *that* Isabel Hasbar," said Lucy. "It was painful, but it was painful in an interesting way. It felt like it was a necessary part of the process, and . . . Wait, I've got another call . . . It's him, I've gotta go."

"Say hello to the Colonel for me," Suzanne said, but Lucy had already hung up. She switched the channel and saw a girl and a boy having sex. The girl opened her eyes and looked over the boy's shoulder just in time to see a man plunge a stake through the two of them.

Suzanne looked away, scanning the horizon of her room. Her house had been driving her crazy lately. Whenever she wasn't in a relationship, her house drove her crazy. First, her curtains didn't shut out enough morning light, so she usually ended up putting pillows over her head. But then, she also thought that she had too many pillows, and that they weren't soft enough. One of the paintings over her bed had a tear in its canvas.

Also, there were two orange soda stains on the white carpet, next to her bed. The cover on her smoke alarm had broken off. There were too many exposed electrical cords she was helpless to conceal, and a large basket of cassettes whose plastic cases had been lost sat beside her stereo. There were just too many *things*. Things growing over the surfaces of her home like a happy cancer.

She turned back to the television screen, searching it as if looking for a sign. A sign of life. Two men were fighting, and one of them went through a plate glass window, and she found herself staring at the bloodied face of Graham Davies, her first in a series of three actor boyfriends. Graham had been the nicest of the three—in fact, he had been her only nice boyfriend, because Suzanne was one of those unfortunate women who did not find nice men interesting. She'd learned her lesson after him. She found undesirables desirable. She sought out unpleasant boyfriends, then complained about them as though the government had allocated them to her. Still, at least she felt like she was taking part in something, even if it was a nightmare.

She changed the channel. Two women in riding clothes were talking on a hill. Suzanne knew one of them. She had done cocaine with her at a David Bowie concert in London. The girl had been wearing a very see-through dress, and she had also been present the night Suzanne started her affair with her second actor. TV was filled with memories for her, a liquid scrapbook. Maybe if she watched long enough, she thought, her whole life would flash slowly in front of her eyes. Now the girl she knew was playing with herself on a bus.

She reached for the clicker again and watched Ronald Reagan getting off a helicopter and waving. He cupped his hand to his ear and shrugged his shoulders while his wife was dragged ahead of him at the end of a dog's leash. You can see why he has her, Suzanne thought. She's angular. With that pointed head and all those sharp edges, she finishes him off in a way, so he doesn't just bleed into the rest of the big picture. She zips him in.

He was still smiling and waving. It's like he's our IV hookup in the White House, she thought. Doctor Reagan, with a bedside manner for a dying nation like you can't believe. Suzanne punched the clicker, and an actor she didn't recognize appeared on her TV screen explaining that there was no such thing as an actor's director. There were actors and there were directors. He was very convincing, but then that was an actor's job. It got very confusing sometimes. Sometimes actors heard that note of conviction in their voices in real life and actually believed themselves. She switched to channel 11, where a movie called *The Tattered Dress* was beginning, then punched up MTV. She watched a Bryan

Adams video, and wondered what life with him would be like. Finally, she switched back to the girl she had done cocaine with. It wasn't a good film, but she was somehow more comfortable watching someone she knew, however vaguely. The girl was describing how she'd had sex with her uncle.

Suzanne looked at her bedside table, which contained a bag of potato chips, some weird health cookies, a box of vanilla wafers, two empty glasses, one half-full glass of two-day-old orange juice, a half-empty can of flat Diet Coke, and a jar of peanut butter. She went for the peanut butter with two fingers.

The phone rang. She waited through the life-indicating three rings and then answered as though she was in the middle of an enormous amount of carefree fun. "Hello!"

"Hello, dear," said a familiar voice. "This is your mother, Doris."

"As opposed to my brother, Doris, or my uncle, Doris?" said Suzanne. "Since we're all named Doris in this family, I suppose it *is* necessary to establish just which Doris this is. Otherwise, it could lead to some highly embarrassing—"

"How are you feeling healthwise, dear?" her mother Doris interrupted in a concerned tone. "Because I spoke to Dr. Feldman just now and he says you might have food allergies. Wouldn't that be wonderful? Then you could just stop eating the particular food you're allergic to and not be in bed anymore. What exactly are you eating?"

"Just foods that lead inevitably to bypass," Suzanne said.

"Don't be smart, dear," said her mother. "Remember my food allergies. I found out I was allergic to shellfish. My lips get all huge and my tongue blows up like a balloon, and they have to give me steroids or something. You could be eating something that makes you tired."

"Could I be eating something that makes me apathetic and insecure?" asked Suzanne doubtfully.

"You underestimate the power of food allergies," said her mother confidently. "I told Dr. Feldman you'd be calling him."

"Just imagine," Suzanne said. "Here I've spent all these years in therapy, and it could have been tuna all along."

Suzanne was watching a black-and-white film starring Joseph Cotten and Ginger Rogers late Sunday afternoon, her ninth day in bed, when the phone rang. She grabbed it on the first ring. "You're on the line," she said.

"What if I were a guy?" said Lucy. "I would think you're desperate."

"I *am* desperate," said Suzanne. "Are you back? I thought you were spending the summer in New York with Colonel Bob."

"New York in the summer is like a cough," said Lucy. "It's like the whole country came here and coughed. Anyway, he went back to his wife."

"How bad do you feel?" asked Suzanne compassionately.

"Not too bad yet, but I always have emotional jet lag," Lucy said. "I just got home and crawled into bed, so that when the impact hits me like a crippling flu, I'll be where I belong."

"I'm going for a world record," said Suzanne. "I've been in bed for over a week. My life is like a lone, forgotten Q-Tip in the second-to-last drawer."

"Who am I speaking to?" asked Lucy. "Sylvia Plath?"

"Sylvia Papp," said Suzanne. "Joe's wife. Why don't you come over here and join me in my not-so-silent vigil?

"I'm going to be too depressed," said Lucy. "I shouldn't drive."

"I'll send a limo for you," said Suzanne.

An hour later, a black limousine turned off Outpost into Suzanne's driveway and Lucy got out. She was wearing her nightgown. She went into the house through the garage, walked back to the huge bedroom, and climbed into the bed. "Actors may know how to act," she said, "but a lot of them don't know how to behave."

"So," said Suzanne, "was it devastating?"

"I don't know yet," said Lucy. "I don't know that you *could* be devastated by an actor. But you know what? It's more insulting that he would dump me because he's not that good an actor. He's more like a TV actor than a movie actor, and it's just not as interesting as being left by a movie actor. I mean, when I was left by Andrew Keyes, you know, it was *Andrew Keyes*, and I got an anecdote out of it."

"You have slept with guys other than actors, haven't you?" asked Suzanne, offering Lucy a bowl of stale popcorn. "I seem to remember you going out with a lawyer."

"Bill Taft," said Lucy. "Yeah. It was *boring*. He used to talk about stuff like clearing miles of forests in Canada. That's what he talked about for *amusement*. I wanted to die in my salad at dinner."

Suzanne reached for the clicker and changed the channel. Their friend Amy Baxter was on the screen in an episode of her series, *Honey, I'm Home!* "What do you think about this thing with Amy and the art director?" she asked.

"Amy will never stay in that relationship," Lucy said. "She chased after him and chased after him, and now she's got him. I think she'll probably stay for a while because she'd be too embarrassed to leave so soon, but have you ever seen anyone look so *bored*?"

"That isn't bored. That's Amy," said Suzanne. "This guy is *fabulous*. He's real smart, he's good-looking, he's nice, and not even that *too nice* thing. He's got money, he's well connected, and he's got great taste in clothes. It's not like she found him under a rock. This is a great guy, but you know Amy. She's holding out for a *greater* guy. Somebody better could move to Hollywood, and if he did, then she would want *that* guy. Amy has to keep about thirty percent of herself in reserve just in case."

"Remember Sam Eisenberg?" Lucy said with a laugh. "She rolled through Sam like thunder."

"You know who would be a real blocker for her?" asked Suzanne. "Todd Zane. She could try to save Todd Zane. That would be brilliant."

"Did *you* ever sleep with him?" Lucy asked.

"Todd Zane?" said Suzanne. "No. Did you?"

"Yeah, I did," said Lucy. "He *is* great. He told me someone told him that he gave head like a girl."

"Really?" said Suzanne. "What does that mean? Good?"

"Yeah, I guess good," said Lucy. She stuck a few pieces of popcorn in her mouth. "I swear," she said. "I think I'm so slutty sometimes."

"Could you go get me a Diet Coke?" Suzanne asked in a small voice. "I don't want to walk by the mirror. My hair is so greasy it looks like it was poured over my head."

Lucy went to the kitchen and came back with two cans of Diet Coke. "The last time I had sex with Scott Hastings—excuse me, with *Colonel* Hastings," she said, "—it lasted three hours."

"You like to have that endless, nightmare sex," said Suzanne. "You use it like a flesh feedbag, you just put some guy on your face and you go into it like ... like I used to go into drugs, I guess."

"Sometimes I think all I want is to find a mean guy and make him be nice to me," said Lucy. "Or maybe a nice guy who's a little bit mean to me. But they're usually too nice too soon or too mean too long."

"I think I'm ill-suited for relationships," said Suzanne, "and this is not a thought that's going away. I mean, I can't date my whole life. I didn't even do it well when I was the right age. Think about it. What kind of a wimpy, pathetic guy would be willing to crawl through the moat of my personality and live in my house, with my stuff?" She opened her Diet Coke and sipped it as if she was sucking poison out of an aluminum wound. "I think I'm right on the verge of accepting that I'm going to live out my life in front of a television." She pointed at the screen. "That's gonna be the last thing I see before I die," she said, starting to laugh. "Rob

Lowe's face in *St. Elmo's Fire*. I'll be in a hospital and they'll be banging on my chest to get my heart started, and I'll be staring over them at the TV screen, and this movie will be on it. It's my destiny, I feel it."

"I know I'm going to get old and be one of those crazy women who sit on balconies and spit on people and scream, 'Get a haircut!'" Lucy said. "I know this, and I don't really fear it. I'd just like to move toward it with as much grace and dignity as possible."

On MTV, a new video came on by a pretty singer whose agent was featured in several scenes. Suzanne knew the agent from her high school days. Her cousin had given him a blow job at a party once, but that was before she'd found Jesus, who knocked those blow jobs at parties right out of her.

"Remember what it was like when you'd be getting ready to jump rope," she asked, "and two people were turning it, and you were waiting for exactly the right moment to jump in? I feel like that all the time."

"I keep thinking that we'll grow out of this," said Lucy.

"Grow out of it?" said Suzanne. "How much growing do you all of a sudden do after thirty?"

"Maybe it's a hormonal thing," Lucy offered.

"Maybe it is food allergies," said Suzanne. "Maybe my mom's right. Maybe this *is* all tuna."

"Could we be having a nervous breakdown?" Lucy asked. "A controlled nervous breakdown?"

"I don't know," Suzanne said doubtfully. "I'm not that nervous, and it's not really a breakdown. It's more of a *back*down, or a backing off. A pit stop. That's what we're having, a nervous pit stop. A not-so-nervous pit stop."

"I feel like maybe I've learned my lesson now," Lucy said. "I want to have learned it. Maybe this could be my epiphany. Maybe Scott Hastings was my epiphany, and now I'll just move into the rest of my life like it was lukewarm water."

"That's the way it works in movies," said Suzanne. "Something happens that has an impact on someone's life, and based on that impact, his life shifts course. Well, that's not how it happens in life. Something has an impact on you, and then your life stays the same, and you think, 'Well, what about the impact?' You have epiphanies all the time. They just don't have any effect."

"Maybe they do," said Lucy hopefully, "only we can't see it because we're in the middle of it. Maybe right now we're at the end of one thing and the beginning of another, but we just don't know it yet."

"I think," said Suzanne, suddenly serious, "that we should agree that we won't get out of bed until we decide what to do with the second half of our lives. This is like life's intermission."

"It could take a long time," said Lucy dubiously, "because we've really made a big mess of it. We're in our *thirties* already. I mean, what's our plan here? I don't feel like we really have a plan yet."

"We could find our plan on TV," Suzanne said. "That's where most people learn about morals and ideals and stuff like that."

"Is it really?" asked Lucy. "Because I watched TV and never got any. Or maybe I did, and didn't know it."

"You were probably watching the wrong channels," said Suzanne.

"Okay," said Lucy, "so our plan is that we stay here and watch television, the *right* channels, and we'll figure out our values. Good plan."

Suzanne sighed. "We have no lives. I think it was Freud who said that the way they determined if people were crazy was whether their insanity interfered with love and work. Those are the two areas. And we have no love and no work."

"Does that mean we're crazy?" asked Lucy.

"Well, certainly we're ... defective. We're defective units. Something broke in our heads, some way we look at things broke, and now we have to fix it. Maybe there's a way to look at things that makes it okay to not have work, or to wind up as maiden aunts. If there is, we should know about it."

"I had a dream last night that I was driving in the dark without any lights on and no brakes," Lucy said.

"I wonder what *that* means."

"I don't need to see a shrink to figure out what it means, okay?" said Lucy, who had never been to one. "I'm out of control. I know that about myself. And when I go out of control, I latch on to something that looks stable, and married men look stable to me. They look like they were etched in air, and they're there for me to make them unstable. I like to try to jar them. Anyway, while we're on shrinks, how's Norma?"

"Norma wants me to lead a life instead of follow one around," Suzanne said. "But she's been away for the past two weeks. I've been on kind of an enforced shrink break, so I thought I'd just go to bed and see what *I* think about all this. I don't want any advice. I mean, I like to talk to you, but I don't feel like you have any advice."

"Thank you," said Lucy. "That's very, very beautiful of you to say. Hey, I hear Jack Burroughs is doing *Ziz! II*. What's the status of *that* relationship?"

"That never was a relationship," said Suzanne. "It was just a theory both of us had for a while. If we'd have had a relationship, we suspected, we wouldn't have liked it very much, so we didn't have one. We just talked constantly about the one we didn't have."

"Who ended the theory?" Lucy asked.

"I finally left," Suzanne said. "I stopped in mid-sentence one day and decided that's where I wanted to end it. You know, I always thought you could work on a relationship, but there's work and then there's *construction* work."

"Guys are great before you know who they are," said Lucy. "They're great when you're still with who they might be."

"Did you ever sleep with Jack?"

"No," said Lucy. "We fooled around once, but someone interrupted us and it just never got continued. We were both real stoned."

"Interesting," said Suzanne. "You never slept with Jack Burroughs, and I never slept with Todd Zane. It makes us unique."

"Do you think there's anyone else out there who's never slept with one of them?" asked Lucy. "Do you think there's anyone who's never slept with *either* of them?"

"Yes, and she'll probably show up soon," said Suzanne. "We're probably having a meeting and we don't even know it."

"Let me just ask you one thing." Lucy said. "Don't you think this is a little pathetic? To just be in bed watching television?"

"It's pathetic," agreed Suzanne emphatically. "I think if you're going to be pathetic, you should *be pathetic*. People don't dare to be pathetic anymore."

"Maybe we shouldn't tell anyone about this until we're really sure pathetic is the way to go."

"I think we should just really explore doing nothing," said Suzanne. "I mean, there are a lot of people who essentially do nothing, but none who are boldly going forward and *really* doing nothing. We'll be pioneers in real nothing. We're the new woman, the Woman of the Eighties, with nothing and no one. Look at it this way. We've spent years fixing up and futzing around and being as vivacious as our nerves would allow, and it got us unemployed as actresses and as dates. So if all that effort got us nowhere, we could just as easily get nowhere without the effort. The goal should be to remove all stimuli and find out what your instincts are, if any. Because living in Hollywood, we haven't used our instincts for a long time. We've used the instincts of our environment. We've seen what other people do and we've done the same in order to achieve their success."

She sighed. "Yap, yap yap, yap, yap, yap," she said. "Let's just hope there are no Third World flies on the wall. If anyone from another culture—from anyplace outside of this specific Hollywood culture—overheard this conversation, it would confirm the worst of their suspicions "

"Sometimes I feel so spoiled," Lucy said, "like something left out too long in the Now-Playing-Everywhere sun. Still," she added hopefully, "I'm very encouraged by this act of hibernation. So, what kind of revenge do you think I can have on Scott Hastings?"

"Revenge may not be a particularly higher consciousness-oriented activity," Suzanne said.

"But it is fun," said Lucy. "Karmically speaking, I agree it's probably very bad, but I obviously already have a large karmic debt. Otherwise, why was I sent to this planet attracted to men that don't like me and unable to get an acting job? What the fuck, I might as well act out some revenge on this guy. Wanna help? I mean, you can't have incredible karma, either—you're with me. Come on, double or nothing on bad karma."

"You're so crazy," said Suzanne, laughing.

"I want to call him and tell him not to call me," Lucy said.

"I did this stuff already," said Suzanne. "Don't you see? We've become smart enough to justify stupid behavior. Like, 'I'm angry at him and I didn't express it, so I turned my anger inward and now it's depression, so in order to feel good again, what I should do is call him and express my anger.' It's like, if we can make it sound smart enough, we're allowed to do stupid things."

"Maybe you're right," Lucy said. "Sometimes I feel like I should hum 'The Battle Hymn of the Republic' underneath when you talk. But I feel bad, because he's sort of famous, and I feel like maybe he'll get more famous and I'll have missed something."

"You're joking," said Suzanne. "You think famous is what, successful? It's not. This guy is a sad, withered guy. He always plays friendly psychotic murderers, and if you pretend something long enough, it comes true. You're well out of it. And besides, he's a moron. This is not a person who acknowledges that other people are right. This is not a person who says, 'Oh, yeah, that's very interesting, you've changed my thinking on this.' This is a moron who says, 'What's your point?' I guarantee you, you are wired up to have a bad call with this guy. You'll get off the phone and feel like a putz."

"Okay, okay," said Lucy. "We'll stick to our original plan. We'll do nothing. The Human Stubble Plan."

"We'll be like those Indian women who go into the forest to have babies," said Suzanne, "only we have no forest, we have no babies, and we're not Indians. Otherwise, the resemblance is stunning."

They slept in different rooms, because both of them were used to sleeping alone in king-size beds. In the morning, Suzanne woke up two hours earlier than she'd wanted to, and she lay there tossing around until Lucy leaned in the doorway and said, "Was there no air in my room, or did I use it all up?" She walked into the room. "Are you up?"

"I'm always up," said Suzanne. "That's what I am. Up, and in kind of a down mood."

"Listen, I've been rethinking this thing," said Lucy, who was eating a piece of toast. She sat on the bed, wearing a pair of Suzanne's pajamas, which were small on her. "I think that if we stay in the house, it looks like we're admitting defeat. I think that if we're starting anew, there should be some kind of energy behind it."

"I would like this all to be easier," Suzanne declared. "Maybe we should live in a university town and teach acting, and be worshipped by all the young kids."

Lucy ignored her. "I mean, you've given yourself a gestation period of nine days now. You know, like nine months, and now it's time to break through these barricades of apathy. Let's hit the stores. We'll buy outfits for the second part of our lives. I've already called a cab. I'm going home to get dressed."

Suzanne thought her bed had begun feeling grungy. "Well, it *does* seem an awful lot like I've just given up. I have to admit, it's been more of a defensive move than a preparatory one." She sat up. Outside, Lucy's cab arrived and the driver honked twice. "All right," she said, "but you have to stay with me while I dry my hair. I don't like feeling that blast of heat in my empty head."

"I'll tell the cab to wait," Lucy said.

Two hours later, they were driving into Beverly Hills in Lucy's Honda. Suzanne definitely felt better being out. While she'd been drying her hair, she'd come up with a new message for her answering machine—"I'm out, deliberately avoiding your call"—and that simple burst of creativity had raised her spirits a bit.

"My mood is lifting," she said, "like a small, heavy plane." She was wearing her combat shopping outfit: a blue cotton dress with slits up the sides, and under it, black slacks with a blue belt. Suzanne only wore black and blue clothes. Her fashion statement was Bruised.

Lucy, on the other hand, was wearing a cream tunic with black pedal pushers. She carried a bag that fit perfectly under her arm, and her hair was done in a French braid. Suzanne's hair was pulled back in a barette.

"I don't understand how you can do those French braids," said Suzanne. "It shows such a commitment to your appearance."

"You're an asshole," Lucy said. "You're so good-looking, and you just don't want anyone to catch you trying to look good. You only want to look good effortlessly."

"I can't seem to outgrow my distaste for doing up buttons and pulling on stockings. It all seems so complicated. I walk into my closet and I suddenly feel like a man. Like I'm a giant man, and it's bursting with some little girl's clothes, and I'm like, 'How do I put all of this on?' and I wonder whose house it is."

"*How* long have you been in therapy?" asked Lucy.

"I've never been in shopping and clothing therapy," said Suzanne. "Norma doesn't tell me how to dress."

"She should," said Lucy. "It's much more basic."

Suzanne was quiet for a moment. "It seems like I want them to like me for my mind, anyway," she said, "so why not let them go straight for it? Why get them to like my legs? It doesn't seem like that's me. I feel like what I look like is government issue, it's pretty much out of my hands. But *I* invent the stuff I say. That's me."

"That's a very clever way to discuss it," Lucy said, turning onto Rodeo Drive from Santa Monica Boulevard. "You're really just lazy about your appearance." She pulled into a parking space. "But the past is the past. We are now future-oriented, and shopping lies before us, glistening like a dream."

They ambled into Bottega Veneta. Suzanne loved the smell of leather, and she briefly considered buying purses in every color. She could envision some day in the future when she would have a yard sale and sell all the stuff she would never use, which was pretty much all her stuff.

She watched Lucy looking at scarves. Lucy looked good, Suzanne thought. She knew how to dress to look thin. She knew how to groom herself. If she had a pimple, your eye didn't automatically go to it. She had pretty good posture, and she didn't adjust it according to her facial blemishes. She even had nice nails, while Suzanne's always looked like she'd kept them short for a typing job and was finally starting to grow them out.

She wandered around eyeing purses, hoping no one would come up and ask if they could help her. If they could help her, they should have shown up years ago, she thought. Even though she was a recognizable personality, she often felt she had to impress shopkeepers with her purchases.

Lucy, conversely, was very frugal. Suzanne watched her haggling with a salesgirl over the price of a scarf and tried to determine what color purse she needed. She found a square black bag, very symmetrical, and as soon as she picked it up a saleswoman who smelled of too much perfume showed up at her elbow and breathed, "Isn't that lovely?"

Suzanne jumped. "Oh, yes. Yes."

"Why don't you look at yourself with it in the mirror? It will go with anything."

"I have a black bag, though," Suzanne said dubiously.

"One can never truly have too many stylish bags of such unique design," said the saleswoman. "This will probably outshine any of the bags you have at home. Look at it. It's *perfect* for someone your size."

"It is nice, isn't it?" said Suzanne. "How much is it?"

"It's very, very reasonable," said the woman, taking the bag from Suzanne and opening it and looking at the card inside. She smiled a kind of sleazy smile, like a Stepford wife.

Suzanne felt a surge of panic as she realized she was being intimidated into an unnecessary purchase, then moved quickly through her indecision. In the short run it was easier to buy it, and Suzanne was always dealing very heavily with the short run. "I'll take it," she said.

Just then, Lucy came up to Suzanne with a scarf around her shoulders. "What do you think of this?" she asked, then noticed the black purse. "Oh, are you getting that?" she asked. "Don't you already have a bag just like it?"

"Yeah," said Suzanne blankly, "but . . ."

"What are you doing?" demanded Lucy. "What are you *doing*? How much is that bag?"

"I don't know," Suzanne said. "It's a lot . . ."

"How much?" Lucy asked. She turned to the saleswoman. "Excuse me, I'm her agent, her shopping agent, and I intervene on some of her purchases. She's in a delirium, she's had a near-fatal illness." She took the bag out of the saleswoman's hands and opened it.

"Four hundred and fifty dollars," she said. "Four hundred and fifty dollars, and you have a bag almost exactly like it at home. I think maybe we should save this money now, don't you, Peanut? Didn't our business manager tell us not to spend money?"

"Yes," said Suzanne.

"Honey, why don't you think about this bag?" Lucy said. "Think about it, and if it stays in your mind like a shiny diamond, we'll come back and get it. Okay?"

"All right," said Suzanne. "Don't condescend to me, though."

"I'm not," said Lucy sweetly. "I'm patronizing you. You are a patron of the store, and I'm patronizing you. Come on."

She took off the scarf and put it on the counter next to the black purse. "Thank you very much," she said to the woman. "I'm sorry that she had a shopping problem."

"You had a shopping break," she said to Suzanne when they were outside. "And now the break is closing, and maybe we'll go put some food in the break, in case it's not closing."

They went to the Magic Pan, which Suzanne liked because they used lots of artificial sweeteners. They served crepes filled with all sorts of things, but things she could recognize as food. She ordered a crepe filled with cinnamon-covered apples with ice cream on it and a Diet Coke. Lucy ordered a spinach soufflé and an iced tea, and then lit a cigarette.

Suzanne felt depressed from lack of purchase. She eyed Lucy's cigarette enviously. "I wish I still smoked," she said. "I shouldn't have given up *everything*. Now all I do for fun is park illegally."

"It's good that you did all that giving up stuff," Lucy said. "Anyway, you did doing-it-to-death to death."

"I do like my additives, though," Suzanne said. "I ask them to add *more* MSG."

Lucy blew out a cloud of smoke. "Don't you have a secret thought," she asked, "that if we got work right now, we'd feel better?"

"I don't know," said Suzanne doubtfully. "I don't think you ever get to relax. I mean, sure, there's a couple of people who could, but I bet they don't. Because by the time they get to where they could relax, they've gotten completely used to not being able to. How do you just suddenly become somebody who relaxes? The kind of ambition you need to get to that place is not relaxing. It's searing. I think there's probably something about living your whole life in a popularity contest—trying to get people to like you who you couldn't give a flying fuck about—that kills relaxation."

"I know what you mean," Lucy said. "I went up for a part in

New York, and I walked in and I thought, 'Remember those clothes that you see in stores that always make you wonder who buys them? Well, here they are. They're on the casting woman.' *That's* who I had to impress."

"Here's a great story," Suzanne said. "An actor friend of mine was up for a job, and the director said, 'You have the job. You're perfect. I just have to go to New York to look at some actors.' And my friend said, 'What are you going to New York for if I have the job?' And the guy said, 'Don't worry. I just have to go to New York.' So of course the guy called from New York and said someone else had the job, and my friend said, 'Well, I don't want the job.' And the director said, 'You don't understand. You don't *have* the job to not want the job.' And my friend said, 'No, *you* don't understand. If you don't want me for the job, then *I don't want the job.*'

"That's how I feel about the whole thing," she continued. "If you don't want me for the job, I don't want the job. If you don't want me for the girl, I don't want to *be* the girl. My want can only do so much in terms of changing what's actually occurring with other people, and I'd like to keep it that way. I don't want to feel that if I had wanted something more, or had said one other thing, or had worn a different dress, or had been more mysterious, or more open, then I would get something or someone I wouldn't get otherwise." She stopped while the waitress brought their drinks, then said, "Remind me. Why did we ever want to be actresses?"

"I didn't want to be an actress," Lucy said. "I was a singer, remember? Then I got an acting job, and it seemed exciting, and, I don't know, the possibilities seemed endless."

"Possibilities shouldn't be endless," Suzanne said.

"They are, though," said Lucy. "There are so many different ways to be famous. You could shoot the Pope and he could forgive you."

"What you don't want," said Suzanne, "is to be known as the person who shot the Pope who he's still pissed off at."

Lucy laughed and sipped her tea. "So," she said, "I called him this morning."

"The Colonel?" said Suzanne. "You asshole."

"I admit it, I'm an asshole," said Lucy. "I left him a message that said, 'Hi, it's me, of the Philadelphia mes,' which was funny. I mean, if I'm going to be an asshole, at least I'm a funny ass-hole." She took one last drag and put out her cigarette. "What am I going to do? Until I find someone else, I'm going to think about him. I have to keep a man in my head. It keeps my posture good."

"And your grammar bad," Suzanne said.

Lucy lit another cigarette. "Oh, you won't believe who I ran into in New York," she said. "Jane Peters."

"Was she with Roland Parks?"

"No," said Lucy, "but she did have the baby."

Suzanne sighed. "She's so beautiful, and she married one of the wealthiest men in the busienss, and they've got this cute kid . . . She's got the perfect life, and she wants you to know it. She walks around like life's helium is in her clothes."

"Tell me about it," said Lucy. "I met her in Bendel's and she went on and on about how great their marriage is, and how their relationship is so solid they don't even have to work on it. On and on. She actually said to me, 'I never thought I would be so happy. If you had told me when I was young that I was going to be this happy, I would have laughed. *I would have laughed.*' She actually repeated it."

"I don't know," said Suzanne. "Maybe there's some kind of joy I've never experienced, where you're just flouncing around and giving everybody minute-by-minute updates on your never-ending glee. I don't know, or maybe she's just relieved that it's not as bad as she thought it would be."

"On the other hand," said Lucy, "you can't expect her to walk around with a glum face saying, 'This is a nightmare. I wish I was poor and living in a little apartment and not working as an actress again.' "

"I think Jane should have a brochure printed up with career and relationship highlights. You know, pictures of them entwined on the couch watching TV, pictures of them laughing gaily with their agents over lunch at Le Dôme, or flying on their private jet to their private Hawaiian island. Then when she ran into any of us who might not be quite so fortunate, she could just hand us a flyer."

"You should tell her that," Lucy said, laughing.

"I sort of did," said Suzanne. "She was going on about this one day, and I told her I'd give her my address so she could send me the brochure. I mean, it's not a *conversation*, you know? 'Roland and I just bought a place in the south of France.' What's my comeback? 'Cary Grant proposed to me the other day'? I mean, if someone tells you they feel bad, you say, 'Yeah, I felt bad once,' or, 'I feel bad, too.' You isolate the area where there's a basis for comparison. But if somebody says she's married to a billionaire and they have this perfect life—not just that they're having a really good time, but that they have a *perfect life*—what's your comeback? 'Breakfast this morning was tough on my kidneys'? *Where is the comeback?* I said to her, 'I don't know what you're talking about.' "

"Still," Lucy said, "you have to admit, if you're gonna sell out, sell out for the big numbers. Sometimes I feel like I'm auctioning myself off to the lowest bidder." She sipped her tea. "Maybe I was dropped as a child."

"You're still dropped," said Suzanne. "I don't get it. You make yourself completely available and de-emphasize everything in *your* life. You put yourself totally at their disposal. A guy should be in your life because of who you are, not because of what you do to get him with who you're not."

"Why don't we open a gift shop?" said Lucy.

"We should open a gift shop?" said Suzanne. "What is this, Non-Sequitur Day?"

Their food arrived. It was the first meal Suzanne had had set in front of her since Mary's bacon sandwich. "I used to think that if

I ate very slowly, I wouldn't gain weight," she said, her fork poised above her crepe. "You know, when you wolf it all down it feels like you've eaten a lot, but a little at a time . . . Oh, forget it." She began eating very quickly.

Lucy laughed. "Your follow-through leaves a little something to be desired," she said.

They finished eating in under ten minutes and drove back to Suzanne's house, where they intended to discuss their evening plans. As it happened, neither of them had any. "It's not like it's a weekend," said Lucy, pulling into the driveway. "That would be really tragic."

There was a package in front of Suzanne's door from her agent, apparently a script. Lucy squeezed her arm and said, "Today is the first day of the rest of your life." They went into the kitchen, and Suzanne got a Diet Coke out of the refrigerator while Lucy called her service for messages.

"What should I do?" she said frantically when she hung up. "What should I do? Barry called. They want me to sub for somebody on *The Richard Collins Show.* Tonight! Should I do it?"

"I don't know. Do you want to do it?"

"If you came with me I'd want to do it," Lucy said. "I have to admit I've been feeling the need to be televised lately. I think maybe I could be funny. If you and I were backstage kibitzing before, then maybe I could just zoom out there . . . I mean, this guy is sort of funny."

"I've heard Richard Collins is funny at the expense of his guests," Suzanne said. "He makes sure he's funny first, and then you get what's left."

"Yeah, well," said Lucy. "Do you know who's on the show?"

"Oh, now we're getting to it," Suzanne laughed. "No, who's on the show?"

"Larry Walker."

"Larry Walker, the painter?"

"Yeah," said Lucy, "it's a late-night show, he gets all these weird artsy types. I've always wanted to meet Larry Walker, I love his work. Portia Lamm has one of his pieces. Did you ever see it? That one with the moonlight shining on the long, long hot dog? Come on, this is like spontaneity."

"That would be a good name for a perfume," Suzanne said. "What about hair and makeup?"

"They said they'd do all that at the studio. Come on, you don't have anything to do tonight."

"Well, I did have kind of a standing date with the bed, but I may have done all I can do there," Suzanne said. "All right, I'll come."

"I'm afraid," Lucy said. "I'm afraid I'll go out of control and talk about Bob."

"Colonel Bob?"

"I'm afraid I'll talk about Colonel Bob," Lucy said. "I'm such an extemporaniac. What if he makes me feel dumb and I reveal everything just to defend myself?"

"Are you sure you want to do this?" Suzanne asked. "Why don't you call your manager and talk to him about it? Call Barry."

"You're so practical," Lucy said. "That's what being in bed so long has given you: a real strong, pragmatic, practical streak. "It's like you *belong* in your thirties."

"Great," Suzanne said. "Go call Barry."

"Wait a minute, let me just be sure I'm getting this," Lucy said. "Are you suggesting that I call Barry?"

"Go call Barry."

While Lucy called Barry, Suzanne went into the bedroom to check her machine. Three messages.

"Funny. Suzanne, this is Mark. Listen, we've got this TV movie here, I guess it's all right, and the guy has written me a note. Apparently he knows you. Anyway, it's a pretty straightforward treatment of a subject I think you're familiar with. It's called *Rehab!* and it's shooting on location in town starting in late October. I'm messengering it to you, it should be there this afternoon.

This guy might . . . He tried to get your number, but I wouldn't give it to him. He claims he knows you . . . Anyway, the script is all right, a little melodramatic, maybe, and they want you for the role of Katie. Two people have been cast: Joe is being played by Bernard Stevens, who was the Skipper character in that black version of *Gilligan's Island* that bombed last year, and Sam is Kurt Hampton. He's new, he just did a television film called *Way Out There*. So it's largely being cast with television people. It has a good scheduling time and it's a fairly credible project, I guess. The implication seems to be that if the ratings are good, they'll do a sequel for the May sweeps. I just don't know how you feel about the subject matter. Give me a call later on today. Bye. 859-4236."

"Suzanne, hi, it's Sid. Listen, remember that creep Alex Daniels from the clinic? The guy who went out and ODed about a week after I left? He called and pressured me into giving him your number. I hope you don't mind, and I'm sure you do, but he said he was working in Hollywood now, so I thought . . . I just wanted to warn you, he's gonna call, and I'm sorry. You can get me at my office, 724-3996. I'm sorry if you're mad, and if you're not, call me anyway."

"Avoiding . . . ? How did you . . . ? Oh, oh, right, you're joking. Uh, Suzanne, I don't know if you remember me or not. This is Alex. We were in the drug clinic together. Alex Daniels? Do you remember me? Anyway, great message. I see you've still got your sense of humor. Are you still going to meetings? I've looked for you but I've never seen you at one, but I mostly go to the cocaine meetings . . . Anyway . . . Do you remember me, by the way? I'm calling because . . . I got your number from . . . I hope you don't mind, but I got it from Sid. Anyway, remember I had told you about how I was maybe gonna write a script? Well, I did, and it's getting made. I've been working on this for a year and this is like the third draft and it's a go project, and I wanted to wait to be sure before I called. I hope you don't mind, but I used your name in the pitch . . . Jesus, I'm going on too long here, sorry . . . I used your name, and also you told me to keep a journal and that really helped. Anyway, I've written a character sort of loosely based on you . . . Well, not that loosely. She's an actress, her name is Katie . . . I hope you're not mad. I hope you're flattered, because that was a very big thing in my life, it had real impact . . . Anyway, your agent said you'd have it today, which is why I'm calling. The network is very excited about using you, although they did pitch some other names, people they said had higher TVQ. But you're obviously ideal for the part. I mean, I did write it for you and, I don't know, I hope you like it. If you have any questions, I can be reached through my secretary at my office at the studio, or at my new apartment in Century City . . . This is going to be so embarrassing if you don't remember me. Oh, my numbers. I'm at 870-6324 or 965-0372. I'm sorry to have used so much of your tape. I'm the guy . . . I pushed you in the swing. Bye."

Lucy came into the room, "Barry said—"

"Wait! I just want to play you this message," said Suzanne.

"We're going," Lucy said. "We have to be there at five thirty. They're sending a car."

"All right, we'll be there. Let me just play you this." She rewound the tape. "Remember I told you about the drug clinic and all that?"

"*Remember the drug clinic?*" said Lucy. "No. No, were you in a drug clinic? It wasn't something you like *talked* about for a while, was it?"

"Just shut up for a second," Suzanne said. "Did I tell you about the guy . . . There was this guy who left, and he went out to some hotel room in the valley and literally exploded, and then he came back. Alex? Did I tell you about Alex?"

"I remember stuff about the black guy," said Lucy. "The disc jockey from hell. And the fat one I met at that Italian restaurant that night. Who's Alex?"

"All right, all right," Suzanne said. "I told you about this guy. You forgot, you have too much of a life. Listen to this." She played back Alex's message.

"He's a total jerk, right?" Lucy said when it ended. "I do remember hearing about him."

"I have to say, he sounds better," said Suzanne. "You cannot *believe* what this guy was like." She held up the package. "We'll read it in the car."

"Who else is on the show?" Suzanne asked, as their limo headed north on the Hollywood Freeway toward Burbank.

"There's Larry Walker, and some author, and somebody else, I don't know who," Lucy said. "I shouldn't be so nervous, right? I mean, this isn't the Carson show."

Suzanne pulled the *Rehab!* script out of her bag and opened to a random page. "Sam says, 'Did you see the new guy?' " she read, "and Joe says, 'I think he's still high on something.' Sam says, 'He says he knows Manson,' and Joe says, 'Shoot! It's safer out there doing drugs than—"

"Do I look nervous?" Lucy said. "I shouldn't be doing this."

"Here's a Katie scene," Suzanne said, flipping through the script. "She's sitting on a big floral sofa, and she's yelling at somebody ... She's yelling at her *father.* 'I'm afraid to tell you how I feel! Feelings are weak, and weakness isn't allowed, is it?' I've *seen* this! This was in that antidrug training film they kept showing us, *Hooked on a Line.* 'You patronize me for having feelings. You're so superior to your own feelings.' He must have taken a tape recorder in with him. Is this *legal?*"

"Let's not talk about this yet, okay?" Lucy said. "Let's talk about Larry Walker and do I look okay? Is this lipstick too dark for television?"

"Let me see," said Suzanne. "No, it's not, but blot it down. That's way too much gloss. The light will hit it and no one will be able to see your face."

"I always see people with lip gloss on television, and I never like how it looks," Lucy said. "But they're always wearing it, so I figure maybe I should. Maybe it's lucky."

"The famous lucky lip gloss," said Suzanne. "That's brilliant."

"I'm really glad you're coming with me," Lucy said. "This is real buddy work. Maybe *you'll* like Larry Walker."

"He's an artist, and artists . . . This is going to sound like a generalization, but artists suffer for their craft," said Suzanne. "That makes me very tense."

"You might think he's cute," Lucy said. "Keep your mind open, unless I like him. If I like Larry Walker, then don't keep your mind open. Close it like a clam. But there are some other people on the show, maybe somebody else'll be cute."

"My dream is not to meet someone on a talk show," Suzanne said.

"What are you, above the talk show?" Lucy said. "I think talk shows are the singles bars for celebrities. Where do you think I met Andrew Keyes? I met him on a talk show in Chicago when I was promoting *Hot Countries.*"

"Really? I didn't know that. I thought you met him at a party, and here I've been going to all these parties looking for *my* Andrew Keyes."

"You're funny, though," Lucy said. "You'd be good on talk shows."

"That's what I'm afraid of. I'm afraid I'd be good, and I'd end up the Joanne Worley of my generation."

"I think you should forget all these ideas you have that stop you from doing things," Lucy said. "That's why you're in bed all the time, because unfortunately you made that one movie where they paid you a little bit too much, and now you can afford to stay in bed."

"I don't see why we're having an argument."

"We're not. All I'm saying is you should go on a talk show every so often. Because you're funny."

"What, everyone has to know I'm funny?" said Suzanne. "Or I'm not funny anymore?"

"No, you should keep it a big bad secret," Lucy said, "so that only you and your bedclothes know. And your clicker."

"My clicker," said Suzanne, "thinks I'm incredibly amusing. It asked me out the other day. I didn't want to tell you."

"Okay," said Lucy, lighting yet another cigarette. "So what should I talk about? Help me."

"Well, don't get pretentious. You know how when you get nervous you get pretentious to protect yourself?"

"Is that true?" said Lucy. "That's weird. You're kidding. You've always thought that? I feel bad now."

"No, I don't mean it bad," said Suzanne. "I think it's good pretentious. Everybody's got their quirks. You just quote William Somerset Maugham when you're nervous. Some people sweat."

"Should I talk about *No Survivors*? I mean, it's not coming out until November, but I can say what it was like to work with Rolf Eduard, and that it isn't a remake of *Freedom Train* like everyone thinks. What else?"

"Why don't you say the thing about singles bars for celebrities?" Suzanne suggested. "Say that's why you're on."

"But can I do that without sounding slutty?"

"Yeah, I think so," Suzanne said. "I mean, don't flirt with the guy on the air, okay?"

"What do you think I am, a putz or something?" Lucy said. "I'm not going to flirt with him on the air. I don't even flirt with them, I let *them* flirt with *me*."

"Why do I feel like I'm the practical one of the two of us?" Suzanne said. "I'm like a ditz in my own life, but as soon as I'm in yours, I have something to do. Cleaning up the mess as you go."

"I don't know, I think I'm good for you that way," Lucy said. "I make you feel like you're stable, when you're completely not."

"This is really revealing about our relationship," said Suzanne. "Who knew we would find out all this stuff on the way to Burbank to do a talk show? Does this thing have an audience?"

"No," said Lucy, "which is why I'm doing it. Otherwise I'd really be sick now. But I can always do these. For *Hot Countries*

199

they had me doing early-morning shows and there was no audience and I was brilliant."

"I saw you on some of those, remember?" Suzanne said. "You were very good, very relaxed. It was like watching Hal the computer."

"That's when I talked about tunneling out of show business."

"That was very funny," said Suzanne. "Why don't you say that?"

"I can't do it again. That was two years ago."

"Who saw it?" said Suzanne. "It was a morning show."

"I can't do it again," Lucy repeated. "Maybe if I get stressed out I'll make fun of my weight."

"I know," said Suzanne. "Tell them you're retaining water for Whitney Houston."

"What do you mean?"

"Well," Suzanne explained, "Whitney Houston is clearly not retaining water. She's obviously getting somebody to do it for her, so let's—"

"God, that's perfect!" Lucy said. "Can I do that?"

"Yes, do that. Do that," Suzanne said. "I can help you on something self-deprecatory."

"Oh, God, oh, God," Lucy said. "There's the studio. I wish you could come out with me. You could just walk out with me like I'm your dummy or something, and we'll never explain it."

"Could you drop us at dressing room B up there on the left?" Suzanne said to the driver.

"All right, I'm just going to let you take over now," Lucy said. "I have a heartbeat as big as the hills."

Suzanne got a Diet Coke from a vending machine while Lucy got her hair and makeup done. It turned out Larry Walker was not going to be on the show—*he* was the cancelled guest that Lucy was subbing *for*—but by the time she got out of makeup she was so self-absorbed she related this news to Suzanne with no sense of irony. Down the hall, the theme music for *The Richard Collins Show* began playing.

"I look okay?" Lucy said.

"You look fine," said Suzanne. "You look great."

"You won't lie to me, right?" Lucy said. "You're going to watch me and tell me how I am, and you're not going to lie?"

"I won't lie to you," Suzanne said. "Look, there's a cute guy over there, the one with the gray shirt. Why don't you go talk to him?"

"I can't," Lucy said. "I'm too nervous about the show, and to add a guy on top of that . . . I can't."

"Oh," said Suzanne, smiling. "Your priorities are sort of juggled around at this point, aren't they?"

"Don't make fun of me," Lucy said. "You can make fun of me all night long, but don't make fun of me now. It erodes my real sense of who I am."

"All right, all right," Suzanne said. "So, who's out first?"

"I'm out first, and then the author, and then I think Emily Frye, that actress who got the movie neither of us did."

"*Top Priority*?" Suzanne said.

"Yes, the girl who got *Top Priority*."

"You're kidding," said Suzanne. "Well, try to be as great as possible."

"Oh, good," Lucy said. "The pressure isn't on. That's good. My buddy."

A tall man came up to them and said, "Lucy, you're on."

"I'll wait for you in the green room," Suzanne said.

"You better," Lucy said. "You better wait for me."

Suzanne walked around the corner and went into the green room. There were several other people in there, among them an attractive-looking man who looked like he was from New York. He was wearing a green corduroy jacket with patches on the elbows, a multiplaid shirt and a tie, and jeans and Hush Puppies. He had brown hair and wore glasses. Suzanne thought he had an air of studiousness about him, of not stability but something near stability. Of calm, almost. She nodded at him slightly and walked past him to another tiny couch, where she watched the television monitor in the corner.

It was quite an unattractive room. There was a big lamp in one corner, three couches, and a shag carpet. A woman wearing a dress with pearls on was drinking coffee on the third couch. She was wearing patent leather shoes with peach bows on them. A young girl who must have been her daughter was holding her purse for her. The girl was wearing a pink sweater and had blond hair down her back. Suzanne glanced briefly at the man in green corduroy. He was probably the author, she thought. He looked like he was wearing a writing uniform.

Suzanne looked back at the monitor, where Richard Collins was still doing his opening monologue. The probable author got up to get some coffee, then came over and sat next to her. "Aren't you the girl who was in *Seventh Tea House*?" he asked. "Suzanne Vale?"

Suzanne was startled and embarrassed, and said, "Yes," as if the question had been an accusation.

"That was very good," he said.

"Really?" she said. "Well, thank you. You liked it? You like that kind of movie?"

"Well, no, I don't really, but yes, I did," he said. "I thought it was a well-made film and I certainly appreciated how difficult it must have been for all of you to be in it. Are you on the show tonight?"

"No," said Suzanne, grateful for his taking control of the conversation. "My friend Lucy is. She'll be on in a minute."

"I read an interview with you once and you were very funny," he said. "I can't remember what magazine."

"Probably in *Omni*," Suzanne said. "So, who are you?"

"Oh, I'm sorry," he said. "Jesse Templeman."

"The author?"

"Oh," he said, surprised. "You know my work?"

"No," said Suzanne. "I knew there was going to be an author on the show. What have you written?"

"Well, actually, I've written a novel," Jesse said. "It's called *The Appetite People.*"

"Really?" Suzanne said. "And you're promoting it, so you must be proud of it."

"I am proud of it, yeah," he said. "I worked on it for quite some time. It's difficult to get a publisher."

"Do you live in New York?"

"Well, actually I've just moved out here," he said. "I've been living in New York, but they bought my book to make a film out of it and I'm writing the screenplay. I didn't want somebody else to do it. I don't know that I'll be staying here after that. Hey," he said, nodding toward the monitor, "isn't that your friend?"

"Oh my God," said Suzanne, realizing Lucy had already been on for a little while. She had promised to watch and tell her how she was. "Can they put the sound on? Can someone put the sound on?"

Jesse leaned forward and turned up the volume. Richard Collins was laughing very hard. Lucy said, "I mean, I'm too old to be in the Brat Pack and too young for my own exercise tape. *What am I?*" Richard Collins laughed harder.

"She's very funny," said Jesse.

"She is funny," Suzanne said. "She was very nervous."

"I'm nervous myself," he said. "I feel dumb doing this, but my publishers . . . you know. Do you live out here? I guess you do."

"Yes," said Suzanne.

"Well," Jesse said, "maybe we could . . . I don't want to seem presumptuous, but maybe we could have lunch or something. Or go out sometime. What do you do to relax?"

"I don't relax," said Suzanne. "It's sort of a therapy goal of mine."

"I see."

"But what I do that's the closest I get to relaxing," said Suzanne, "is I drive around and listen to loud music."

"Well, maybe we can take a long loud drive sometime," he said.

Suzanne looked back at the screen and saw that Lucy wasn't there anymore. "Oh my God, I've gotta go find my friend, she's gonna kill me," she said. She scribbled her number on the flap of the envelope *Rehab!* had arrived in, tore it off, and gave it to Jesse. "This is my number," she said. "Good luck on the show."

"Thanks," said Jesse. "I'll call you sometime."

Suzanne rushed past the tall man who was coming to get Jesse and saw Lucy running down the hall toward her. "Did you hear what I said about my *father?*" she asked hysterically. "He's gonna kill me. He's never gonna speak to me again."

"No, honey, it was fine," Suzanne said calmingly. "You were funny about the Brat Pack thing—"

"Did I have lipstick on my teeth?"

"You were fine," Suzanne said. "But what did you say about your father?"

"I thought you said I was fine," Lucy said. "Were you watching the wrong channel?"

"You were fine," Suzanne assured her. "I saw everything but that. I looked away for a second—"

"At what?" Lucy demanded.

"I was talking to a guy," Suzanne said. "The author guy."

"Did he think I was good-looking?" Lucy asked. Suzanne nodded. "And you didn't hear the father thing? Do you know what I said about my father? That he was a giant whale and I wasn't sure he was actually my father. I called him my alleged father."

"So?" said Suzanne. "He's got a sense of humor, doesn't he?"

"My father? The Republican *nightmare?*"

"Well, are you counting on his will for anything?"

"Don't be funny about this," Lucy said. "Oh, all right, be funny. The show is over, you can make fun of me now. So, you didn't think it sounded slutty when I said I went on talk shows to meet guys?"

"To meet guys, no," Suzanne said. "You didn't say to blow them, did you?"

"You wouldn't know," said Lucy. "You were busy cruising the green room."

"I was not cruising the . . . I was talking to . . . You *tell* me to do this stuff."

"I don't tell you to do it while I'm on TV," Lucy said.

"Oh, it's scheduled around your career now, my talking to guys?" Suzanne said. "Let me just tell you this one thing. You look great and I gave the guy my number. It's been a breakthrough night for both of us. Now we can go and have some French fries and doughnuts and really live life."

They walked out of the building and got into the limo. "What's his name?" asked Lucy, settling into her seat, and Suzanne talked about Jesse all the way back to Hollywood, thinking the whole time, "He'll never call me.

"And if he does, what if he's a murderer?"

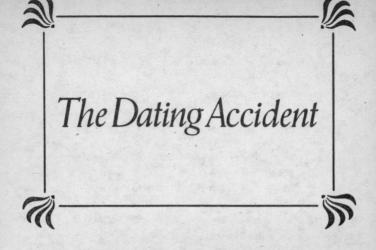

The Dating Accident

Suzanne was dreaming that she was hanging by her hands outside the window of a speeding car with her hair flying behind her. Driving down a street and flying through the air. It was frightening, terrifying, but as she sped along it became almost exhilarating. She passed through the danger into the creamy filling of *Wheeeee!* and then woke up, her heart beating very fast. She had the strange sensation that she actually had cried out, "*Wheeeee!*" but she saw Jesse fast asleep beside her and knew she hadn't.

They had been living together for almost a year—though he'd kept his apartment—and she was still always a little surprised to find him there in the morning. She liked to study him when he was asleep—he seemed unarmed somehow without his glasses on—but she could only engage in this activity on weekends. During the week Jesse got up at seven to write. "Look at him," she thought. "He looks like somebody you could go up to at an airport and say, 'Could you watch my bag?'"

He remained curious to her. She knew she cared about him— her latest analogy to Norma was that he was a wounded Confederate soldier and she was this sweet Yankee woman who'd found him on her lawn—but she wondered why. It was as though she doubted her own judgment, which in fact she did. For years her judgment had told her to take drugs. Why should she think her logic had improved that much in just two years?

What did she see in him? He said that the sky was "bucolic"; she asked him what "bucolic" meant. He said he liked Steely Dan and the color black. Well, so did she. What did that make her? He drank coffee black, or sometimes with a little cream. What did *that* mean? She felt like she was on a scavenger hunt, searching for clues as to who he was and what he wanted from her. She had no idea whether, if she found out, she would give it to him or not.

Was Jesse a good man? she asked herself. He probably was, because he bored her to death sometimes. "You think that if it isn't dramatic, nothing is happening," Norma had told her. "The idea is to get old *with* them, not *because* of them. Pretend it's an act- ing assignment. Act like someone who *enjoys* the quiet that can be found in a mature relationship. Act normal, and see if some feelings of normalcy don't eventually follow."

"Normal. People don't get much more normal than us," she thought. "We're prototypes for the new normal line of people who were designed to pave the way for the nineties." She realized that she and Jesse were getting serious. Serious. She hated the sound of it. "I joked myself into a serious situation," she'd told Lucy.

"You've backed into normalcy via Cambodia," Lucy said, "so you can appreciate it more. It's like you applied for a weird life and got a regular one by accident."

Lucy liked Jesse. She thought he was good for Suzanne, that people would take her more seriously if they knew she was going with "an author." For a while she even considered finding herself an author, but one who was, as she put it to Suzanne, "maybe just a little famous, like John Irving or Philip Roth."

Then Lucy met Lowell Stephenson. When *No Survivors* came out, she received a lot of attention, so when she went to Seattle over Christmas to make up with her father for the things she'd said about him on the talk show, Lowell—the head of New Age Studios—recognized her on the plane and struck up a conversation. She was seeing him fairly regularly now.

Sometimes the four of them would go out together. Lowell even cooked for them once. "This is *exactly* how I like it," Lucy had whispered to Suzanne while Lowell was perfecting the salad dressing. "Breadmaker and breadwinner all in one."

"How did we ever end up as parts of couples?" Suzanne asked, as they watched Lowell show Jesse how to sauté shrimp.

"Think of it as an experiment," Lucy suggested.

"Does one of us have cancer?" Suzanne had asked Jesse on their fourth date, after they'd sat in her house talking for eight hours straight.

"Pardon me?" he said.

"I just wondered. We spend so much time together, it's like you have a twelve-hour shore leave, or we're cramming for a state exam on one another, or . . ."

"Cancer," he said, nodding. "That wouldn't have been the analogy I would have chosen."

After their fifth date, he hadn't called her for six days. Suzanne was stunned. She forgot what he looked like. "Smoke in a room, that's what he is," she told Lucy. "Smoke in a room." She started thinking about him as the guy she liked who never called her again.

"What's the matter?" Michelle asked her.

"I've been in a dating accident," she announced dramatically. "A terrible, terrible dating accident."

It became Suzanne's favorite phrase. "Ask me what's the matter," she said to whomever she talked to.

Then he called, and again she was stunned. "I didn't think I'd hear from you again," she told him.

"Why?" he asked. "I told you I was going to New York and that I'd be back on Monday—today."

She had forgotten, but because of this mistake he had become more vivid to her, more real. They'd had a crisis in common—though, to be sure, in Suzanne's mind more than anywhere else—and they'd come through it. They had survived the dating accident together, and on their sixth date they had total endless nightmare sex. "Big Kabuki Sex," Suzanne called it.

"This is interesting, isn't it?" Jesse remarked during a rest stop, then said, "That sounded odd. I just didn't want to frighten you with affection." Suzanne thanked him, and wondered if she should say that she, too, thought the sex was interesting.

Instead, she said, "I called someone the other day, and his message gave the number of his car phone. I left my home number and said that if I wasn't there, I could probably be reached in my crop duster."

"I consider it a kind of defeat to call someone in their car," Jesse countered, stifling a yawn.

"Do you want to stay over?" she asked, her chest tight.

"I really should go. I'm writing in the morning, but I—"

"Okay," she interjected quickly. "Okay," she said again, this time quieter.

"I'd love to, though," he said, nuzzling her affectionately. "You're so calm, so still."

"I'm like a peaceful flesh rock," she said moodily.

"You took the words right out of my mouth," he said ironically. He turned her toward him and put her head on his shoulder. "What's the matter?"

"Nothing."

"Which nothing?" he asked.

There was a beat, after which Suzanne said quietly, "You're leaving me."

"I'm not leaving you. I'm leaving to write. I have to—"

"It's okay," she sighed. "I'll get over it. I'm getting over it already, look." She was silent for a moment, then said, "My hand on your chest looks like a flesh shell on a hairy beach."

"Do you have an alarm clock?" Jesse asked wearily.

She had had relationships before. Well, people had had relationships with her. Eventually, she would always end up on drugs, and there were only two roles you could play with someone doing drugs: you could either do them, too, or you could object to doing them. Or both. In any case, the relationship then became, in part, *about* drugs, and then it was just a matter of time until the drug part wore away whatever it had been about before.

Jesse had done coke twice and found it wanting. Occasionally he smoked dope, but never around Suzanne. Her only other relationship with a nondruggie—that is, with someone who wasn't taking drugs while she was involved with him—was her nonrelationship relationship with Jack Burroughs. Suzanne had recently heard Jack had begun free-basing again now that *Ziz! II* was such a hit, but then, that *could* just have been a rumor.

She was horrified at the surges of sentiment that rose up in her. She fought the tenderness, kept it down like nausea. When she finally started saying the barest of nice things to Jesse, they were accompanied by facial expressions more appropriate for swallowing cough medicine. It was like a punishment to fit the reward.

She explained to him that she hated "the L word"—that she always felt like she was under some kind of obligation when she heard it. "Why do you tell him these things?" Norma had asked. "One day you might *want* him to say this terrible phrase."

To Suzanne's surprise, that day came. She began watching his mouth, imagining what it would be like if he ever said the sentimental trio. One night while they were kissing, he looked into her eyes, his expression almost sad. After the briefest moment—she hadn't even realized they were gazing at each other through *pounds* of air—he cleared his throat and looked away shyly. "I wasn't going to say, 'I love you,' I swear," he said. "I know it looked like it, but I wasn't."

"He's smart," Lucy said. "You *told* him it freaked you out to hear all that mushy, romantic, *great* stuff, and so now . . ." She shrugged. "Hey, why don't *you* tell *him*? You love him, or at least you do have great big cheerful feelings for him."

"You think I should tell him I love him?" Suzanne said.

"Why don't you write him a note?"

"What if he showed it to people and laughed?" Suzanne said.

There was a period early on, when she knew for certain he liked her a lot, that was decidedly unpleasant. Suddenly, everything he did annoyed her, everything he did after liking her.

The Sleeping Giant reigned. Jesse held his head too still. He walked like a burglar. He touched his hair a lot, and he chewed too much gum. It was prissy to be so smart, he wasn't that smart, why was he that smart? Who was he, anyway? Why had he been available? Who had put him up to this? The Russians? That was it. The Russians had trained Jesse to impersonate a great guy on a date in order to penetrate Hollywood through Suzanne Vale. Well, she could see through their game. Did they think she was a fool? Maybe they should try being apart for a while. Maybe they should see other people. Maybe there was someone better.

All this would go on and on in her head, and she would just clench her jaw until it subsided, trying to keep the withering contempt out of her eyes. She refused to let the Sleeping Giant win. This was a nice guy. He didn't deserve the horror that hid inside her. She held on, and after a while those feelings began appearing less and less frequently, like reverse labor.

Suzanne asked her mother for some "relationship advice," to which Doris replied, "For what age?"

"Thank you," said Suzanne.

She wanted to walk up to couples in the street and find out what their relationships were, as if that would somehow help her determine how hers was going. One Thursday she spent the entire afternoon in the Bodhi Tree bookstore. She discovered two things: you should communicate openly with your partner, and red meat is bad for everything, including relationships.

She also found a book about the trend in world history of westward migration. Suzanne figured that meant that eventually—probably right after she was dead—all the intellectuals would finally get to L.A. She imagined them arriving just in time for her funeral, and talking about how they wished they could have gotten there just a little bit sooner, because they had this incredibly salient point they wanted to make to her so she could carry it into the afterlife. At this point, though, she thought, it appeared that the intellectuals were only in New York, and the people they wanted to fuck were out here in L.A.

"I think we have compatible kissing styles," Jesse said one afternoon, brushing her hair off her forehead.

"You have a very soft mouth," she said darkly. "Why is that, do you think?"

"Probably because I chew so much gum," he said. The Sleeping Giant was strangely silent. "I like everything about you," Jesse said, stroking her hair. "That probably bothers you, doesn't it?"

"No," she said, smiling sweetly, "because I don't believe you."

He was suspiciously nice. He had to be hiding something. "You leave him alone," warned Norma. "He's fine. *You're* the weird one. You just don't know what to do when there's no trouble. You're looking for something to fix. Watch out you don't fix it till it breaks."

"You sound like a bumper sticker," Suzanne said.

"Don't sulk."

"Am I sulking?"

"You're sulking because you've lost your favorite toy," Norma said, "the exploding man. Now you have a nice gentle man, and you want him to explode."

"I don't—"

"You're having a normal relationship," Norma said firmly. "You don't feel normally about it, but that's another step."

"I don't wonder if he's a murderer anymore," she said.

"*Very* good."

"I think he's a narc."

Jesse did the thing Suzanne had always imagined her ideal mate would do: he read the paper. The whole paper. He was stunned that she had never done this.

"That's a guy thing to do," she said, by way of explanation.

"I hardly think it's the province of one particular gender."

"So, you tell me what's in the paper," she said. "Like it's gossip." Sometimes he did. He told her what was happening in the world that he belonged to and she visited.

She postponed reading Jesse's novel for the longest time, until Lucy finally volunteered to read it first and sort of test the waters. When she finished it, she was quite enthusiastic. "It's real good. Go ahead and like him," she told Suzanne. "It's about a bunch of obsessives—one of your favorite subjects. It's funny. Read it."

"Is it smart?"

"Smart? Yes, it's smart, funny, all that," said Lucy. "It should even make a good film. I might ask you to sleep with him an extra time to get me the part of Leslie."

So she read it, and was relieved to find that she thought it was very good. Even the Sleeping Giant seemed to like it, except for a couple of the sex parts.

She was calming down about her career. She had worked three times in the last year. She had done a small part in a movie called

Mood Swing and a limited run in a Los Angeles theater of a play called *I'll Buy You a Cherimoya*, and had costarred in a terrible TV movie called *Cut to the Chase*, which also starred Lucy's ex-lover, Scott Hastings. (Neither of them ever acknowledged that they knew Lucy.) She felt show business was not her life now. It was becoming *part* of her life. Lately, there had even been times when she regretted not having studied criminal psychology, after all.

She had seen Alex recently, at Wanda's funeral. Suzanne was with Jesse and Alex was with Amy Baxter, the star of the sitcom *Honey, I'm Home!*, who had played the part of Katie in *Rehab!* Rumor had it Amy had fallen in love with Alex during filming, and had left her boyfriend to move in with him. Amy was standing near Wanda's family weeping, and Suzanne wondered if Amy had ever met Wanda. Stan and Julie were also there, along with Carl (who was now a therapist at a halfway house), Carol (who was now pregnant), and Sid (who was now dieting). It was a strange little scene.

Afterward, as everyone was walking to their cars, Suzanne and Alex paired off for a moment. She congratulated him on his network job and Emmy nominations, which Jesse had told her about.

"Listen," Alex said earnestly, "I *begged* them to use you for Katie, but . . ." He shrugged. "They said your TVQ was low."

"Forget it," Suzanne said. "Amy was *perfect* for it. Very understated."

"Wasn't she brilliant in the swing scene?" Alex enthused, as he watched Amy talking to Jesse and reapplying her makeup.

"Brilliant," Suzanne agreed.

Carl and Sid joined them. "You kids feel like a meeting?" Carl asked. "We're going over to the eleven-thirty Gardner."

"If Jesse drops me, can one of you drive me home?"

"Sure," said Sid.

"I really can't go," Alex said. "Amy and I have a *real* meeting—I mean, a business meeting—at Trader Vic's at one fifteen to discuss *Beyond Rehab!*"

"Don't sweat it, man," Carl said. "I make my living out of being an ex-junkie, too."

Suzanne and Jesse drove out of the cemetery behind Carl's car, which had a bumper sticker that said EX-HEADS GIVE BETTER HEAD. Suzanne looked back and saw Alex in the parking lot talking excitedly to Carol's husband Rob, who, Suzanne knew, had just signed a production deal with Lowell Stephenson. "He's probably pitching an idea about a model who ODs in Hollywood," she said.

"A vehicle for Amy," Jesse said.

When they'd first started seeing each other, she'd been unable to remember anything he said. She'd wondered if and when his words would stick, and what the sentence would be. Then, in the space of a week, she'd recalled three sentences of his. Random ones, but it was a beginning. First there was "I talked to my friend Roy on Friday—I told you about Roy, didn't I?" Then, "I run five miles a day." And there was something else about chili dogs, but she couldn't remember the exact phrase. She was also making strides toward remembering what he looked like. She'd have a sudden image of his face while waiting for the light to change, or sitting in the bath.

Sometimes she disliked the sight of his feet, or the glint of his glasses when the light hit them at a particular angle, or the sensation of hearing him use a word that she didn't know the meaning of. But then she'd smell his soft Jesse smell, or he'd read something to her about some South African riot, or she'd watch him bent over his typewriter making a correction, and she'd think, "He's mine. I *own* him." Or, in a healthier vein, she'd feel a sense of belonging, a corny feeling that embarrassed and thrilled her. She felt like a What's Wrong with This Picture? element in a Norman Rockwell painting.

She wasn't sure exactly when he'd started calling her Gail, but it was pretty soon after he'd moved in. She called him lots of things, ranging from Joseph to Sir. It was their understanding that she called him so many names because he was so many things to her.

Sometimes she would go to him to discuss the notion of happiness. "Remember in *Ethan Frome*," she said earnestly, "where they're sledding in the moonlight? Where they're wailing with laughter in the glistening snow? That's what I think happiness is." She stared at the floor in front of her.

Jesse removed his glasses and wiped his eyes. "More than anything," he said, "it's probably just the absence of pain or anxiety." He squinted across the desk at Suzanne. "What does Lucy say? Did you ask her?"

"She said it's a penis the size of a wastebasket, which hardly covers absence of pain, unless you like cystitis."

"Which apparently she does," Jesse said. "So, Lowell has a penis the size of a wastebasket."

"How did we get on this subject?"

"Happiness," he said, his glasses once again on and his hands folded in front of him. "Have you eaten today?"

"I think so," she said vaguely.

"You'd be happier if you ate, don't you think?" he asked.

"Maybe."

"Want me to fix you a peanut butter sandwich?"

Suzanne smiled. Maybe she was just hungry.

One morning, while driving to the gym, she suddenly panicked. "I'm going to die," she thought. "I'm going to be killed in a car crash." Her hands gripped the wheel and she slowed to the speed limit.

Suzanne was convinced that now that something nice and regular was happening to her, she was going to die. Whereas she used to hasten her death through substance abuse, she now feared for her life because she had reason to live it. She had felt the hot breath of irony on the back of her neck for years. Now she was breathing irony, filling her lungs with invisible irony, its buoyant dread charging the atmosphere, moving in like a cold front.

She predicted her death flippantly to Lucy, so that in case it actually did happen, at least someone close to her would know that she knew. She didn't want them to think she was one of those putzes who died unwittingly. She could hear Lucy telling people, "She predicted it—she knew somehow. What a talent."

Gazing at him now across the abyss, she felt as though she was somehow displaced, but she realized now that she'd always felt that way. She'd thought she felt that way because it was true. Now she saw she felt that way because it was *her*.

She moved out of bed carefully, so as not to disturb Jesse. He stirred and opened his eyes. "Was it something I said?" he asked groggily.

"You're suffocating me," she whispered lovingly. On the way to the bathroom she had an idea. She'd make Jesse some waffles. Waffles and muffins and bacon and . . . That was probably enough. Oh, and orange juice and coffee. Coffee with cinnamon in it.

Maybe she shouldn't make waffles, though. Her slapstick tendencies had a habit of rearing their ugly heads during waffle preparation. Still, she wanted to do something nice for him. She'd been staring at him for half an hour, and now she'd sort of woken him up . . . All in all, she felt she owed him waffles. That big waffle gesture was the only one that would do. She smiled at her reflection, filled with the enthusiasm of bold resolve.

Twenty minutes later, on the way to the hospital, Jesse said, "But why waffles? I don't even really like waffles."

"Look," said Suzanne stoically. "It's already starting to blister." She held up her left hand, with its domestic scar across the knuckles where the waffle iron had landed.

He shook his head in bewilderment and patted Suzanne's head. "Isn't this the emergency room where . . . they know you?"

"Yes," she said, smiling slightly. "I should open a house account there."

"They should at least give you a quantity discount," he said, heading south onto La Cienega. "What was the last thing? The dog bite?"

"The dog bite," she said cheerfully. "Unless you count the time I had to take Lucy to have her IUD removed." She held out her hand to him. "It hurts," she said, with some surprise.

"You're a brave girl."

"Soul," she corrected him. "I'm a brave soul." She sighed. "This is what I get for trying to be the cooking half of a couple."

"Gail, don't be dramatic," Jesse said. "You've made meat loaf and spaghetti several times without incident."

She was quiet for a few moments, then asked meekly, "Don't you have your dudefest tonight?"

"You mean am I leaving you alone with your hand tonight?" he said. "No, Gail, I'm staying with you."

"Oh, goody," said Suzanne maturely.

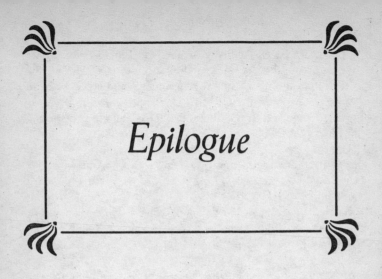

Epilogue

DEAR DR. BLAU,

Of course I remember you. Who else would have sent me a stuffed animal exactly like the one he gave me after he pumped my stomach, only twenty times the size? When you gave me the little one three years ago in the hospital, I thought it was a thumb of some kind. Now, though, in its enormous form, I see that, of course, it's a dolphin. How great. No one's ever given me a giant pink dolphin before. How did you know I've always wanted one? You must think I'm very inconsiderate for not acknowledging your first letter sooner, but I've just moved to a new house, I'm rehearsing a play, my grandfather died, and I'm inconsiderate.

I hardly know where to begin in response to your question about "what I've been up to for the past two and a half years." Suffice to say that the last time I did dope was the last time I saw you—and nothing personal, but I don't want to see you or anyone else standing next to me with a hose ever again (unless we're standing over flowers in a backyard).

Sometimes I feel like my life ended and I'm still here. Other times I feel so calm, I swear I can hear air moving slowly over the earth. I still eat junk, I don't exercise enough, and last week I had a cigarette. But I figure if I had to give up everything I put between me and my feelings, I'd stand at the center of my being and howl like a lonely old dog.

Unfortunately, I am not "available for dating," as you so quaintly inquired. I am presently living with someone, and have been for over a year. I guess I like it. One of the hardest habits for me to break is taking the right things the wrong way. If I was available, though, I would definitely consider you as an escort, since even after I'd thrown up on you, you said you found me "interesting." For that I am truly grateful.

I had what I call my triumphant return to the Cedars Sinai emergency room a while back for a burn, but I didn't see you there.

Your psychodrama group sounds intriguing, but I think I'll stick to conventional therapy for now. I still don't think I feel the way I perceive other people to feel. I don't know if the problem lies in my perception or my comfort. Either way I come out fighting, wrestling with my nature, as it were. And golly, what a mother of a nature it is. Sometimes, though, I'll be driving, listening to loud music with the day spreading out all over, and I'll feel something so big and great—a feeling as loud as the music. It's as though my skin is the only thing that keeps me from going everywhere all at once. If all of this doesn't tell you exactly what I'm doing, it should tell you how I'm feeling when I'm doing whatever it is.

Thanks again for the dolphin and your letter. I hope this finds you well and still on the right side of that hose. I have to sign off or I'll be late for my shrink. I'm expecting a breakthrough any decade now.

Happy New Year,
Suzanne

P.S. That night in the emergency room, do you recall if I threw up something I needed? Some small but trivial thing that belonged inside? I distinctly feel as though I'm missing something.

But then, I always have.

ACKNOWLEDGMENTS

There are no words to express adequately my gratitude to my friend and editor Paul Slansky, but if there were words, they'd have to be multisyllabic and shrieked from high atop a roller coaster in appreciation and glee.

I would like to thank the following for their support and inspiration:

Gloria Crayton, Mary Douglas French, Ilene (she knows why) Waterstone, Buck Henry, Melissa Mathison, Mike Nichols, Maxene and Ray Reynolds, Constance Freiberg, May Quigley, Richard Dreyfuss, Beverly D'Angelo, Bill Reynolds, Beatriz Foster, Amy Edmondson, Charles Wessler, Blair Sabol, Chana Ben-Dov, Arnold Klein, Cindy Lee Zucker, Al Lowman, Patricia Soliman, Richard Hamlett, Brian Frielino, John Burnham, Jim Wade, Edwin Jack, Donald Roller Wilson, Bill Wilson, and Harper, Sean, Linda, J.D., Simpson, Albert, Roger, Begley, Grip, Lennie, Arlo, Harrison, Henry, Lester, Mo, Evelyn, Maggie, Penny, Ted, Moses, Carolyn, Evi, Thom, Nikki, Shimkus, M.G., Reigo, Bleeaz, Mira, LaVallee, Henley, Erika, Renee, Hyjean, David, Howard, Tom, Lynne, Drew, Toni, Carol, Leon, Kipper, Philip, the alumni of the Century City New Beginnings Rehabilitation Program, and Joan Hackett.